With *Head Full of Traffic*
fiction collection that is w
the often-precarious line between surreal expressionism and more
traditional horror themes. Ames is clearly a writer on the rise, and *Head
Full of Traffic* is a collection readers of dark, thought-provoking fiction
do not want to miss.

-Greg F. Gifune, editor, *The Edge: Tales of Suspense*

Ames's stories are firmly rooted in an ordinary world, where
extraordinary things happen; a world that is only separated from ours by
the thinnest of walls. In his hands, something as comforting as visiting
the carnival, hearing an ice cream vendor, or going on a hike becomes a
journey into nightmare, where past, present, and future collide with a
power that will have you looking over your shoulder and turning on the
lights.

-Barbara Roden, editor, *All Hallows*, Journal of the Ghost Story Society

Brian Ames's writing style makes it easy for the reader to experience his
stories with the characters. I highly recommend *Head Full of Traffic* for
any bookshelf. "Several Appearances of Stuart" clearly illustrates
Ames's gift in making the reader experience the story with the character.
This ghost story will haunt me for years to come.

-Diana Cacy Hawkins, editor, *Whispering Spirits*

Head Full of Traffic plunges the reader beneath the surface of everyday
life. The ordinary becomes twisted & unfamiliar. Different rules apply.
It's survival of the strangest. In these stories, Brian Ames combines
elements of various genres—suspense, supernatural, & slipstream—and
then mixes in ideas from literary fiction. The end result is thought-
provoking & wildly imaginative. Indulge yourself with this electrifying
collection.

-Nan Purnell, editor, *Lunatic Chameleon*

I'm not sure which is more disturbing: Ames's exceeding eeriness, or the suspicion that he's holding back... If "Feeding Time" is a shadow of Ames's future work, it's a creepy shadow that's unlikely to go away. And we're glad. *Head Full of Traffic* is bedtime stories for those afraid to go to bed and those who want to be.

-Asher Black, editor, *MYTHOLOG*

Brian Ames writes sneering, kick-in-the-teeth horror with a working-class edge. From road crews to corporate offices, from fishing vessels to fruit orchards, Ames's blue-collar stories evoke the fleshy, banal, and slightly hallucinogenic horror of the human experience.

-Dru Pagliassotti, editor, *The Harrow*

Head Full of Traffic

Brian Ames

Pocol Press
Clifton, VA

POCOL PRESS

**Published in the United States of America
by Pocol Press.**
6023 Pocol Drive
Clifton, VA 20124
http://www.pocolpress.com

Publisher's Cataloguing-in-Publication

Ames, Brian.

Head full of traffic /Brian Ames. -- 1st
ed. -- Clifton, VA : Pocol Press, 2004.

p. ; cm.

ISBN: 978-1-929763-01-6

1. Fantasy fiction. 2. Horror fiction.
3. Short stories. I. Title.

PS3601 .A14 2004
813.6--dc22   0403

Cover art © 2004 Ken Meyer, Jr.

ACKNOWLEDGMENTS

Emanations in the form of grateful, glowing ectoplasm go out to the editors who first published many of these stories. Stories in "Head Full of Traffic" have appeared as follows:

"John Lee Hooker undead," in *Lunatic Chameleon*; "Carnival," in *Indigenous Fiction*; "Feeding Time" in *MYTHOLOG*; "The Geomancer," in *Seedhouse*; "Istvan the Painter," in *The Edge: Tales of Suspense*; "A Widow's Tale" as "The Brick Men" in *Hobart*; "Several Appearances of Stuart," in *All Hallows* and *Whispering Spirits*; "Head Full of Traffic" (originally titled "Traffic") in *The Harrow*, "●," in *MOTA: Truth* (an anthology from Triple Tree Publishing); "Poles Apart," in *Monkeybicycle*; "No Weapon Formed Against Me Shall Prosper," in *Barbaric Yawp*; "Lamentations" (as "Lamentations of the Gods") in *Aphelion*; "Tableaux of Murder" (as "Halflight") in *Timber Creek Review*; "Cumberland Plateau," in *RE:AL*: "Grandpa's Orchard," in *Darkness Rising* (an anthology from Prime Books); "The Hummock King" in *MYTHOLOG*; "Flexor" in *Lunatic Chameleon*; "We'll Leave the Light On," in Britain's *UNHINGED*; and "The Spokesman" in *Strange News*.

cross helt up don' scare me none, baby
ain' 'fraida my r'flection no mo'
necklace a garlic just stank, tha's all
an' I'm right on t'other side a yo do'

boom boom boom boom

don' wilt inna sun like collards, sugar
heah me tap on yo winda pane
pump it up real nice n sweet now, mama
gotta jones for yo lovely vein

a-haw haw haw haw
hmmm hmmm hmmm hmmm

stake inna heart won't make it, honey
don' sleep in a big pine crate
cause I'm mad bad Vlad, dad
an' it's yo blood I moana drank

boom boom boom boom
whoa, yeah!
a-haw haw haw haw
talk that talk, walk that walk
hmmm hmmm hmmm hmmm

—*John Lee Hooker undead*

Table of Contents

CARNIVAL

"On the road that leads to destiny, one will walk."

"Weebs, you gotta getta loada this."

Weeb's good eye structures bow-legged Skimmy, who's hitched a thumb back over his shoulder. From the cockpit of the roller-coaster, Weeb's cornpone face scrunches while his lazy eye twirls – he sweats in the afternoon humidity, balloon thighs sprouting the ride's gear-lever. It's been a staggering day of chainratchet, buck and pull of carriages, scaffolding twists. Squealing, snotty teenagers and the smell of livestock. The clouds have dropped to inches above the two carnies. It traps county fair sweat above sawdust, makes gagging probable. Night-time comin', and if Weeb knows anything in that fricasseed cortex a his, he knows this: Nightfall brings out the druggies, the drunks, the dealers, scoffs, super-skanks, cornholers, tattlers, bad dreams.

"Whuh?"

"New jar over at the freak tent," Skimmy elaborates.

Now that's somethin'. Weeb pulls the gear forward to lock as a cart-necklace shrieks into the station. "Gotta pull this gear," he explains.

"Ah fuck it," Skimmy says. "I'll spell ya. I'll pull the gear for a while — you go over and see."

Weeb seems to undulate for a few seconds, puzzled whether he can leave his post. Whether the showmaster, Palp, will have his ass for it. His lips curl up into a grin, hulls of corn between dishplate teeth. He pours himself, rather than climbs, from the cockpit. Exchanges places with Skimmy. Rolls off in the direction of the freak tent, pendulant, his T-shirt-hoisted gut leading, all three-hundred-eighty pounds clearing the way like a great, perambulating hill. He moves like a hippopotamus out of water, that hairy navel peering out like a second good eye. It scans fairgoers cyclopically as Weeb waddles.

He calls them skanks – all of them. The fairgoers. Can't wait to wrap their lips around cotton candy, buttercobs on a stick, licorice whips like red or black snakes. Snow cones — Weeb know what's in snow-cones. One day he saw the snow-cone jockeys pissing into plastic jugs of the flavored syrup. Everyone he passes got they tongue on a snow-cone — he's thinkin' a that piss in the syrup. *Heh heh.*

Weeb twaddles down the fairway, stops at the Corn-on-a-Stik for a buttery cob from Maisey. She leans out over the counter, hands him a dripping yellow treat, vends up a wink. Her eyes suggest she may come over to Weeb's trailer and play Go Fish or War with him tonight. Drink some corn whiskey and slap fat. He separates himself from the

1

cornstand, forgoing a paper napkin. He moves on, passing skanks aiming their squirts in the water-gun game, one tall skinny skank swinging the hammer for his gal. The weight travels up its tracks, falls short of the bell. Melted butter drips down Weeb's fingers and wrists as he approaches the freak tent. He stands at the entrance and sucks the kernels, lubed-up dowel in his pudgy fist.

"Hey, hey, lookie there," Zee-Buck greets. Zee-Buck's on ticket collection shift for the tent. "Lookie the head on *that* one! You in the show or what?"

"You can gimme some head," Weeb retorts, and both snigger through nasal caves. Weeb likes Zee-Buck, likes even better the freak tent. "Skimmy said you gotta new jar."

"Yap."

"What it got in it?"

"Dog head."

"A dog head?"

"Yap."

"So what, a dog head. Get a dog head any day a the week."

"Naw, Weebs, this is different. This is a kinda dog-man head. Just the head too, cut off right at the neck."

Weeb was pretty sure he wanted to see the new jar. Now he knows. This sounds great – he wants to see it right now. "I'm on it," he declares, "my pants're full with it." He squeezes through the crowd-counter. Its arms rotor and click twice as he wedges through.

The freak tent is a happy, happy world.

There's the three-eyed lamb and the calf with a fifth limb sprouting from its fuzzy brisket. Both honest-to-God bona fide items of taxidermy. They are mounted on burnished stands — little brass plaques set on the bases document their heritage — birthed on this-or-that farmer's ranch in such-and-such county, Iowa or Nebraska or South Dakota. The two-headed baby in a jar floats in fluid, strange particulates attendant. Its four eyes are squeezed shut as if the deformed infant struggles to leak a tiny double shit. Other jars stand in a row, skanks crooning and wincing, crowded around — a two-headed cottonmouth, a rat with three tails. The rat looks like it's swimming through frozen gelatin. There's a tiny bubble in the jar's milky medium, just escaping the rodent's whiskered muzzle. Weeb thinks maybe the little beastie wasn't quite dead when they plopped it in goo.

A gallery of historic freaks runs along all four walls, portraits of bearded women, Siamese twins, alligator men, limbless torso-people, triple- and single-eyed triclops and cyclops, an Asian man with a lit

2

candle sprouting from his scalp. In one corner, there's a shrunken-head display. The tiny eyes are scrunched closed, sutured rudely shut.

But this afternoon most of the skanks crowd into one corner, furthest from the tent's entrance. Weeb knows it must be the new attraction drawing them. And it draws him as well, in a way he could not possibly explain, with a strange sort of call Weeb can't hear but, instead, feels in his stomach, down there with all that corn. A dog's head ain't that big a deal, he thinks. But still, it's a callin'. And a man can't ignore a callin' like this one.

De-kernelated cob and stick still enfisted, Weeb parts the skanks like a shoat Moses would separate the halves of a sea. There, on the far shore, up, out of the depths, is the new jar. It's brown inside, whatever it is – Weeb can see only that much from here. He penetrates skank-waters, they fall away from his greatness and abundantness as from a rolling juggernaut. Weeb stands before the jar, pinwheeling pupil at 33-1/3 rpms, good eye wide as a punkin' pie.

It's a dog, it's a man. He can't tell. The head floats in brine, neck flayed in flaps. Fur and skinflaps at the truncation float like slick, still parchment. That's one helluva neckjob. The round face suggests a man, but the doggish is there too — longish nose, fur, unlidded eyes mostly dulled, cloudy iris. The tips of canines fold back the boundary of black-gray lips at two points. It's a man's face, *heh heh,* but muzzlish. *And is that, Weeb, a glow kindling there in the depths of those opaque eyes? Is the filmy pastiness of inert vision dissolving in fluid as you stand there as if in lipid worship?* The jar-eyes rock Weeb — the barely balanced sphere of him — on his feet-balls. They clear up good and stare out at him. Except it's more than a stare. It's a gaze that suggests sentience, comes knocking with a bad-dog memory. Weeb feels pregnant with this offspring: Dread.

For Weeb knows something new now. Somehow, he knows he has *experience* with this dog. History. He and this dog go way back. This is a Rhode Island dog. Weeb remembers Providence, squeaks *Uh-uhh* barely audibly, drops cob, holds negating palms up and out at the jar. Like a bag of beef tongue, Weeb piles to his knees between skankwater columns. The whole carnival shakes with his fall to earth, and those waters close around him.

"Weebs!"

He hears Zee-Buck's voice, feels Zee-Buck fanning him.

"Weebs, wake up you big ol' bitch."

Weeb has a neuron left, and it fires its synapse. "Whuh-hell?" he demands, rolling on his side, farther, onto fours. Stubby blowfish man, he swoons there like a Jello quadrapod.

3

"You passed out, big boy."

The head, the head. It has colonized him, left bitemarks across his mind.

"Where Palp get that head?" Weeb demands above an escaping strand of spittle that dollops sawdust. There's silence. "Anybody could answer!" he bellows.

"Shee-it Weebs, calm down. Palp get the head from a little girl last night. She came 'round to the office and sold it to him."

"What she look like?"

"Well... I don't know. Palp said she was just little. Could hardly see how she could heft the jar. He didn't say no more'n that."

Recall flaps in Weeb's mind: He's a newby, running the Round-Up in Providence, R.I. The show's been up and down New England for three months, but he just hooked up in Hartford after hitching north from the circuit in Lewsiana. There's this little gal, no more'n twelve, thirteen, wispy skinny thing. His momma woulda said to feed her pork, grits and butter, anything fried. The Round-Up's geared in and spinning, starts its orbital cant. Then the tenor of those skanky squeals changes from dizzy glee to shock and terror. Weeb looks up.

This little gal is rag-dolling all over the ride, bouncing from strut to strut — she's a ricochet princess, come outta her straps. Weeb shuts down the ride, moaning *o my god o my god,* the diesel motor clutches out. And she's laying there busted up near the hub, draining blood out her tiny ears. That little head, hair the color of sweet corn, dappled with red. That extraordinarily pretty, pouty death mask, strangely unravaged by her random tossing.

Weeb remembers he didn't check straps. *That's part of the job, you asswipe. Check the straps for all patrons.* But Weeb's been letting riders worry about their own damned straps for some time — that's why he got canned down South.

Weeb recalls his rush to bust the strap off before the inspectors turned out. While the skanks coo and mope over the dead girl, Weeb slips off and yanks — all his weight behind it — that mo-fo mesh strip out of the steel crossbar. The rivet gives hard, grommet blowing out to sharp brass burrs. Then he rejoins the group and the show boss is there asking, "What happened Weebs, what happened?" "Strap musta blew," he says. His lazy eye spins like a top as he explains, again, same straight story for everyone. "Strap musta blew, I said it a hundred times, I'll say it again." This lie exactly matches the verdict of the inspectors.

The officials move off and she's ambulanced away. The show-boss shuts down the ride for the night — they'll have to hose down the blood in the morning. They step off, and Weeb seems shook up good.

4

And they notice a doggy leashed there on the temporary fencing. The big some-bitch is looking them over, back at the ride, back to them, back to the ride. Suddenly, the pup has the stare of an animal left behind, and the show boss says, "Oh shit, it's hers, it's her dog."

The abandoned dog gazes the show boss and Weeb over, settles on Weeb for a long while that feeds this into his pork-pie head: *I know I know I know I know.* Woof.

Weeb had started the boozing, but sleep was a continuous nightmare of her. So he took mouthfuls of speed to keep awake. And he ate and ate, so that in spite of the speed and insomnia, he bloated into a massively dense object, part Jovian gas planet, human only at the last, innermost core of him. He left that show, ended up in this one.

"I gotta get outta here, Zee," Weeb gurgles.

"Sure Weebs, sure."

"I gotta go lay up."

"Yeah, big boy."

"You tell Palp I'm sick, tell Skimmy he gotta run the coaster. I'll put in double time tomorra."

Weeb gropes sawdust and finds a doughy purchase, pushes up that bulk and stands. But before he departs the freak tent, he has a last look at the jar. The eyes have gone cloudy again. *Nothin' there. Never was you fat fuckin' fool.* Still, there's somethin' new upstairs. Those bitemarks. Teethholes, is what it is.

Weeb stumbles from the tent into a spectrum of late afternoon carnival light. Starts the long, unbalanced wobble to his own trailer. But like an infection that won't stop running, the dog-man head has left a virus behind. Those holes up there in Weeb's gray matter start a-leakin', and the first pusey drop floods him as he walks up near the merry-go-round.

The horses slip their poles. Wicked ponies, mad and no longer impaled, show big bucky teeth. And they're all over the little riders, *heh heh.* Horsebites for everyone, those steeds nip big fleshy gobbets outta the skanks' backsides and shoulderblades. Shake some a them girl skanks by the hanks. There's no end to the screaming and spray. Then there is — an end — and Weeb's staring at this universe's merry-go-round, calliope-grinder music wheezing from its mirrored core. Kids go up and down clutching poles. *Nothin' there.*

Weeb utters a surprised whimper. "No, sir," he shakes his head. "Nosir, nosir, nosir." His utterance is like a big, corpulent mantra of refutal. Suddenly he wants badly to cower undercover in his trailer, get there before night falls and the whole fair goes magic. But twilight is

5

falling fast, a dropped plastic tarpaulin over the sky, night coming on quicker than a bodybag zipper.

Weeb passes the funhouse, stops short as Palp cuts in front of him trailing Maisey by the hand. The show boss and the Corn-on-a-Stik girl enter the hall of mirrors. Weeb combats an urge to follow, but reasons he can't even fit through the goddamned doorway, much less navigate the speculum maze inside.

Weeb staggers away from the Fun House, swivels that cornpone head when he hears tearing metal. Carriages of the Octopus rocket into space, occupants trailing one long scream. To his right, up against one of the Port-a-Potties, a carnie's smacking a skank's head with a ring-toss bottle. The glass slowly reshapes the skank's melon with each blow, as if his head were fashioned from children's clay. Soon the carnie's ministrations bring the skank to his knees, and over prone, where the carnie continues reshaping the back of his head. And then an enormous roar, a catastrophic signature of metal separating from metal, and the ferris wheel slips its mighty axle and rolls off toward the parking lot, the countryside. The fair's fence crumples in its sparky path. The giant disk rotates over bucketsful of shrieking occupants, neon tubes exploding along radial struts, and it folds and collapses through itself with a groan like a behemoth giving violent, failed birth to abomination.

Little messages from the dog-man head, welling like abscesses in those teethholes. Oozing out for fun fun fun.

Weeb blinks, totters — all is unchanged. The Octopus whirls its riders into gleeful dizziness. A skank scores a ring over the neck of a Coke bottle — the carnie points to the first-level stuffed prizes. The Ferris wheel spins slowly, royally. Two lovers in its topmost bucket suck each others' tongues. The last of twilight fades. It's a world of neon and shouts and pipey music. Weeb thinks he must get indoors. It's like when he was a little fart in Lewsiana — his momma would stick him down-cellar, in the 'fraidy hole, when tornada warnings would bellow. This is like that, he thinks, looks up at the low, starless sky.

Weeb crosses through the grounds with no more of these terrors. It's as if they, for the moment, have exhausted themselves — a calm after violent, carbuncle eruptions. Skanks give him a berth — they see a bloated tear-streaked grotesque with one spiraling eye carom, as if by random, over dirt and sawdust. He takes shelter in his own trailer.

After the carnival closes down for the night, Weeb's drinking hard, bewildered by the dog-man head's toothy visions. Maisey comes by, but Weeb's in no mood to receive visitors. Not even for fat-slapping, not even for that. Cause he knows, somehow, that mo-fo dog-man head is watching and waiting. There may be more than that final synapse left — Weeb can in no way be imagined to possess intelligence, but he's thinking hard now the best he can. But this... this... is so, so damned confusin'.

He's knocked back his seventh or eighth belt of corn whiskey, feels the urge to piss. Stumbles out the door, down his steps, into shadows to find — underhanging his vast distension — his little feller and drain. He freezes, good eye detecting an unfamiliar shape.

He sees her through the arms and mechanisms of the Tilt-a-Whirl. Her perfect face. The pretty, pouty Providence death mask stares pasty-eyed through him from above sallow, pale clothing. She's maybe forty, fifty yards off, but her features are unmistakable. Weeb curses, places a hex on her in the form of an oath, swears by the dog-man head's name, "I am sick a this shit!" He shouts across the Tilt-a-Whirl, "You ain't here, *heh heh.* You know you ain't. Jus go back inside a that dog-man head, now, 'fore you catch cold." He taunts her. "Run along, now, little Providence girl. Go find yo' doggy." Yet she stands, still as a cipher — her eyes are like baleful maws.

"Shoo!" Weeb cries, breaking into drunken tears. "Move off!" He doesn't realize he's pissed himself, doesn't pause to think it's 1 or 2 a.m. and he's hollering loud enough to wake the damned. Yet no one wakes, no trailer lights snap on, no one hollers, "Shut the fuck up, Weebs!" It's he and she alone at opposite poles of the Tilt-a-Whirl, pale ghosty dead girl and pee-pants, roly-poly spin-eye Weebs.

But then, just as Weeb begins to imagine she might fade into nothing, or that he might blink and she will evaporate like the horrific mental implants sent by the dog-man head on Weeb's earlier cross-grounds wobble, she moves. The girlshade lifts her pale arm and beckons, from the shadows, a beast.

A humongculus shape lumbers toward her, it looks like a great ursic lifeform. It stops at her heel, turns to follow her gaze and rotates toward Weeb. He can't imagine what it is, this massive mammal. There is no shape in his nubbly databank that precisely corresponds. She points toward Weeb, and the humongculus starts a long, intent lope around the circumference of the Tilt-a-Whirl. Too late, Weeb understands why the form wouldn't register. Beheaded, stumpy, swarthy, stinking, the beast moves like a bustling monolith. The headless shadow bears down on him.

Weeb has maybe five seconds, no more. Up in that blast-furnace cornpone head a his, he thinks *Bullshit,* and he's gonna beat this mo-fo's beasty-fuckin' trunk in, right now, *heh heh.*

"Come on, you big bastard," Weeb snarls. "Come an' get it."

7

It's well-muscled, with veins and sinew visible under fur in the halflight. A nubby tail emerges from above its buttocks, Weeb can see it bounce as it rounds the last corner. He's not afraid to fight this dog man, this bear. Weeb Remembers Jacob wrestling the angel from his Sunday School teachings in Lewsiana. He's gonna wrastle this big bastard. He'll bite this bad boy's fucking balls off.

They meet like colliding planets. Arms lock, limbs, tendons, teeth, blobby fat stored as energy for a mighty grappling. Two mo-fo ogre mammals. Freak show.

Weeb and the humongculus wrastle for a thousand years. They're still wrastling.

You don't even have to listen to hear it.

FEEDING TIME

The first night Mary saw a shape in her bedroom she simply pulled the bedclothes up higher and peered at it from under cover. The response of a child, really, who has no framework or conception of what to do. She lay next to Magnus, her husband, and felt anxiety crawl on her. The shape, discernible only as an anthropomorphic shadow in weak light cast from their radio clock, stood in the corner next to the armoire. It had assembled there, sometime before she had wakened, and waited. It didn't move, nor did it further resolve. The shape simply remained motionless, and that was the most unsettling thing about it.

As Mary perspired into the sheets, her mind raced with what to do next. Should she try to rouse Magnus? The shape – she assumed it was an intruder – would know immediately that it had been discovered. It might execute whatever grim purpose it had resolved for this night, this household. Yet to wait, in fear, under the covers, seemed ridiculous. She must do something.

But she did not, and the radio clock changed numbers as moments passed. She began to wonder whether the shadow was a trick of small light, an outline cast from streetlights and, somehow, oddly diffused and refocused through the draperies. The fact that it didn't move, just hovered in the corner – that it took no action – was peculiar. And it didn't disturb the cats, which slumbered at the foot of the bedspread, waking periodically to groom their own inky fur.

She had a moment's notion to address the shade. She would speak, in only a few seconds. Yes, she would begin an interrogation. *Who are you? What are you doing here? What are your plans?* But she found her voicebox frozen, dryness seizing it shut. It felt as arid and clutching as the muscles surrounding her stomach, as the low sinew that borders entrails, where dread manifests itself as gripping, clenching cramps. Nausea colonized her, and she felt that she must rise, maybe vomit.

As she stared longer, it seemed as if the shape slowly developed unrefined facial characteristics. But then these proto-forms would slip into obscurity so quickly Mary wondered whether they were actually there or products of her stimulated imagination. The shadow was, in ways, like an unfinished, occluded painting. A still life in the corner of her room that remained without motion, without sentience and, after a long while, without point. It was meaningless, this diffusion there, Mary decided. *Nothing.*

Resolved, as though her denial had rendered it thus, Mary's fears eased. She and the form coexisted as well as could be managed in the darkness. In the absence of explanation, this was fine, she thought. The shade would either act or not act. Morning light was only a matter of waiting, and this she could do, now.

Magnus shifted in his sleep, rotated above the mattress, drawing the throw off of her. The sudden exposure caused her to gasp audibly, and her husband mumbled a low, indiscernible segment of a dream-sentence. The shape vanished.

Later, when light finally had bridged the long night, Mary poured coffee into mugs, adding a spot of the Beefeaters' to hers. Magnus joined her in the kitchenette, burned his tongue and lips on his first sip.

"Stiff brew, dear," he said.

"Good morning to you, too," Mary said.

She had wrapped herself in a robe on rising, stepped across the room from the mattress to inspect the abandoned corner. Nothing had stayed of the shape itself, nor did any evidence of its nocturnal presence remain. The corner of the room was undisturbed, floorboards and the corner of a carpet unremarkable.

"You look tired," Magnus observed in the kitchenette from behind coffee steam.

"Trouble sleeping," she said. It would not do to disclose the source of her insomnia at this point. Magnus was extraordinarily skeptical, an atheist – or at least vigorously agnostic – a disbeliever in anything he could not directly see or handle. That there might be some logical explanation for the intruder's presence the previous night had evaporated with the shadow itself. This left Mary with only the unexplainable – which would be impossible for Magnus to deal with. Instead she pulled up a dining chair, hovered over her own coffee mug with dark sacks under her eyes.

"I'm sorry," he said. "Any reason?"

"Dreams." She spoke almost in a whisper. "I dreamt oddly all night."

"About any particular thing?"

"No – nothing I can clearly recall."

And over the course of her day, after Magnus gripped his lunch bucket and exited for work, she determined that, yes, of course it had been a dream. About nothing, indeed, that she could clearly recall.

By the time Magnus returned, she had swept the house's carpets, ran three loads of laundry and hung them to drying, fixed herself some lunch, watched the telly for a few moments, and prepared a lamb chop supper. Her day had been unremarkable in all respects, so that when they retired, she barely had a memory of something disturbing from the

10

prior night. She settled into the bedclothes with the lamp on, thumbed through a copy of *Punch* while Magnus read from a war novel. After a while, she noticed he was softly snoring.

"Magnus, love," she whispered. He stirred. "Magnus, put your book away. You're sleeping."

Her husband started from his doze, emplaced a bookmark. "Yes," he agreed. "Sorry, I must have fallen off." He removed his reading glasses, set them and the novel on his bedstand. She too abandoned her reading, snapping off the lamp after an inexplicable glance at the corner of the room next to the armoire. Darkness settled upon them. She moved on the sheets until she was next to him and waited to fall asleep.

Later, she saw that the form was not masculine, as had impressed her the previous night. Or if it was manly, it was diminutive. She had wakened, again, for no apparent reason other than to scrutinize the intruding shadow, which had moved nearer from the corner – toward where the door opened onto the hallway. Closer, as it was, she still could not make out any features. But of one thing she was convinced – this was not a burglar or rapist. If it were, it surely would have taken action last night. And it seemed benign at this point. The shape simply stood and, Mary assumed, stared down upon her.

Still, shock and fear returned. Her skin resumed its clamminess from the prior night, pinpricks of gooseflesh erupting along the surface of her limbs. She lay absolutely still, breathing shallowly. Her skin felt as if an anthill had emerged through the mattress, spilling its crawling contents across her body.

The shadow gained some resolution through closer proximity to the dim light of the radio clock. It seemed tainted by the deep red. She decided for sure, after straining in the dark for a while, that it was feminine. And then a horrific thought occurred to her – it, *she,* knew Mary was awake. *She* knew Mary was watching. This opened up an entirely unexpected problem in that, Mary feared, there would be some sort of expectation of interaction. Two beings could simply not coexist in this way without some manner of intercourse. As Mary waited, she became more and more convinced that she would break the stalemate, would address the intruder.

But how would it respond? With intelligence? Friendliness? Mary lay gripped by indecision. She thought it more likely their interaction would be characterized by some kind of malevolence. This thing was not an angel or guiding spirit, otherwise it surely would have disclosed, by now, its intent. No, this thing seemed baleful, morose, a lost thing. Sorrow or abandonment seemed to emanate from the shadow.

11

Mary's mind raced and she felt a spasm in her colon. She heard the hammering of her own heartbeat against the pillow, temple pounding an admonition across fabric. The skin on the drums of her ears seemed to stretch and warp as the sound of her blood pumping became universe-filling. She must know what this creature is, what it intended, or soon she would be adrenaline-flooded. If nothing was resolved, and the damned thing just stood there, she might soon become incapacitated.

An instinct borne of rising panic mechanized her – she nudged Magnus with full purpose. He called out into the dark room. The form at the door instantly began to dissipate, so by the time he had rolled over and snapped on the lamp, there was only a vacuum where it had, only an instant before, stood.

"Christ, Mary," Magnus said through the congestion of a deep sleep rudely terminated. "What is it?"

She sucked her explanation back before it escaped. At this hour of night, Magnus would be wholly unsympathetic. If seventeen years as his wife had taught Mary anything, it was that, roused, Magnus wasn't a very appealing fellow for some time. He required a number of swallows of coffee and a bit of muscle stretching before he could scarcely draw two meaningful sentences together and form a thought.

"I had a bad dream, dear. That's all."

His command and the dousing of light came simultaneously: "Go back to sleep." She lay in the dark and listened to his breath become even again. The shape did not reappear for as long as she waited, so that in spite of her insomniac fatigue and emotional imbalance, she slipped into sleep as well. Indeed, when the alarm pinged into soft morning light, she was surprised, and barely recalled with any clarity at all the night's transpiration. She only remembered that the shadow had now, somehow, twice visited on consecutive nights and that it seemed, after the two nights, to bear no harmful intent.

Nevertheless, over the course of the day Mary became resentful. How *dare* this being enter her life uninvited? What had she done to bring down upon herself this confusion and unease? It was unfair and made no sense. And this fact, as she completed the day's tasks, evolved from a sense that equity was not being served into a fully profound anger, so that she was furious – slinging dishrags about the kitchenette and handling the pots roughly – by the time Magnus returned from the job site.

He sensed she was displeased, but in spite of indirect – then direct – queries, could not derive the source of her displeasure. A man suited more than Magnus to a hands-off approach to life could not be found anywhere; in accordance with this, he retired to the living room to

12

watch the news. She must be in the early clutches of her pre-menstruals.
This could explain almost anything, he thought, grinning at the telly.
And this he could abide, seeing as how he thought of himself as an ugly
man, and Mary as lovely – beyond lovely. How a nail-driving, smudge-
potted bloke such as himself had scored her was beyond his ability to
explain.   It was enough for Magnus, he reminded himself, that so
beautiful a woman had consented to spend her life as his companion.
And he sensed that, in an overall sense, he made her happy.

Later, the warbling of the telephone burst the silence of their
room. As Magnus fumbled with the handset, Mary saw the form at the
foot of her bed dissemble. The caller was Rory, Magnus's foreman,
telling him to report to a different work site this morning. Mary looked
at the clock – it read 4:10, an hour and five minutes before the alarm was
due to chime. In her mind, she performed a momentary but painstaking
recombination of the shape as it had stood, closer yet than the two
previous nights. In the second after the telephone had wakened her
spouse, before Magnus had lifted the receiver, the intruder had stood
there over the twin lumps of their sleeping cats, astonishingly defined.

She had been nude, a woman, most definitely. Mary had seen
the outline of her breasts, hair softly cascading over small shoulders onto
their rise. The shape of her had been exquisite, goddesslike, with a flat
stomach and a carefully trimmed pubic thatch at the locus of slim, milky
thighs. She recognized the shape as her own – it was as if she beheld
herself from a mirror in a darkened bathroom. She puzzled through this
as Magnus concluded his conversation with Rory: "Very well, then,"
she heard her husband utter, "see you in a while."

At this moment, as Magnus replaced the telephone in its cradle,
she chose impulsively to disclose the reappearance of the intruder.

"Magnus," she said. "I've been seeing something."

"What?"

"Something ... there." She pointed in the general direction of
the armoire, the door, the foot-end of their bed. "A woman. She...
she's... coming in here. At night."

"Mary," he began, and searched through drowsiness to make
some semblance of the meaning of all this. "Mary, dear, what are you
talking about?"

She regretted her disclosure. The timbre of his response made
her feel idiotic, and she was so tired. She became defensive.

"I don't know what the hell she is, or what she's doing..."

"Love," he said, adopting a fatherish tone, "you're dreaming,
like the other night."

13

"No, Magnus – I know dreaming from not dreaming, and this was *not* dreaming."

He looked at her from his stack of pillows. She watched him struggle with her credibility, watched him think on it for a silent moment, watched his decision made and spread across his rough face, his brow, his thick, pursed lips. He suggested she make an appointment to see Dr. Coombs. It produced in her an instant infuriation, like a firework.

"I'll not have you mock me," she said. "I'm tired and wrecked, you stupid git. She's coming in every night, and I haven't said anything to you like I should have done from the beginning, but like I'm already regretting I *have* done just now."

"Mary..." he said.

But the fusillade was too great. "Don't be a bastard," she said.

"Now Mary, sweetheart, don't bust my milk..."

"Just shut it." She turned from him and pulled up the covers. Magnus clicked the lamp off again, and they both fumed for an hour – Mary not even so much as glancing at the foot of the bed but recalling the woman's eyes, her own, almond-flecked brown, but void – until the alarm insisted they rise.

During the ensuing day, Mary was unable to let go of the eyes. It seemed, to her recollection, they had been depthless in a way that didn't suggest deep cognizance but, rather, emptiness. She gazed at her own eyes constantly throughout the day, until doing so became a minor mania – to check her gaze every fifteen minutes or so, and see whether she could discern content therein. But she seemed unable to differentiate, looking at her own stare in the house's various mirrors, what made a gaze meaningful and content-filled as opposed to blank.

She drank again to mask her confusion, so that by the time Magnus returned Mary tottered on the edge of drunkenness. To his credit, Magnus sought emendation for his callous manners of that early morning, but she was disconsolate. Instead she almost violently heaped fish and chips on the plate in front of him, having failed to blot the oil from the fried fillets. Her spoonload of mashed peas slapped onto the ceramic like dropped shite. Nothing he could say could mitigate her glare, so after he tried and retried a few times, he simply fell silent, forking in his supper.

They fell into bed later.

"I'm sorry for this morning," he said. She moved next to him, asked to be held. Then their nightshirts fell away and she placed him inside her for a good, long, delicious while.

14

She woke with the face of the intruder inches from hers. With wide-eyes, Mary silently begged her own consciousness to convince her she was dreaming. She squeezed shut her lids so tightly she felt their ducts fill and tears well up behind them. Against the back of her eyelids, the afterimage remained: her own face was recognizable, but it was spectrally pale, the white deriving from within the shape but discolored in the red of the radio clock. *Please go away, please,* she thought.

Mary lay on her side curled like a small girl. The face – *her* face – had been at mattress level, as if the being had risen from the bedside, perhaps from underneath the bed itself. She recalled all the tales intended to frighten children where monsters and ghosts, banshees, swell beneath the bedsprings and rise in the night. And then she realized that, indeed, she was frightening herself in indulging this line of thought. If she kept shut her eyes, the vision would go away. She was never more sure of a thing.

So, of course, she was then compelled to look, to open her eyes and verify that the woman was no more complicated than a dream.

Her face stared at Mary, vapid gaze crossing the inches between them with no more meaning than blowing ash. The intruder's face didn't blink, betrayed no acknowledgment that Mary's eyes were open or closed. Lines on its skin, crow's feet at the corners of the eyes and furrows on the forehead, appeared deep and canyonlike. The pupils were like bottomless holes. And the lips were void of color – they shared the same neutral whitishness as the rest of the woman's features.

Mary shrunk from it, her skin again tingling with horripilation. She inched closer to Magnus on the sheets – her movement disturbed one of the cats lounging at her feet. It stretched and settled.

And the shape rose, the neck ascending above the sheets' horizon, then the breastbone and swell and cleavage, and Mary thought she would see her own familiar breasts in only a second. But when the visitor stood, the stone shapes of gargoyles emanated from her bosom.

In place of her breasts, beasts.

Mary shrieked. The visitor stood next to the bed as Magnus started, the eyes of the beasts of her chest flashed and Mary knew, then, that this was the seat of sentience for this visitor. Screaming, she experienced an instant revelation, clutching her bedclothes – those beasts, forged at the place from whence a woman nurtures, were not benign.

The woman – viewed through the veil of Mary's terror as nothing more than a host vessel for the fiendish breasts – vanished as Magnus pushed himself up and alert.

"God, Mary, for fucksake..."

15

"She..." Mary gasped through an immolation of fear, "She had monsters for tits."

Mary could not recall an instance where she had sleepwalked since she was a child. Yet she was doing so, this night, in her own room, the one she shared with Magnus. She didn't know where her nightclothes had got to, and thought it was strange that she understood she was, at this moment, walking in her sleep. She would have expected to be dreaming or unconscious, but she was not.

She approached the bed with its cats at the foot. They remained silent, a pair of dark dollops at the feet of two sleeping forms. *Who is this, in bed with my Magnus?*

Yet where circumstances should have rendered her well beyond inquisitiveness, she was oddly calm. She rounded the mattress to her side, noted the glow of the radio clock spilling an arc of redness onto the white sheets.

She pulled the covers away from the woman who lay there. Mary's breasts began to swell and undulate. She felt in them scratching and the sharp unsheathing of granite teeth. *Something wants to get out.*

She sat gently on the bedside, the mattress giving a small bit under the weight of her. She pulled her calves upward, scooting her bum toward the woman, placing her feet delicately under the covers, then pulling the spread up and over her. She began to consume the woman, until she had made the woman a part of her, so that Mary lay alone next to her husband.

As she was finished, she moved on to Magnus. Her breasts fed upon him as well, until they were full and nourished and had resumed their daytime shape, and he was gone. Then she slept.

16

THE GEOMANCER

I asked a *feng shui* man inside my head for a look around. He stood, neck swiveling, eyes peering out across epicanthic folds at the trail left by a woman who had rode her horse through. He let his fingertips rest on a dusty porcelain urn, caressed a small wood box.

"The arrangement here is no good," he confirmed, making brief eye contact with me, then quickly glancing away.

He was a beautiful man, my age, middle thirties or so. He claimed to have worked on buildings in Hong Kong, Shengdu, a couple in Ho Chi Minh City. Then he had come to British Columbia, completed a job there for the new Hong Kong and Shanghai Bank towers in Vancouver, caught a bus south to Seattle. I asked him what he thought of the new Mariners stadium. He shook his head: *Hopeless.*

He stepped to the urn, lifted it, blew dust from its cap. "Don't open that," I said, and he quickly set it back where it had rested, on a brainshelf. Inside was the captured sound of a solitary guitar string. It had plucked itself, a single note, every two minutes inside my closet, inside its case. I'd laid in bed, the roots of my hair standing, needles poking up through my skin, asshole puckered. Terrified and frozen deep in the night, eleven years old, my guitar stroking itself in the closet. It was a memory clear only as a frightening suggestion. The urn held an archetype for all things that had never been explained, and that, for one reason or another, I lived in fear of. I wasn't ready for him to peer in there yet.

The *feng shui* man was watching me watch the urn, watching me remember the sound. "There is very little of the dragon's pulse here," he announced. He meant *ch'i*, the flow of balance across time through this interiorscape. He meant *yin* and *yang* were out of whack in this sticky place. He looked away from me then, studied the shape of the land.

"What is this?" he asked as we stepped, together, onto sand. A shoreline disappeared to our left and right, and fog rose out across the water.

"A lake," I answered.

"Of tears you have refused to shed," he surmised.

I couldn't answer, just nodded: *Yes.* He sniffed the air, held his chin high and sifted for air currents. His flat nose scrunched in the stagnant air. "*Sha*," he pronounced, a single syllable, staring at the water's surface.

"What is it?" I asked.

"Bad vapors," he answered, turning from the shore to re-examine the trail left by the horse. "And what is this?"

17

I looked down at the bare earth at our feet, which was the palate of my mouth. It was torn up with shoeprints, those iron U's, wrecked, dirt thrown everywhere in huge gouges.

"She rides through here all the time," I complained. "I'll be focused on what's at hand, but then my attention is sapped by the sound of approaching hoofbeats and it rises and rises and then she's riding through." I shared with him this picture of her, a bareback-riding, raven-eyed sylph.

He noted that she trailed black hair, that she whispered lies as she cantered by.

Then he nodded, encouraging me to disclose more. The *feng shui* man was clearly pleased; up to this point I had answered him in single words, or two- or three-word clauses. "Tell me more about her."

"One day she asked me to re-shoe the horse," I recalled. "She brought the horse out and it was muddy up its legs and belly. I thought of being down there in all that mud with the stinking animal, holding its caked fetlock up in the cleft of my calves and shins. I thought of its mud and filth on the fabric of my jeans, and I packed my shit up and said, 'Next time you make an appointment with me, have your horse cleaned up before I get here.'"

The *feng shui* man nodded. "She is a secret arrow," he said, "an inhibiting, noxious course. You must free yourself of her."

"I want to," I lied.

"What is in that box?" he pointed at a small, ornamental receptacle that rested in another cortextual fold.

"I can't remember," I answered, somewhat truthfully, though I suspected it was one of two things. One: a severed salamander, head and body, which as a curious boy I had separated with a scissors, believing it already dead. But blood, red like my own, had oozed from the reptile's fresh stump and its tail had twitched once before I dropped it in horror. Or two: the fisted pigeon. This small bird had lost its claw at a train station somewhere near the Italian-French border. I had seen it hobbling across ties and rails — all claw and stump — had reached down to feed it only to receive its deep, infected bite. "I don't think it's anything important."

"I need to have a look," he insisted.

"I don't think it's necessary."

"Do you want my help or not?" he asked. I capitulated with a nod; he lifted the hinged lid and a small sound escaped, an audible release of alarm long caged. I cowered as this stagnant exhalation hovered there in front of him for a moment, dissipated in wind. "You are free of this box," he said, overturning it, now empty.

18

I didn't feel any better. I told him so.

"You will," he promised.

"You can clear this place?" I asked. "With *feng shui*?"

"Maybe... with *kan yu*," he corrected. "*Feng shui* just means wind and water. *Feng shui* is only a component of *kan yu*, in which we concentrate on features that surround this place and seek to understand how *ch'i* flows through here — *if* it flows through here — in terms of time."

"You don't know for sure..."

"Within reason, some improvement is possible for all places — even this," he said. "You can't put much more *ch'i* in a place where *ch'i* is weak, but you may be able to reduce *sha*."

I thought maybe the *feng shui* man was an impostor. Perhaps he was nursing my desperation, offering me a suck at a non-Western breast. He knew I was skeptical, but also that I had reached the end of all my own resources.

He knew I wanted, and didn't want, *this*.

We descended a tight staircase; the wet walls crowded in and enveloped us, and the stairs spiraled down in gulped circles through my throat into my chest. The meat that surrounded us undulated with heartpulse. I knew he was surveying for sinew that might conduct *ch'i*, features of internal topography we could exploit, reorient. *A mountain*, I thought. He was looking for the broad *yang* of some internal mountain from which a strong line of pure *ch'i* flowed. We emerged into a cavern, which opened up around us like a dome. The *feng shui* man stood with his hands on his slender hips, stared at the center of a frame mapped onto the north wall.

It was a picture of a boy's eyes as they evolved through his ages, small. There in the picture, then, was the curl of his red boy's lips, and his little boy's nose as he softly aspirated *Daddy Daddy* and would never find him, me, ever. He was simultaneously an uncertainty and a certainty, a shade of culpability, fatherless, cast aside. And his eyes pled for the embrace of a father. Their pupils and irises tattooed onto the walls of my heart a black accusation of abandonment, and the *feng shui* man witnessed the beating of these sticks, these mallets of question.

"Neither is dragon pulse found here," he stated in clipped, tight diction. I knew he had begun to regard me with distaste, as if my appeal for his professional evaluation had suddenly expanded, that he should thus begin to take inventory of my character. He pointed again at the picture, at the notion of the head of my illegitimate son. Now framed in an airplane window, the boy watched as his country and its lights receded below.

I had grown confused and told him so. I begged him, at that moment, to promise me that relief was possible.

"I think you will have to experience a total rearrangement," he concluded. "But there isn't much here to work with, mostly bad vapors and inhibiting courses." This was all the succor he could offer me, this beautiful man from China with his compass and texts. I had invited him in. Then I began to consider him an intruder.

He stood in front of me, looked directly at me, barked like an animal or a drill instructor. He demanded to know whether I was willing to do whatever it took to rearrange, to have the proper balance of *yin* and *yang,* to further balance the five elements: *Water! Wood! Fire! Metal! Earth!*

It all came out of him like horseshit in a parade.

Finally unable to hold back any longer, I enumerated the reasons why what he suggested was impossible. I went on, and my tenor rose a pitch, then several more, and then my harangue was like the sound of a jet airplane engine, until he gripped my shoulders with both of his perfectly manicured hands.

"Stop this jeremiad!" he shouted. "You will have to begin uniting yourself in harmony to that which is around you."

Then I killed the *feng shui* man, cut his throat and dumped his body in a drainage ditch. I remember I snarled, *"Ch'i THIS!"* as I slit his neck and abandoned him there. No one was going to fuck with this splendid arrangement. *No one.* My blood hammered and his blood coated me, and I knew I had done nothing — *nothing!* — wrong.

After roaming my torso a while, I returned to the corpse. I dragged the *feng shui* man's body to the door of my upper intestine, watched the blood at the slit coagulate and saw that my stomach acids already were working at the edges of him. Then I waited for him to pass.

The rising thunder of approaching hooves caused me, finally, to look up.

ISTVAN THE PAINTER

The first time Dierdre posed nude for the university art seminar, she felt as if insects were crawling up and down her bare skin. She had entered the old conservatory just after nightfall and reported to the instructor with butterflies in her stomach.

"Are you nervous?" the instructor had asked in a disinterested way.

"Yes, very," Dierdre said.

"Don't be. These are students of the form. You're no more to them than a bowl of fruit."

Students gathered a few minutes before class. The instructor led Dierdre through a maze of easels to a partition, where she exchanged her clothing for a robe. Still tense, but excited, too, Dierdre strode to the dais at the center of the room and stepped up. This seemed like an easy thing two weeks ago when she responded to the advertisement in the university's newspaper. Now she stood, robe clutched around her, feeling entirely different while students took up their posts behind canvases. Then surprising herself, she let the garment drop around her feet.

The conservatory was not well lit. The instructor moved around her in a circle toggling on lights from various angles. He explained to the class that this was to emphasize shape and curvature. It would make it easier for them, he promised, to memorize the form.

The Form, Dierdre thought. Her thighs, her ass, her stomach, her breasts, her shoulders. The way her biceps rose, then gathered at the elbow, then widened again at the forearms before her wrist. Her neck where her hair, pinned, usually cascaded. All of this is *The Form*. No more than a bowl of fruit.

The instructor approached the dais.

"I'm going to move you into several positions," he said. "I want you to hold each for about three minutes."

Dierdre nodded. She felt chilly, felt what she thought must be the raising of gooseflesh. She wondered whether the students would detect its minuscule mounds in the lights. The instructor asked her to put one foot in front of the other as if she were mid-stride. He said to raise one hand toward the clock and place the other on her hip. She heard her heartbeat in the sides of her head.

Dierdre held her new position, moving only her eyes across the faces of students. It wasn't long before she noticed none of them looked at her — at her face, that is. They aren't here to learn to paint faces, she reasoned. Still, how odd for none of them to even glance at her, to make

21

even the remotest, chance eye contact. Near the end of the first three minutes, she felt a sort of tingling or movement on her thighs. It was like the crawling of hundreds of tiny legs on her skin. She thought, oh God, it's my period. She felt herself redden at the notion of the students watching blood trickle down the inside of her legs. Then she thought no, it would be too early, two weeks too early. Still, she was relieved when the instructor approached again to change her position. She stole a brief glance at the fork of her legs. Nothing, of course.

He turned her so she faced another quadrant of the room, had her raise both arms and lace her fingers behind her head. It struck her it was a pinup pose, and she smiled a little, just for a second. He said this pose would be for five minutes.

Dierdre watched the students work. She surveyed the features of each, watched how people's looks of concentration vary like fingerprints. She watched brushes dip on palettes, the mixing of colors. From behind the canvases, she saw them bulge with the pressure of brushes, like an animal moving under cover.

Then she noticed the student at the back row, near the curtained window. He was looking at her. Not at her body, not at the bowl of fruit, but at Dierdre. All the way through to her eyes. He was watching her.

Do you know who I am?

No.

He held his brush motionless, his palette upturned but still. Where normally she would be rendered uncomfortable with sustained eye-contact, would have swept his gaze briefly then dropped her eyes to her feet, Dierdre held the man's gaze. Like two engaged in a communion, they watched each other, unmoving. She felt it again, the insistent skin crawling. But it was deeper this time, as if the legs of tiny insects burrowed through her sinew and meat, rising occasionally for air at the surface. She fought an urge to reach between her legs and scratch. Still, the man stared directly at Dierdre's eyes. Infrequently, he would swirl his brush on the palette and make an application to the canvas, still weirdly maintaining his eye-lock.

Do you know who I am?

Stop it.

Dierdre decided he was handsome. Dark haired, dark skinned, elegant of cheekbone. His nose was broad, but strong, not fat. She thought he must be Russian or Baltic. Slavic maybe, some measure of eastern European heritage flowing through him. More than handsome: delicious. His eyes were like candleflame. Beautiful. She was still staring at him when the instructor called time and reconfigured her.

22

"How are you doing?" he asked.

"It's harder than I thought, still like that."

"Sorry, this one's another five minutes."

He placed her back to the staring man, had her bend one knee forward and thus cant her pelvis to that side, fold her arms and lock them under her breasts. He turned her head over her right shoulder, tilting her chin slightly up. She supposed all of this was so the corner of the room she'd just been facing could now learn to paint asses. She could tell her neck was going to be stiff after this one.

She could see the man staring at her, still, from the corner of her eye. Early into the pose, she felt tiny animals burrowing, the scratchy urgent feet of rodents, of centipedes, the lighting of flies. Spiders walked from the cleft of her buttocks up her lumbar ridge to weave webs across her shoulderblades and leave egg sacs on the nape of her neck. Muscles tense, she felt the beautiful man's eyes hot on her, the heat of them like rough contact.

Do you know who I am?

Please, stop.

When Dierdre thought her neck muscles would surely spasm, seize up and freeze in the odd over-the-shoulder position, the instructor called for a break. She slumped to her robe, rubbing her neck with her palms, kneading the flesh there. She gathered the robe about her, looked for the gorgeous Slav. She might have found the courage to ask him what he thought he was looking at, and did he like what he saw. How much more courage would she need, having just stood naked in front of thirty university students for a quarter of an hour?

He was gone. She looked around at everyone and couldn't find him. Thinking she may have missed him go through the door for the men's room or the water fountain, she found, instead, the instructor.

"That man," she said. "The one who was painting over there."

"Where?" the instructor asked.

"There, at the easel next to the curtain."

"Yeah, OK."

"Who is he?"

The instructor fumbled with a folder in his hands. Drew a class roster forth, checked a chart on which he had sketched the room and placed surnames next to easels on the paper. A sort of art-school seating chart, Dierdre supposed, to let him get to know his students' names faster.

"Laszlofi," he said. "Istvan Laszlofi."

"Oh," Dierdre said.

When break was over Istvan Lazslofi did not return. Dierdre was placed in a half dozen other positions, and lit from two dozen other angles. The clock hands swept arcs toward nine o'clock, and the instructor dismissed the class. Dierdre put her clothing back on and walked home after signing a university timecard. Not a bad way to make forty dollars.

Dierdre dreamed fabulously that night, dreams with colors and flow and delight that seemed, at the moment she woke with a great pain in her stomach, to merge in blood red. She staggered to the bathroom, still moaning, as she had in her dream, *Please, stop,* doubled over the toilet, but couldn't bring anything forth. The pain, at first as if she had been gut-punched, waned and then vanished entirely. She got back to sleep a half an hour later and didn't notice until she soaped herself in the shower the next morning two tiny wounds, one each on either side of her navel. Two decimal pinpricks whose new scabs dissolved in the water flow and bled anew for a moment before she toweled off and they clotted again. Dierdre hoped they would heal before she had another posing session.

Two barely perceptible scars remained athwart Dierdre's bellybutton a week later when she posed nude the second time for the art seminar. All week she had Istvan Lazslofi on her mind, the penetrating gaze of his gorgeous European eyes. Throughout the week she wondered often of him, what he might be doing, where he might be. She found herself, out walking or on the way to the grocery, thinking she might meet him by chance. She would see whether he recalled her, whether he had an explanation for the intensity of his stare.

She also discovered throughout the week prior to her second posing that she was tired all the time. It felt as though she was at the height of a heavy menstruation, as if iron and energy had been vacuumed from her. She thought her skin looked pale, her lips bluish in the fluorescent reflection in her bathroom mirror. Her muscles, normally finely toned, were sluggish and sore. Still, these were odd moments, forgotten in the sunshine of day and the thought that Istvan Lazslofi might, again, behold and paint her form. Over the week Dierdre developed a conceit that she might be more than a bowl of fruit to him. He might, in fact, be warm for *The Form.* How else could his persistent stare be explained?

When she mounted the dais the second time and allowed the instructor to manipulate her posture and limbs, Istvan was there, behind his easel, staring. A slight smile tugged at his full lips. They struck her as very red, wide, pulpy. Oddly so for a man — almost feminine. As if vessels of hot blood pumped just beneath their slick surfaces.

Where Dierdre had grown chilly during the first posing, tonight she felt warm. Between the second and third pose she asked the instructor about the heat.

"Never can tell in this building," he said. "Always too hot or too cold. Never just right."

He configured her again, a pose full-on to Istvan, arms akimbo, feet and legs parted slightly. It was a simple pose and could be held for a long time, balanced, with a stable foundation. She spent several minutes trying to imagine what she looked like from his perspective. Did her breasts, for example, seem firm and high? Would he be charting the curves of her inner thighs, the nest of her mons, a glimpse of labia? She imagined his eyes were hands, that he grasped her as he grasped the brush, that he swirled inside her as he mixed paint.

Warmth like an oven spread from Dierdre's core. She thought of bedding him, of riding him with a rolling, sliding pelvic motion. She thought of herself below him, squeezing his upper arms as he slammed into her. She thought of his beautiful face buried between her legs, of those Slavic eyes still gazing, gazing.

Do you know who I am?

Oh God, please...

Dierdre thought of those full red lips on her pale neck. On the river pebbles of her nipples. She thought of him kissing her belly, tongue lapping her navel.

She felt a drop of dew roll down the inside of her thigh. Felt herself blush, that before a class of university students her vagina had grown moist and heated. She felt washed in her own horny scent, felt the heat rise into her chest and onto her face. Sweat broke on her brow. Her nipples shrank into themselves, and she glanced at Istvan, who was grinning. God have mercy. *Those teeth! Like a dog's...*

Dierdre grinned back stupidly. Her smile was like a fake covering, a façade. Dierdre felt him swimming into her. That pulpy smile and those Slavic eyes nailed her, drove a spike upward into the center of her, splayed her on a debauched altar. Dierdre knew, and she knew that Istvan Lazslofi, the painter, knew she knew.

Istvan Lazslofi had raped her.

Of course, Dierdre had been willing. The thought of him on her, in her, had been welcome. She had stood on the dais drawing him, compelling him forward. Indicating the way with her pelvis canted, hips thrust outward. He had colonized her mind completely the week prior,

25

and whose fault was that? She could have driven him from her thoughts, an exercise of will over pleasure, but she persisted.

Now, she knew, something of his swam into her.

Dierdre was exhausted the week between the second posing and the third. And she wondered whether she would make it to the third, her cycle approaching. She laughed — it was a race! She hoped the period would win, that she would have to call the instructor and offer a lame excuse. It would not do at all to pose nude before the university art seminar trailing a string. But she also hoped it would delay, that she might coo and gasp in the gaze of Istvan Lazslofi again. The bastard.

Again she wondered, wherever she went, whether she would run into him. Hers was a small town, mostly campus. It made all the sense in the world that they might happen upon one another, at a café, in the library, waiting to cross a street. She had a notion that Istvan was an evening person, one of those people who stays indoors most of the day, only venturing forth after nightfall. Her eyelids fluttered through thin daylight, muscles aching like they'd been cored by drill-bits. Dierdre wondered whether she had a flu bug.

Of course there were the wounds on her belly. Same as before, so similar she wondered whether they were actually the same set, that somehow they had burst and reopened like seed pods. She'd stepped from the shower after dreaming of his teeth on her, bites like fire-needles on her skin, little twin scalpels separating flesh in razor-clean punctures, to discover her white bath towel blotting blood. At first she thought she was early, but looking down discovered a pair of rivulets cascading from her flat stomach, blood cataracts that rose from the twin holes at her bellybutton and disappeared into the V of her pubic thatch.

On the day of her third posing session she wakened to nausea. It was exactly as if she were hung over from drinking too much booze. Except that she hadn't — Dierdre never drank except for an occasional glass of Chianti on a date. She wondered again about the flu, about the wounds on her stomach, closed, for the most part, over the past few days. She baked and sizzled over the thought of seeing, no *staring*, back at Istvan Lazslofi this evening. Tonight Dierdre would be the aggressor, see how he'd like that. The thought was delicious and deeply fatiguing.

He was there when she mounted the conservatory's dais. He was there as the instructor formed her limbs and torso into shapes. He was there, only he, as if the other students and the instructor had faded into vapor. His torch eyes, his blood lips, those teeth *oh God*, filed to points, and the nails of his hands.

Do you know who I am now?
I don't want to know.

26

He was alone with her, kneeling in front. His mouth suckled her navel, nails grasping her hips, pulling her near. She felt him drilling there, fluid coursing between them, filling her like a balloon then draining her like a pump. He was like one of those transfusion devices that cycles lifeblood. Except she felt this exchange of fluids was deeper, more fundamental than that. Life-giving, no, not life-giving — more like an amniotic death. Istvan Lazslofi uttered phrases upward, gazing between the cleft of her breasts into her. His eyes, aflame once, were like faceted lead crystal. The calving of icebergs.

The instructor broke this rapture with one word.

"Break," he said.

The art seminar materialized around her, and she stared dumbly at the spot where Istvan had probed her. Dierdre's robe lay undisturbed, still draping one of her feet. She glanced up, saw the back of his head as he exited. She stooped for the robe, clutched it around her and fled the room. She emerged into the long hallway that led to the staircase, and saw him walking away. His pace made no sound.

"Istvan! She shouted.

He turned, gathered her in his sight. She stepped toward him, pulling the robe tight across her front, across her stomach.

"Yes," he said. "You know my name."

"The instructor told me."

"Nice of him."

Dierdre tilted her head sideways like a puzzled dog. Close, as now, Istvan was stunning. She couldn't imagine not melting into him, telling him *no, please don't.*

"You've been watching me," she said.

"I'm painting you, yes."

"No, not my body, not the shape of me, but *me.*"

He seemed to consider this, and a white flame like the tip of an acetylene torch seemed to strike at the core of his pupils. He smiled pointed teeth. She had a flash glimpse of an unsheathing, and then it seemed normal again, the hall, the sound of students opening and closing the door behind her.

"Do you know who I am?" he asked.

"Yes."

"Then you know what I've done."

She was silent for a moment. And then a wave of new nausea washed her, tugged at the base of her throat and drew her cheeks taut against her skull. She was pregnant. She carried the seed of Istvan Lazslofi, somehow. She felt hot tears coursing her face. This cannot be, she moaned inside herself, knowing that of course, it was. She found it

27

incongruously hilarious that she had been worried about racing her menses to this night, found herself giggling in the midst of her tears. All the time Istvan the beautiful horrific European standing before her above waxed linoleum.

"I won't have it," she said.

"You will. You can't help it. You want it."

"No, women have choices."

"Not you," he said. Istvan Lazslofi grinned hugely, barred his fangs over those moist glottal lips, showed her his big bad motherfucking teeth. "Not you," he repeated. He turned, continued down the hall, and Dierdre stood shaking with the sweat of loathing. The robe stuck to her like a shroud.

The instructor was at her side.

"Dierdre," he said. "It's time to resume the class."

Mutely, she followed him through the doorway. But where she would have proceeded straight to the dais, she veered to Istvan's easel.

His work was in no way skilled. There was no particular grasp of the use of color, or shadow, no sense that he understood curvature and shape and *The Form*. But Dierdre was not there to critique his deftness with the brush.

Before her on Istvan's canvas was the shape of a woman nursing, crudely rendered, but unmistakably Dierdre. At her breast, an abomination, an insectoid thing both man and bug. She saw that its needle teeth gnawed the nipple. She saw the imprints of fangs set about the navel. She saw the lacerated flesh of her hips, where his hands, his claws, had clamped her belly close to him. And she saw him, Istvan, peering out from behind her, low, so that his eyes and lips and teeth gaped around her thigh. She saw that one claw emerged from between her thighs and wrapped her leg, nails dimpling pale skin to the breaking point.

But mostly, there was his offspring. Her offspring. The issue of them both.

"Mama," it seemed to gurgle.

ICE CREAM MAN

There is a sun so vast and bronze and weighty that when it bears down on people just trying to get by it does so unrelentingly and without mercy. This is the sun that shone upon a subdivision in a suburban neighborhood in the southwest corner of Washington state in 1981, and in doing so tracked a moving white object that formed itself around the young man Roger Hart, who piloted the white moving object. From a speaker affixed atop the white moving object emitted a carillon of simple and juvenile bell music. The music, although synthetic — that is, not the product of any actual bells, but rather an amplified music-box offering the sounds of bells — nevertheless had moved irrevocably into Roger's head so that never mind how long afterward, no matter how distant in the future, whether the sun fell behind hills or became cloud-occluded or vanished while the sky spat rain or snow, for a hundred seasons, as long as he lived Roger would hear that bell music. *Oh My Darlin' Clementine* is a song familiar to most people; it was one of those songs. Then there was *Turkey in the Straw*. Also the theme song from a popular children's cartoon called *Popeye the Sailor Man* rang from the speaker atop the white moving object whose wheel Roger grasped in his palms. And while this story is not about the bell songs or, necessarily, about the white moving object, I just want to give you an idea of what Roger had to deal with on that day. I suppose it could be argued that this story is about the bell music — at least its everlasting imprint upon the mind of Roger Hart — but the synthetic music was only part of this. The other parts we shall deal with shortly.

Roger drove an ice-cream truck across asphalt. Heat in waves shimmered over the streets. The ice-cream truck was really not a truck but a motorized tricycle, with two tires and an axle on the back and one tire connected to the steering column on the front. Yet everyone — all the operators — called it a truck. The engine, which was scarcely larger than a lawn-motor engine and only a bit more powerful, ran with a governor. The governor prevented the operator from driving at speeds in excess of 25 miles per hour. This for the sake of general safety and the fact that cornering in the tricycle-truck any faster than that doddering pace risked upset. The operator's nest comprised a seat covered in a durable rough fabric that brought burlap to mind, and was open sided so that the road slipped slowly by as the tricycle tinkled its way through the neighborhoods. Over him was a broad carapace, on which was mounted the speaker. On both sides of the vehicle were painted the words **ICE CREAM MAN!** in red blocky letters like those found upon ambulances. Also, there was a menu of the available confections: Cherry Bomb!

Drumstick! Ice Cream Sandwich! Lemon Pop! Frozen Root Beer Float! Each option included the exclamation point, as if the names of these cool, flavored novelties should be shouted or cheered emphatically. At Roger's right hand on the floorboard, next to the governed accelerator pedal, was a chest that held the icy treasures. A cash pouch and chrome-plated change-counter were around his belt.

The 1981 summer sun that baked Roger's ringing transit of the neighborhood had burned the skin of his biceps and forearms — which stuck out from the short sleeves of a pressed white cotton vendor shirt — the day before. For this reason, the skin stung sharply with the sun on it. He had applied salve that morning, and its peculiar odor rose to him stronger than the odor of the oily engine puttering under him or the burlappy seat or the heated tar of the asphalt he traversed. Roger wore a paper sergeant's cap with the brim already damp. He motored, and the ice cream motored alongside him, and he earned money this way — a summer job — based on the number of confections he sold. There was one price. No matter which novelty a customer wanted — Lemon Pop! or Cherry Bomb! — the price was 35 cents. Children would hear Roger's bells and spill out of the houses to either side from behind banging aluminum screen doors under silver-grained shingles so bright as to render Roger's sun-shot pupils like the points of pins. They would abandon lawn sprinklers whirling over browning dandelion-flecked lawns or catapult themselves from swing sets, all with coins in their hands for him. The children would come up to the side of the moving white tricycle with **ICE CREAM MAN!** painted after the fashion of ambulances on its side and engage him in their first, early acts of commerce. For every 35 cents Roger collected, he earned 7 cents.

In a day, he might make $10.05, if all applicable taxes were considered.

But in the same way this story is not about the bell-sounds (but possibly about their imprinting on Roger Hart), neither is this story about his sunburned arms and their attendant smells, nor about children merrily leaving off their summer distractions for a moment in pursuit of those frozen treats. These specifications are merely peripheral components in the memory of the events of that blistering day, and even then, only perhaps.

The neighborhoods through which Roger motored at no greater than 25 miles per hour for no more than $10.05 per day could be described, at least by one who considered only the surface details, as uniform. All the houses were of the same boxy shape and general configuration, with gradually pitched roofs, front doors without any windows in them, sidewalks that curled under large panes fronting living rooms across flowerbeds and lawns to driveways and single-car garage doors. Each house had a mailbox on a wood post above the curb next to the driveway. There was a dearth of trees. Diversity might be expressed in the shapes of juniper shrubs, an interesting branch of driftwood lying decoratively on bark chips, a row of pansies, or whether the hose was neatly coiled next to the spigot or had been left unfurled across the lawn, grass growing up around it. Usually cars were in the driveways, not on the street itself, so as to aid the postman going box to box.

In all of this uniformity was, however, one stretch in one neighborhood that could be described as anomalous. Not because the homes or mailboxes or hose-coiling habits were any different, but because there were few children on the block — almost none — and a house where the lawn had not been properly watered so that even early in summer its grass was sear and brittle with patches so desiccated that bare ground appeared. Not that Roger had observed this, although it may have registered as an oddity in some blanketed nest of his mind. Again, looking back, these details about this house would be manifested only as part of the constellation of that arid, burning, bell-tinged day.

When a bleeding woman staggered into the street, Roger yanked the wheel to the right.

Despite its slow pace, the tricycle's momentum lifted high the rear tire, the axle forming a growing angle with the road. The truck rose askew. Roger tried to correct for balance with his body. He struck out with his right arm and leg, and dislodged the ice chest. Its lid flew free, followed by ice and ice-cream novelties. The right rear tire and the vehicle lifted higher then paused as if sentient but indecisive, then flopped back down on its shocks with a jar. Roger's head struck the left side of the cab and he saw, for an instant, black and swirling platinum. Lemon Pops! lay in his lap, Drumsticks! on the floorboard. Ice, fast melting on the street, and the woman, now with her hands held up to her gasping mouth as if she had caused this, drained blood as brilliant as Cherry Bomb! juice in rivers down her forearms.

O My Darlin' Clementine's refrain jingled into the impossible middle of the day. Roger and the woman stared. They appeared to each other as figures in a mirage. For Roger, this took a short amount of time to clear. When it did, he saw that the splashes and streaks were not limited to her raised arms but also stained her bright yellow blouse and fell from the corners of her mouth and came out her nostrils and that the tips of her blond hair appeared to have been dipped in it, and that at the core of her eyes was either nothing or the most whole and unmitigated horror. She lowered her hands eventually, then opened her mouth and Roger saw that it was a maw. "He broke my teeth," she said.

31

For no connected reason except that sometimes events that shock us cause our minds to jump, as would the stylus of an old phonograph if bumped, Roger flashed on the rare, odd occurrences of his routes. One afternoon a number of days past, he had rounded a corner and saw a woman sunbathing on a chaise lounge on her back porch. It was just a momentary glimpse, made possible through moving angles. She was rising from the lounge clad only in bikini shorts. There was a slight breeze and her hair flew to one side. Her naked breasts bent the overhead sun's rays in the way twin beacons might direct ships, and then were lost as the angles collapsed into retrograde and the house moved to block his view. She may or may have not known of Roger's unwitting voyeurism, and he drove on. Another time — it might have been as recently as the beginning of the week — he passed a house with the garage door rolled up. In the dark recesses of the garage two men sat on a couch and passed a joint. Roger watched them toke as his tricycle lumbered past, and they watched him, and they did not come out to buy ice cream.

Roger stared at the bleeding woman and despite a rising urge — borne of a loathing whose origin in his soul he could not have traced — to flee, he instead killed the truck's engine with a flick of his fingertips across the key. The bells rang on their stupid tune for a moment before he shut them off as well. "Ma'am?" he said, and his question had everything in it. He noticed now that she was wearing a navy blue skirt that was in disarray. The blouse tailed out of the waistband on one side. His eyes traveled downward to her legs, and the nylons were torn in spots and also spattered with bright, red dots. Further down, one foot was still in the nylon stocking but the other was bare, with the stocking frayed at the ankle.

"He broke my teeth," she repeated. A bit of blood like the tiniest drop of wine welled at the corner of her lips then spilled over and dangled on the lengthening string of itself to her cupped hand.

"Who?" Roger said. "Who broke your teeth?"

He saw her swallow, imagining the copper taste of it. Besides blood, she was also dropping tears, and he saw her chest heaving and realized that all along she had been gasping and that when she had spoken, it had come out like desperate retching between huge gulps of air. He thought that her eyes spun and went up, that she might faint hard onto the pavement, that she had gathered everything left inside her to tell him not once, but twice, that someone had broken her teeth. "Just... stay calm," he said. "Tell me if I can help you." His temple throbbed.

She took an enormous, tranquilizing breath and turned slightly back toward the house. "In there," she said. "My boyfriend's in there."

Her words set upon him a discordant note, one whose dissonance Roger could not quite place. Of course, he had no time to think all of this — as much as we read on an entire page flashed through his mind, because he was an intelligent and analytic young man — but in the shortest period of time imaginable he considered all of the following: If her boyfriend was in there, why was she out here alone? Why wasn't the boyfriend out here helping her? Ah — because *he* had broken her teeth. And she was fleeing at this moment, propelled into the street with such anxiety so as to render her oblivious to his approach, his music. She was fleeing, and the teeth-bashing boyfriend might be shortly in pursuit. Yet was not! And all this blood on her, and her clothes undone, spattered, and in tatters. All of these thoughts were the firings of sparks in Roger's head, and though his circle of logic closed quickly, it also took a very long time and in this rose and fell and changed pitch, as would the bell-box atop his tricycle, heard from a house. On approach the notes would sound at a certain key, but as the scooter putted past and receded, the register would drop. It is the same with starlight, red- or blue-shifted.

"What?... how?" Roger's tongue twisted across all sorts of interrogatories, but for some time, in his confusion, never got past the first word. He was for the first time in his life a stutterer, and could make no proper beginning. For a second or two, he looked up at the sky in case this might shrink the thickness in his mouth. As he tried to speak again she began to tremble and wave her hands with near-hysteria. The jerking of the yellow in her blouse caught his eye and his head snapped to level. He had not noticed before her skin was so white — nearly the color of bleached paper or the enamel of the ice-cream truck's carapace. The blood on her was so fiercely brilliant that he only now noticed she appeared as if all blood had been drained from her, that her lips, though thick and pulpy, were the same color as her skin. She dropped to her knees and clutched fistfuls of her blond, bloody hair in both hands next to her ears and screamed, and at first the scream was just a long series of juxtaposed shrieks, her guts aflame, and from this Roger discerned that she was screaming "My boyfriend's dead! Sweet Jesus, he's dead!" over and over again.

"Oh, God," she then said. "Can't you help me?"

And Roger Hart stepped from the tricycle.

Frequently people will consider a circumstance and wonder what sort of alternative histories might have led elsewhere. How many options, courses, parallel universes there might be soon runs to the infinite, and metaphysics is served up again, and this dwelling on substitute possibilities becomes banal and quite possibly maudlin. The

33

Road Not Taken and so forth. Roger may someday indulge this conceit. Come to think of it, he probably does today, in fact, when he tosses awake on his cot at night. He may go as far back as the street-corner he turned on just before this encounter and wonder what would have happened if he had simply skipped this street on this day, the street that had few children and rarely brought him their coins. He may go further, back to that morning when he arrived at the warehouse with the other operators to begin his shift, entering the bay where the ice-cream trucks that were really motorized tricycles were arrayed — thirty or forty of them, at least — in the semi-dark like tombstones on a clear night with only as much light as the sleekest crescent moon could cast. What if he had started five minutes later or earlier? What if he had traded routes, which operators sometimes did to combat the boredom of an entire summer spent crossing the same grids of houses?

Yet he had not. He had come here, to this place, at this appointed time in the history of the world, to this shrieking bleeding woman, and he had willfully stepped from his tricycle to aid her. But would you believe that this story is not even about all of this? That, again, these things are just the funky sideshows or warm-up acts (as is *everything*, a metaphysician might point out, leading up to the end of the world)?

"Please help me," she said.

He pulled her to her feet. The blood on her slicked his sunburned arms. He regarded this with some revulsion but leaving the silent tricycle in the street, not considering that he may have left it as a beacon, followed her up the walk to the house. She shuffled and staggered as if she were drunk — she may well have been; Roger never heard one way or the other — and they paused at the screen door. The wood door behind it was ajar and he saw through the bug mesh the corner of a sofa and an alcove with glass trinkets placed in it and the opening of a hallway. "He's inside," she said. "Down the hall. In the bedroom."

It did not occur to Roger to stop her and ask whether she had summoned the sheriff. It seemed that she simply wanted him to see the dead boyfriend, and then maybe place the call. Perhaps something in her explanation needed his corroboration, at least in her unraveling mind, and that the help she required was one of witness and validation. If the boyfriend had struck her, yet lay dead himself, then there was much to account for. The woman summoned Roger down the hall with a tug at his hand, and the walk was long and the end was as distant as a range of mountains on the horizon. Roger's sneakers shifted slightly with each step on the plush carpet, which too was dappled with blood, and on this long walk he began considering the source of the blood on the woman, whose panic seemed to have abated somewhat and whose demeanor had evolved and now was purposeful, almost businesslike. He began to question his recollection of her mouth moments before. He had stared into it — had there been teeth? She had said her teeth were broken. She said it more than once. There was no doubt that he had seen blood falling from her lips and from her nose.

The boyfriend's torso, head and arms were on the bed. His legs and feet and lower back were off the side on the floor. It appeared that he was kneeling with the mattress for support, and his arms stretched as would a supplicant's. There was a terrible gash on the left side of his skull, and shards of deep-green glass of varying size in his red-matted hair and as islands in the maroon pools gathering next to his down-turned cheek. Roger saw the neck and lip of the wine bottle, intact but jaggedly truncated, lying nearby on the bunched-up blanket. Some of the green glass was broken but knitted together by a paper label, and this mass rested a foot beyond the boyfriend's head, at its current zenith, also in blood. A spray pattern fanned across the exposed sheet and one of the two pillows onto the bedstand, with one or two droplets on the wall behind it.

"Hit me one too many times," she said, and Roger turned to her and saw that there *were* gaps in her mouth. He observed that she probed them with her tongue, even as she pointed at the body of her lover and shook uncontrollably, her tongue popped in and out of those raw cavities — she couldn't keep it out of them. But her words, nevertheless, now spilled around and through them: "The bastard, said he was gonna fuckin' kill me, the drunk pig. I had to... he turned away from me for just long enough and I had to before he turned around again." She dissolved into sobs. For the first time Roger saw that the top buttons of her blouse had come undone and that cleavage appeared there but was restrained by the front hasp of her brassiere, and that this too, was red. Is there nothing in all of this not covered in blood? he thought. She tossed aside her hair and breathed in deeply, swelling her chest so the entire, slightly revealed operation pressed against the bright yellow fabric, and Roger wondered for an instant about this, trying to recall whether the buttons had been undone quite so low outside in the stunning heat of the day when she had first blundered into the street dripping her boyfriend's blood and mourning only for the casualty of her smile. She had not, in those moments outside, drawn attention to her chest. It was impossible for him to reconstruct, for she pointed insistently at the corpse. It was a command for him to look again.

"See," she said. "The wine bottle."

35

"You smashed his brains out with it," Roger said. Indeed, was that white cranial bone and something grayish, the hue of white laundry too often mixed with coloreds? And of course red, red everywhere too.

"I said I *had* to!" she shouted. Roger looked from the boyfriend's bludgeoned skull back to the woman's eyes, and the horrifying emptiness or whole, unmitigated horror that was there in the street was replaced in a coup by fierce, blue flame such as that which would squirt from gas jets. "Look," she said, "I swear." And her fingers pried apart her lips, making a macabre and hideous mask of her face and, bringing her heaving breasts a foot and then another foot closer to him, she showed Roger a gaping, gasping hole with a tongue rolling like a ship and the palate ejecting the hate of sure justice and, yes, there, teeth uprooted and absent, and another broken at half-mast. Roger held his hands up as if to ward her off. "I believe you," he said. "I do."

Then there was a moan behind him.

The woman's fingers flew from her mouth and the rims of her eyes expanded so that each of her eyeballs appeared spherical and exposed. Dread frazzed up Roger's spine and smacked into the back of his neck. He whirled, and beheld the corpse again living, attempting to untangle itself from its own collapsed heap upon the mattress and, gaining focus and momentum and its feet, then bellowing at the both of them — its killer and her erstwhile rescuer, accuser, desirer, this innocent uncomplicated man attempting to do good, to be helpful, to fix her breasts with his stare and make them rise and rise and rise, this fresh-faced boy with his white paper sergeant's hat still unaccountably on, this *dumpling*, this **ICE CREAM MAN!**, this doppelganger for you and I, this Roger Hart. And the hull that had been the boyfriend, having lifted its body from death, blundered across the room toward them. The bell-sounds that came from his throat were not the gay chords of *Turkey in the Straw*. His eyes locked on Roger's and they shared a brief, knowing communion before failing behind cataracts of outrage. His mouth formed the same words hers had — *Help me...* — although there was no actual vocalization but, rather, a silent copy of a plea, and the man's breached brain collapsed inward into itself. This is the same thing that happens to a star in deep space after it goes supernova.

Wasting not a single second, the woman sidestepped the boyfriend's blind reach and even as he sank again to the sticky carpet in his void-minded, skull-rocked misery and began to die again, she snatched from the table at bedside the lamp and wielded it as a hitter would a ball-bat. She went to work, bringing it onto his head with fury. The cord whipped from the socket and snarled around her arms, yet she

36

lifted and drove the light home. A curtain of red mist, as if sprayed under pressure from a nozzle into warm air, blossomed.

And somehow it came to Roger — maybe in the afterflare of the boyfriend's nanosecond of sentience — that the bleeding woman had told him not the truth but a lie, that the fabrication she first visited upon him in those first startled moments of their encounter, over the asphalt where his sweet novelties and confections now melted in their cellophane wrappers, had followed him up the walk through the screen door down the long hallway in the same manner the sounds of his bells followed him to bed each night. This false witness then had lodged in that tempting valley under her blouse's topmost buttons and her blood-smattered bra hasp. This lie had now gathered bones and sinew and hair, then unified into a form and shouted from the top of a hill of vengeance, and now he, Roger Hart, not the blood-killer-bitch, owned and commanded it.

Roger sprang to restrain her. His sunburned, red-slicked arms reached to intervene, taking the brunt of her final swing with the lamp. Its shade having collapsed and fallen torn apart to the floor, the bulb burst and presented a tightly grouped bundle of knife points. The whole operation carved complex lacerations down his chest. The doctors later would stitch there for hours, re-knitting flayed skin and subskin. He risked his wrists and fingers, wrestling the lamp from her crazy grip, and she spun and descended on the mound of her boyfriend with only her body as a weapon. And without really thinking it through, for rationality had fled all of them — the boyfriend long since, of course, and the woman for sure now, too — Roger pulled her away from him, his hands at her bleach-pallid throat and then clenching the carmine hanks of her hair in his tight palms. To make her stop, to make all of this stop, this heat, these streets, this moving white object, the brassy mass of the sun, *Popeye the Sailor Man* tumbling in his brain, Roger squeezed her head in his soon-to-be-cuffed hands and forced the back of it onto the table at the bedside. He forced it there, on the beveled corner, flesh on oak or birch or cherrywood — some variety of hardwood to judge by the result — and not once just to make the blood-bitch stop but again, and more, and again, until blood was indistinguishable from his sweat and the sergeant's cap had popped off sopping. When he stopped, the only dry place was the inside of his pockets.

She who he first wanted of all women, now a simulacrum of that desire, stared again with that disturbing emptiness he had first met, by chance, in the street of your subdivision, your neighborhood, just two or three blocks away.

37

But neither is this story about any of these things. Can you guess what it is?

When Roger Hart was a child he used hear the bell-tones of the ice-cream man coming up the street. The scooter's motor made a putt-putt sound that made his little mouth water. Those days were so warm and lovely, and he would play the games of children and skip up to the side of the ice-cream man's conveyance and have a grape-flavored Popsicle or a Fudgesicle or an ice-cream sandwich. Sometimes he would bite the icy confections, chewing the ice then gnawing and sucking on the splinters of the stick, for on those days he was greedy for every bit of taste he could excise from the treat. Other times, though, he was patient, slowly licking the ice so that each bud of his tongue could savor the delicious juices. Think of the way you'd imagine Adam and Eve taking the fruit into their mouths, the utter and unabashed succulence of it. In the same way, on those days, small Roger would lick and palpate the sweet treats with every part of his mouth, and their colors would run onto his lips and tongue.

There were a few days when the small son of Mr. and Mrs. Hart took his Popsicle in his pudgy fist and gobbled it in only a few more bites than you would use to eat a potato chip. On those days he would get a brain-numbing headache that would last no more than twenty or twenty-five seconds.

But you know how good those feel.

A WIDOW'S TALE

A widow in Thessaloniki telephoned the brick man after the earthquake. Could he come quickly and fix her chimney? The brick man said she would have to take her place in a long queue of requests. Though the quake had been only a small temblor, it had cracked scores of chimneys and retaining walls so that the brick man had more work than he wanted (and he was a man who normally wanted a lot of work). The widow protested. Even so, the brick man at first refused to advance her on his list.

The widow cajoled, then pled, then begged. Still the brick man, like the bricks with which he worked, would not bend. He held fast to his list. But when the widow finally sobbed into the telephone his heart softened. When she wailed that something had come loose and had to be put back, his hard baked-clay heart surrendered its hard-baked position. The brick man capitulated: he would try to stop after the day's calls and make an estimate of what could be done. She gave him her address on the outskirts of town and hung up abruptly.

When the brick man arrived it was almost dusk. A breeze off the sea soughed through the branches of olive trees alongside the dirt road, and the hills were veiled in shadow. He stopped his van. He saw that her home was not one of those modern constructs from the newer neighborhoods of Thessaloniki but was, instead, old — perhaps a hundred or two-hundred years. Wires went from the pole at the road to a knot at its eaves. And indeed, the top of the chimney was missing. In a heap now, the brick man presumed, at its base. The brick man lit a lamp. He stepped up the walkway to her door. The air smelled of salt and dust. He knocked.

Despite her great age, the widow's hair was raven-black. It hung well-brushed and with an unnaturally brilliant sheen to well below her waist — almost to the backs of her knees. Her face was like tanned animal hide, eyes poking forth as would a zealot's. Her lips were a crack indiscernible when shut, but like a vast, roaring maw when active.

"Come here," she said. "Have a look at this mess." She motioned that he should follow, and stepped off her stoop. The brick man held up his lamp and followed her under the wire around the old house's corner. As he had guessed, bricks lay unbound in a broken pile. She pointed at the chimney. As his lamplight played upward, he saw a jagged fissure that started about the level of his forehead and separated the brickwork all the way to the top. There he saw again that the top of the chimney was ruined. The bricks that lay at his feet were, no doubt, complemented by an equal number that had fallen through the chimney and now blocked its flue.

This all amounted to bad news for the widow. The whole works required rebuilding. It would take a long while. And the widow would have to part with many more drachmas than she probably could afford.

As he was formulating this assessment she laid her thin hand on his forearm. With the opposite she pointed at the crack.

"That's where he got out," she said. He saw that there were tears forming at the corners of her eyes, and although she was laughing, they spilled over and down her leather cheeks. "You have to catch him," she said, and her eyes sparked. "Put him back in!" Her head hinged back on her neck and she cawed. The tips of her hair touched the fallen bricks at her heels.

The brick man refused to understand. The widow was really quite macabre, he thought. She had called for brickwork. Everyone in the entire town was uneasy after the quake, but he had taken special pity on her plea for quick service. Her voice had seemed desperate on the telephone. What's more, he had broken his own rule — calls serviced in their order — so as to calm her. Now he stood before her while she cackled like a crazy hen. And because he dwelt so intently on his own present circumstance he did not notice that the widow had ceased behaving bizarrely and now stood silently alongside him observing the crack. He heard her speak, but it was some time before he understood.

"Have you had a supper?" she asked again.

There was light inside from her electric lamps, but no fire of course. The room smelled of old smoke, not altogether unpleasant. The crust of her bread was hard, but its heart was delicious. She explained, as he buttered his slices and tasted her wine, that many years prior her dead husband had been a Cabalah-master. In fact, if the brick man were here in daylight, she promised he would see the ruins of her dead husband's synagogue behind her old house.

Her husband — a rabbi — had died when she was very young, before they even had made babies. But she studied his texts and allowed herself to become a witch. Did he believe this? she asked. The brick man nodded and chewed the delicious bread. He drank from his wine cup and nodded. Her eyes threw fire.

She claimed that when her husband died she gathered clay and made a golem. She integrated its form and whispered incantations at the clay, life-words that would invest the golem with her husband's soul and mechanize it. With her hands she inscribed symbols over it through the dead, still air, and the mass quickened and rose and walked about. And

40

did the brick man believe this? Yes: he asked for more bread. Yes: he pointed at his empty cup. She filled him again.

The golem husband was companionable at first, but as her knowledge of the secret arts grew she found it doltish and slow. After some time she could no longer abide its presence without experiencing new distaste. Forgetting that she was the agent of this strange, surrogate life, she resented its cold, clay, stupid stare, the splaying of its fat digits, the hulking roll of its steps. And, of course, its fundamental inability to perform what husbands must.

She studied her dead husband's books for the spell to recant life. When she found it the widow practiced on insects and birds until she had it right. Then she cast it on the golem husband and it fell to sleep. Afterward, the widow crushed its form with a large hammer and further ground it, during the course of months, into mortar in a stone bowl with a stone pestle. With the vigor of a sorceress, she had erected the exact chimney she had shown the brick man this very night using bricks and the mortar of her golem husband. And did the brick man believe even this?

He nodded, but he was drunk from the wine, and his guts were full of the bread.

"When the earthquake came, he got out through the crack," the widow said. But there was only the sound of her aged voice, unless the brick man's besotted snores were counted as well. She went to her dead husband's shelves to consult, once again, his old manuscripts.

There was an unprecedented heaviness to his waking.

The widow saw the brick man move. Perhaps she had gotten something wrong the first time around, she thought. Maybe this one would be better. Maybe this one could catch the other one and put it back in the bricks.

Later, she watched them crash together in a field, behind them the blue and light-dappled Bay of Salonica rimmed by the olive hills of northern Hellas.

Idiots, she thought, shaking her hair. Fools.

Their bodies crashed together like undulating earth, the violent slipping of faults, two great automatons fractured at the corners. Stone chips flew from their congress like bullets. A salt-tinged breeze off the bay carried their huge, tectonic grunts to her.

Imagine this! Her only offspring launching themselves together in a field on the outer edge of town. Both loose.

41

Unbeknownst to her, at that moment, a single strand of her hair turned gray. A phenomenon that would spread, in the coming days, as her golem-husbands wrestled, until her hair was a white shawl over her head — white as ash — and then fell to the ground at her feet.

And worse, as her hair falls and their grappling union grows increasingly fraternal, are those bargains they are making in the midst of their groans? Collaboration, as their granite muscles stretch and strain? A whispered agreement of revenge between them, brothers of stone now, with purpose and momentum to unite them.

The widow's falling white hair makes a pile of ash she may heap upon her bald head, begging later at the mineral feet of her transformed husbands. And all of Hellas will not be big enough for her to run and hide.

SEVERAL APPEARANCES OF STUART

"Jesus Christ, Son of God, have mercy on me, a miserable sinner."

Each day began at the Pluscarden cloister with these twelve words of humility. Each day I could remember since entering after finishing the sixth form, this day, each day in the future. It was a mantra particularly helpful to me, since the rest of our prayers were to comprise the intercessories — that is, prayers for *others*, rather than ourselves. That is what all the brothers did. And that is what I was to do.

When I first came here as a novice, fresh-faced, eighteen, with a tattoo of dark fear in my heart, the abbot caught me praying for myself. It was a simple request of Heaven, really — to be rid of the unbidden visions that had plagued my sleep for two years — surely God was capable of and amenable to this tiny want. But the abbot gently admonished me, familiarising me with the aforementioned Jesus Prayer. Then he made me make a penance.

"I will inform your brothers that you require intercessory prayer in this matter," he promised. "That's the way it's done."

I can't pray for my own needs; others must be plagued with them and thus, in the sharing, bond one with the other. I am similarly tasked with advocating Holy Relief from their childhood trifles. For instance, I must lift up the heavy heart of Brother Simon for acts of perversion visited upon him by an astonishingly wayward male neighbour. And Brother James requires an advocacy in the matter of his mother's and father's pensions, which have been suspended by Her Majesty's tax authorities. We intercede on behalf of peace for the whole world. But we may not, on our own behalves, beseech Our Lord. Such a prayer is inherently selfish, greedy. It is the prayer of a carnal believer, which we, as monks, must eschew.

But the temptation often is great. And it was with especial will, at first, that I resisted. When I arrived at Pluscarden Abbey, only a short four weeks had passed since Stuart Lund's most recent appearance.

To this day, I remember when a lorry killed him. I can put my mind into every angle of that summer day. I am able to visualise the precise location of sun-cast shadows, and recall the fact that it *was* sunny, a rare enough meteorological condition in our corner of Scotland. I can hear the blaring klaxon as Stuart darted out between parked autos, chasing after his mongrel dog into our Aberdeen street, then the screech of tyres and the indescribable *whunk* of impact. In later years I would dream of Stuart's gymnasium shoes, spinning in a great arc of sadness, as they separate from his ankles, from the shock and energy of contact.

43

The sneakers and their attendant laces whirled, rotating through the deep spots of my dreams before I came to Pluscarden. (I am confused over the matter of whether I actually saw this detail — the whirling of the shoes — during the actual accident, or whether my memory fabricated this image deep in my brain stem, storing it there for later use, then belched it forth to my sleep's detriment.)

The lorry ran Stuart over when I was eight years old. Or, to put an exactness to it, the lorry ran *under* him. The vehicle hit him mid-shins with authoritative force, so that as his shins snapped and he ricocheted off of the grillwork and bonnet, his upper body bounced in the windscreen like an oversized bug. Now that I think of it today, I'm sure this did happen: his shoes did this whirling thing I mentioned. My head did not fabricate this detail; no, I witnessed it. This is a great mystery, as great as any sacrament, how the shoes flew into space spinning. He was lifted out of his shoes by the power of the truck, but they too — the gymnasium shoes — were lifted by a force I didn't then, and don't now, comprehend.

The uncertainty of this aspect of Stuart's demise has plagued me throughout adulthood. It troubled me deeply when I entered the order, filling me with such intensely desperate longing for explanation so as to be humiliating. But I never received one; that is, no explanation ever came. I am left to surmise, and to ask my brothers to remove this burden from me. And to secretly and rarely — yes, I will admit it — ask Saint Benedict or the Blessed Virgin or even Christ Himself to banish those images from my sleep.

I made all kinds of bargains with God, redeemable if He would only remove the notion of Stuart's spinning shoes from me. I suppose, ultimately, one of my bargains with Him resulted in my coming here, to remote Northern Scotland, to this Benedictine cloister — not that we are any great distance from my home in Aberdeen. I was hoping that the magic of Christ, the magic of this remote, Scottish monastery set up against the forest, the enormity of this full Catholic immersion would keep the specter of Stuart, finally, from me.

Aside from the recurring dream of the whirling shoes, Stuart otherwise periodically troubled me from the ages eight to eighteen. By this I mean that he appeared.

The first time, we were conducting a funeral for one of Angus's dogs, a wire-haired male who had eaten some rotten garbage on a midnight prowl. Some bacteria had harried him down, and he died with howls and moans, brown eyes fading as we all stood in a circle. Angus wept up until the moment Iain, from across the downs, shared a scheme to hold proper burial services. Then the dog's demise became an

44

entirely different thing — an *opportunity* to engage our small selves in a very grown-up rite. Funerals were a vast ambiguity to us, an adult's function. So, without the leave of the adults in our lives at that time, we undertook services for the dead cur.

We spaded up a hole under an old ash tree, having borrowed one of my father's shovels from a shed on the back corner of our property, and laid the beast aside. As Angus intoned a few somber words about the loyalty and friendship of the dog, and its efficacy at chasing unwanted animals and persons away, I glanced up. I saw Stuart standing off from the group, next to a copse of other ash trees. He looked at me, and then at the hole, from maybe thirty or forty yards away. I looked down at the hole, then back at Stuart, but by then he was gone.

I nudged Stacy. "Did you see him?" I asked.

She looked at me. Then her eyes followed the point of my outstretched fingers, which trembled in a small, uncertain fashion. She shrugged her shoulders as if to respond, said nothing. I stared at the edge of the woods, let my arm fall to my side and felt a wash of cold over bare skin. My scalp tingled with the imagined stimulation of hair follicles that must have been standing at rigid attention. I looked at the other children, but there was no sign of anything out of sorts. All of them were paying attention to Angus and the sack at his feet, which contained the earthly remains of his dog. We dropped the sack in the hole and shoveled dirt over it, and I kept glancing at the spot at the edge of the woods where I had seen Stuart.

Then my father and I were searching for dry wood in highlands during the summer, stuff we'd section, split and stack in cords outside the house for the following winter. It was sweaty work for my dad, wielding the chain saw, stopping the engine periodically to prime the chain with oil and then having to strain against the rope pull ten or fifteen times before the motor would fire up again. We were permitted to cut only wood that had fallen in the previous spring's windstorms — never anything live — so we spent hours deep in the forest cutting and packing the logs.

I had been permitted, for two summers at that time, to do some of the cutting myself. After having been adequately oriented as to the safe operation of the saw and instructed to keep the whirring chain out of the dirt, my father freed me to assist him whenever the ache in his back would grow too acute. He would stop to drink cold tea and drops of sweat would fall from his brow as I struggled with the machine.

The operation of the saw still was a novelty that second summer. But when I made it through a downed trunk that had been particularly challenging to sever, looked up and saw Stuart standing next to my father, I dropped the spinning blade to my side, nearly cutting my leg in half, releasing its biting teeth straight into the soil. It kicked out of the ground, its propelling motor coughing once then dying. My father shouted a blasphemous phrase, not comprehending the entity next to him. I dropped the saw — which only made him angrier — and pointed.

"Whuh?" he said, following the direction indicated by my index finger, finding nothing.

"Ss... Sstu... *Stuart*," I explained, believing he would understand why it had been imperative to forget his careful tutelage and drop the moving saw blade onto dirt. Of course, a single episode of grinding highlands soil for half a second was not going to dull a blade too profoundly, but my father did not happily suffer lessons that appeared to have gone unlearned.

"Stuart, indeed," he said. He believed that I was diverting attention from my folly with the saw in order to avoid chastisement. He demonstrated his belief with an ash switch, cut from the log I had, moments before Stuart appeared, been busily, happily, *safely* bifurcating.

Another time we had gathered to play a game of football on the grounds north of the gymnasium. The afternoon was gritty, the air compressed with smoke and ash effluvia from a font of Inverness stacks to the west. The wind from that direction was utterly contaminating, and autumn's chill worked through to our marrow. The trees had dropped their leaves, and everything was brown, even the turf. The only thing that colourised our world that day was the jerseys we wore — in the colours of Aberdeen and Inverness and Leeds.

I received a pass from one of the fore guards, dribbled upfield, jockeyed with the goalie, and kicked the ball into the net.

A cry of triumph — that which flows everywhere from the throats of teenaged combatants for contests unimportant but won — filled the leas behind our town's school buildings. My comrades rushed toward me for congratulations, and as they lifted me onto their backs I spied Stuart near a corner of the building. He stood next to the brick structure looking at us, looking at me, unmoving.

"Put me down!" I shouted over the cheers of my teammates. "Let me down!" My commands went unheeded; the team couldn't hear me over its corporate enthusiasm. By the time they stopped turning me, and my neck ceased to swivel as if mounted atop a visceral caster, and I again was able to focus on the building's corner, there was nothing. No Stuart, nor an afterimage, nor even a suggestion of his form.

I now realise Stuart made several appearances before the actual dreams started. I can almost pinpoint the night of the first dream; I must have been sixteen years old, just shaving on my own without the instruction of my dad.

One morning as I bent to rinse lather from my chin and cheeks over the sink next to the loo, I sensed a change in proximity behind me, a hovering presence there and a strange alteration in the pressure of the air. As I lifted my head, water drained down my neck and chest. I raised a towel to dab the moisture away. In the mirror, Stuart stood directly behind, between me and the closed door to our hallway. He peered over my shoulder into the core of me, and in his gaze there was an unmitigated emptiness, a North Sea of *nothing*.

I spun, and in the spinning lost my footing, collapsing onto the closed toilet. And I encountered, there in the tight confines of a small Aberdeen water closet, empty space.

It was that night when I first dreamt of the spinning shoes. And it was two years later I sought respite at Pluscarden. Two years — give or take a month — until I began my negotiation with God: I will come *here*, to Pluscarden, to a house of the Lord's service, if You will deal with Stuart.

The life of a Benedictine monk is rarely perturbed by anything out of a normal routine. Our days went as follows: We rose at 4:30. We retired at 8:30. In between, we prayed, worked, chanted, read scripture, attended choir, wandered through the cloistered areas of the abbey, made repairs to the structure, attended vigils, lit candles. This was a school of service to the Lord. Once in a while, we engaged in meaningful spiritual growth by agency of a direct conversation with the abbot.

We were able, between all of these proscribed pursuits, to have brief fellowship with our brothers. It was during those times when we could share, in a limited sense, some of the desires of our own hearts, so that intercession might take place — one for the other — on behalf of each of us.

When I arrived at the abbey at eighteen, I explained Stuart's recurring appearances as visitations. I did not consider them spectral or ghostly. But I was certain they were not temporal, not of this world. Rather, I believed them to be a manifestation of spiritual warfare, the battle we believe has been and is waged every day between Our Lord and the great deceiver. Brother Micah agreed, observing that as the Holy Father of Rome pronounced in the *Vita Consecreta*, spiritual combat is an element of monastic life that has been neglected. I think the notion excited him a little, to have a real working problem of ethereal skirmish here before him, in the person of myself.

I was surprised in a pleasant way when it occurred to me that, after seven months at Pluscarden, I had not again seen Stuart. And very few of my nights had been a torture of dreaming. And after seven more months, then seven times seven and more, I forgot about Stuart, even in my deepest dreams. I can appreciate now that I had begun to take this relief for granted. It may even be possible that I began to believe this: my painstaking service at the abbey, my success at the intercessories, the tonal quality of my lifted voice in the nave during choir — the *beauty* and quality of my service — meant that God the Father and Son and Holy Spirit *owed* me this relief.

And I was thus free of Stuart Lund, either by visitation or dream, for twelve years.

I became comfortably accustomed to the life of a Benedictine monk lived on the north shore of Scotland, a stone's throw from the North Sea, with its attendant moist autumns, winters and springs, as well as summers that seemed to last only moments. Deep fog and high grass were customary, and I believed that no other life could be as serviceable. Weeks and months went by without a thought given to the unfortunate Stuart Lund, or the arc-path of his shoes.

In my thirtieth summer a novice named Brother Isaak came to live at Pluscarden. He was a strange young man, a boy who shook as if palsied. He seemed nervous as he went about his initiations, as we engaged him in discussion about monastic life. His eyes would dart left and right, or up at the high timbers that formed beams to hold back the roof. As I reflect on it today, it comes to mind that Isaak often looked as if he believed the roof was about to collapse, as if some force pressing from above was about to stove in our church.

Word started to circulate that Brother Isaak had been discovered sleepwalking through the dormitories, that the abbot had found him in a strange state between waking and sleep on one of the transepts. Apparently when he was wakened, he had no recollection of leaving his quarters, no memory of dreaming, just the same disquieting explanation — or rather, lack thereof — an expression of surprise and bewilderment that he had slipped the confines of his own rooms. The abbot collected us, the rest of the cloister, and instructed us in intercessory prayers for Isaak, revealing only this: at the conclusion of the most recent incident of sleepwalking, Isaak had been wakened from a frantic sweat repeating a single name: *Stuart*. Later, after weeks of the brethren's prayer, Isaak sleepwalked again, woke from night terrors on the grounds outside the priory, screaming *Stuart! Stuart!* at the starless night. We confined him in the infirmary, and he whispered the name of my boyhood friend until sleep overtook him.

A few days afterward, I saw Stuart behind the altar in the apse. Filtered halflight fell down like gauzy material through coloured glass and I saw him emerge from the shadows there. I was sweeping in the nave, and I dropped the broomhandle and collapsed to my knees. Stuart looked at me and through me and around me, then seemed to move closer — across the bema and truncating the line of the transept, and then he stood exactly in front of me and I lifted my hands like a supplicant. When he reached out to accept my offered palm, I saw that he suffered from stigmata, the signature of Our Lord's passion on mortal men or their afterimages. The wounds were large and open, draining.

I looked up from his hands, and he was gone.

I sent a note to the abbot. I intended to abdicate my vows and recuse myself from the order. When he summoned me, and I was ushered into his clerestory office, Stuart sat at his desk.

I sank to the floor and prayed, and it was an honest prayer from my guts. It was not an intercessory prayer, but rather solely for me, for ultimate relief, and it was a pitiful, begging, cloying cry to heaven.

Stuart and I left Pluscarden two weeks later. As I entered the order, I left it — with nothing. Since, we have wandered north Scotland, found shelter in barns, under culverts, in mercy houses. We have been as far south as Stirling, but headed back north before reaching Glasgow, crossing highlands and lochs. I wrote all this down in a small tavern in Wick, checking the spelling and details with him. I have told him a hundred times if five, now, how I am sorry I dropped his mongrel's leash. He seems to have forgiven me.

I've a mind we should hire a boat to the Shetlands; I share this notion with Stuart. He nods: *Yes.* There, no one will bother us and we can get to the business of dreaming, again.

Good. Stuart agrees.

49

HEAD FULL OF TRAFFIC

Randy is seeing the car for the second time now. It's one of those small, late-model Plymouths, blue, and for the second time in less than an hour, it is passing this spot.

Randy's crew is digging trenches for conduit. The conduit will carry sewage. The locals aren't happy because the county is forcing them to convert from septic to sewer, and they've had to absorb the cost. It means, sometimes, they try to get precipitously close to the workers with their cars.

But this car is not too close, just a repeat. It happens once in a while. Randy will notice the same car driving slowly over the roughened road. It's someone running errands in the neighborhood, or maybe the driver forgot something at home, returned, and re-launched his or her commute.

The electric window slides down as the Plymouth crawls past. Although the sun is shining, its light seems to dim for an instant. The driver stares at Randy — there is no acknowledgement, no half-smile. Just a stare. It strikes Randy as purposeful. Makes him take a step backward, wonder for a second what he's done, whether the driver recognizes him from somewhere. This happens too — people will recognize him, outfitted in a bright orange vest, hardhat, reflective fabric stripes. Usually they will nod a greeting. But this driver's face harbors no familiarity — certainly no friendliness — and passes.

It's hot and dusty. Heat from the asphalt and non-stop parade of engines and exhaust mean Randy breaks a sweat even at 9:30. The sun is already pushing down on him and the rest of the crew. Engine noise from the earth-moving equipment — the trencher, grader, roller — belches into the morning. Randy, in walkie-talkie communication with his partner at the other end of the dig, switches his sign from SLOW to STOP. It's a pattern he repeated hundreds of times yesterday, and will do so, yet today.

He watches the bumper of the Plymouth recede as the driver accelerates past him. "Screw you, too, buddy," he mutters, and blinks back into the sun.

An hour and a half later, the Plymouth shows up again, from the same direction. This time the window's fully down, the driver staring at Randy from a stop. It's the second car in line, waiting for Randy to flip the sign from STOP back to SLOW. From a different angle, the sun casts shadows under the cars, but is it less sharp, less *black*, under this car? The driver is looking at him again — glaring. *What?* Randy thinks. What's the deal? The driver's stare is mean, malevolent. His face is red and weirdly contorted, almost like he's at the onset of a stroke or an attack of apoplexy. The lips pull back to reveal sharp, dirty teeth and a swollen tongue. Then the lips purse and mouth an angry "You." Just that one word, but it means *You: that's the deal.* Maybe the angry driver is an area resident, pissed about shouldering the sewer cost.

Randy forgets where he stands for a second. His walkie-talkie hisses dead space — then his partner's airy voice: "Randy, what's up. *What's the deal?*" He looks up, down the length of the trench, at his partner in the distance. The road is empty next to the dig, his partner's sign flipped to STOP at the far end. "Oh," he says. Depresses the thumb-key for the walkie-talkie, speaks into it, "Sorry," as he flips the sign. The driver passes him. The man's forehead looks like it's about to explode. He shows his teeth again, champs them together as he passes. His neck swivels so he can eyeball Randy all the way through the sign. Randy has a clear impression the sun dims again, and that somehow this angry man and the momentary onset of wan light are connected. Angry over the sewer or not, this guy blocks — or does he *absorb?* — the sunlight. Randy wipes a drop of sweat rolling on his temple, glances up at trees. He could swear their branches dangle further, higher over the road crew. Imagines they grow woody fingers, no, claws.

But it's the fourth passing of the Plymouth that really starts to shake him up. The driver is in full bloom, now, or rather his forehead is. The man's pate seems to have ruptured, a bloody crack opened up there like a magma fissure. Blood lava is dripping down the side of the guy's face and still, he's staring. Randy is stunned, steps back again as the trees crowd over him with sharp talons. The sun is right overhead, but the Plymouth casts no shadow, and the man clacks those Nosferatu teeth together. Between gnashings, that tongue pokes like a snake, all of this in half-light. Randy experiences a moment of vertigo and lost focus. *You you you you* the driver speaks, blood running down his shirt.

Randy collects himself, thinks the man needs help, an ambulance. "Hey buddy," he starts, but the Plymouth moves on in the line, through the site, and disappears down the street.

Randy.

What the hell was that?

"Randy."

I mean what the...

"Randy!"

"What?" Randy nearly screams. He turns around and there's Jack, his foreman. "What?" he repeats, calmer.

"Break time, man," Jack says. "Geez."

"Yeah, okay," Randy says. He removes his hardhat, hands the sign to Jack. He's having trouble making his eyes work in tandem, has pain at the core of his stomach he isn't sure his sack lunch will cure.

"You all right?" Jack asks.

"Yeah, I'm tired. It's the traffic — I just got a weird look from this guy, that's all.

"Locals," Jack says.

"Yep." Randy looks up at the talon branches growing.

Randy sits in the bucket seat of the grader and picks at lunch from a brown sack. He wonders about the man in the Plymouth, and his appetite drains. He spreads apart the two halves of his sandwich, peanut butter and strawberry jam. *Look at that*, he thinks: *Blood and guts on white bread.* He closes his eyes in the high-noon heat — the temperature is well above eighty now — and sees the man's splitting forehead, knifepoint teeth. He rises from the seat, climbs shakily out of the cab, down over the roadblade. Throws his nearly full lunch bag into a refuse barrel. Cars wait and pass, raising dust. He breathes it in, dirt and heat, closing his eyes against the sting of sweat.

Back on the line at 1:00, his stomach is turning from lack of food and unease. Ten minutes later he spots the Plymouth at the end of a line of cars. It has returned to the queue from the same direction — he looks twice down the long snake of automobiles to make sure it's the same one. Yeah, light blue, that's the car all right. The line of vehicles is long, and the Plymouth is way back, thirteen or fourteen cars away.

Randy feels like his guts are being raked by a scythe. Then he has an idea that might stave off... what? He doesn't know. It resolves in his head like the blow of a hammer against skin, makes him giddy for a second. He depresses the talk button on his walkie-talkie — "Hey, Ron."

Ron comes back to him, from the other end of the site. "Go ahead."

"Hey Ron, check out the guy in the blue Plymouth, he's right there in front of you."

"Which one?"

"Behind the big silver car, the sedan — it looks like a Cadillac or a big Olds or something. The Plymouth behind it."

"Yeah, okay."

"Guy in that car look all right to you?"

There's a pause that seems to last longer than it should. Randy hears the limbs over him creak and swell, the impatient friction of branches rubbing in a tiny breeze. The rustling of leaves.

"Affirmative," Ron reports. "He looks fine."

52

Randy's still not so sure, and the pain in his stomach blossoms, spreads to his upper torso, up the ganglia in his neckpipe, slaps his brainstem and leaches into that hardhat-shelled cortex. "Okay, thanks," he acknowledges, flips his sign. Stares down the line to Ron, who flips also, and the cars gently accelerate like a wakened adder.

And here comes the car. Randy notices the inside of him failing — a despair made tangible. He feels *concentrated*, like he wants to jump through his skin. He lifts a hand in front of him, notices it shaking. His skin is coated with perspiration, high fat sun blistering down. The driver of the Plymouth gets closer. Randy is able to resolve his shape — its shape, its form — and he, it, is no way in hell fine. No, the being behind the wheel is a ghoul, a shroud of sappy blistered skin wrapped around a gasbag of a head. The crack in its pate has widened, opened up and suppurating. The world goes dark, like twilight, and black ichor runs from its headwound. The being's eyes are milky white, occluded by cataracts. They look like dirty dense eggs, and roll wildly back up into their slips, but then train and focus: there's no question they stare at Randy with rage.

He thinks, *no no*, and its mouth — a fleshgash of peeling lips — blows words at him like fetid bubbles. They leap off those knife teeth like acetylene flames. It speaks his name, *Randy*, in an indecipherable, low language. The vocalization escapes like a swarm of hornets. Randy, in a deep place of him that broaches the terror and clearly understands, interprets the being's utterance. He is being called.

No, *selected*.

Randy has a distinct impression that he has misinterpreted the rage emanating from the bloated head, that, for an instant, it is pure longing. Yes, it is — it's *desire*. The Plymouth creeps closer. Randy gags on a fuggy wall of putrefaction, greasy meatrot pulling what little of the sandwich he ate up his esophagus. He gulps it back, holding out as his stomach lurches. The trees bunch and counsel, crowd over him in the dark dripping syrup and blood and semen and aphids, lifefluid from those claws, cloying together, and they echo the being's call.

"You're the one, baby," it summons.

"No," Randy responds, from a vacuum.

"Oh, yessss!"

The gasbag head passes, blowing sputum and a cloud of black air, and Randy's knees crack, sag, liquefy. The world rushes onto him — he collapses like a sack of dead animals. His sign stands upon its pole for a second, balancing on its own, then topples. The walkie-talkie clatters on the pavement, falls over the lip of the trench, Ron's transported voice breaking silence — "Randy! Randy! You okay?"

53

Randy comes to with the road in his mouth, grit on his tongue, his gums, teeth. His fellow crew members have drizzled cold water on his face, wiping his sweaty hair with damp cloths.

"You okay?" Jack's asking. "You passed out on us, man."

Randy cannot yet speak, the ghoulish impression still burning on the backs of his eyeballs like a cattle brand.

"It wants me it says I'm the one," he mumbles.

"You got the heatstroke," he hears, the voice of Ron.

"No," Randy moans.

They help him up from the freshly turned dirt, assist him to the side of the road. Two or three of them carefully settle him against a tree trunk, keep forcing him to drink water. His head is swimming at first, but clears quickly. Jack is asking whether he wants to go home, whether someone can drive him. Randy can't afford the sick time, not even an afternoon. Nor does he want to leave his rig, or have someone else drive it. He'll stay, he says. He'll be all right in a few minutes.

"It's just the heat," he agrees. Just the heat.

Then it's three in the afternoon. Randy's back at his post, waving cars along, toggling the sign in concert with Ron. The diesel signature of road-work equipment vibrates behind him as the cars slow and stop, then start again. The sun is heavy, but he's drinking plenty of water. He's convinced himself that, yes, it was an episode of heatstroke, or heat exhaustion anyway. He did stay out late last night, after all, maybe drank one or two more beers than he should have. Quitting time nears, and he feels remarkably well.

But his well-being clacks to the deck as he sees, once more, the blue Plymouth approach. Same car, same direction, same oily trees swooning over him. Light is sucked away from the job site like a riptide, a midnight black descends and headlamps snap on, synchronously, a trail of pearl beads up the length of the trench. They blind him. The Plymouth pulls up.

The driver is a bone-man, all cloven cranium and jawbone tilting wildly atop spine links. "Howdy!" the skeleton greets. "I told you you're the one!" Its lilting exuberance flies in the face of the low utterances it emitted as a mouldering gasbag. Randy takes a step back in the darkness while the trees crowd overhead to observe and rain corpulent fluids.

"Huh-uh," Randy gasps, shaking his head. He rejects this, this moment, this bone man.

The mandible hinges open — inside it's a blast furnace. Pointy teeth pop like corks and blast at him like bird-shot. Randy takes another step backward, ignorant of edges, of boundaries. The skull laughs, *it's fucking hysterical*, the sockets glow like the headlamps only deep, deep red. There are malignant rubies set in them.

"Uh-huh," the skull shrieks. "You're the one. Yessss."

Randy still shakes his head, reaches up to pull off his hardhat, flings it at the Plymouth while backing away. It clatters off the Plymouth's quarter panel, spins on the black roadsurface. The sewer trench, on whose lip he has teetered these last few moments, opens like a chasm. Ozone and smoke leap from it, and the odor of impatient fire whirls in a cloud. The trees are singing, a barky, sappy chorus of corrupt heartwood. Limbs grow liquid, snake-like tendrils. They slap at his ankles like viney asps.

Bone man throws its skull back against the headrest and screams laughter, slaps its fingerbones against the steering wheel. "Yessss!"

"Noooo," Randy loses balance, topples, falls and falls as the flames lick his clothes, his orange vest melts like plastic, burns his jeans, smoke, brimstone, he flies through blistering open air and never, ever hits. The bone man rips open the door of the Plymouth, leaps in after him.

Jack is worrying about lawsuits as he stands over the trench, ambulance siren blaring from down the road. But it's too late: Randy's skull is fractured against the concrete conduit seven feet down in the ditch. His blood oozes down across the circumference of the pipe, drops onto dirt in a little drip-metered pool.

Ron's down there with him, pushing gauze into the head wound, fighting tears. He holds up the saturated compress, hands streaked red. The bandage looks like an excised organ, a heart.

"No, man," Ron says, "there's no pulse. Nothing."

MAURICE THE BASTARD

Long after I had finished doing what I do for a living and had entered the realm of sycophancy, I got this telephone call from the boss of Maurice the Bastard. The voice on the other end of the line belonged to my boss's boss, see, Maurice the Bastard being my supervisor, or "coach" as they say.

"Come on up here, I gotta special project for you."

Now *special project* can mean one of two things. One, you are either being sent to pasture, as in early retirement while continuing to collect a paycheck, or two, you really *are* going to be asked to do something special, so you'd better do it well, or you'll be sent to pasture, etcetera.

"What can I do for you, sir?" I asked. *How may I kiss your ass today?*

"Just come up. I'll tell you in my office."

I replaced the handset, secured my terminal, swiveled out of my chair and headed for the elevator with the first sheen of sweat in my pits. The hair on my neck stood up some.

On the great circle route to the lift, I passed Maurice the Bastard's secretary's desk. She glanced up from a moon-pie lunch she was consuming over a red-hot paperback, eyeballed me over her glasses rims. "Where *you* going?" she demanded. I ignored her just to drive her crazy. "Hey!" she called down the carpeted corridor, a screech monkey, a chattering starling. She spat the phoneme glottally, umbrage spilling out of her throat as fat as hemoglobin from a cut.

Her presence here was another in the long list of evidence against the competency of my boss, and so, ambling toward the elevator after ignoring her caused me to further reflect on Maurice the Bastard. If someone asked me how my boss was, or whether he was intelligent, a picture would assemble itself in my mind: You know when you go get a haircut and the hair clippings fall down that bib and across your clothes? Those clippings collect on the tiled floor then some hominid comes along and sweeps them into a neat little pile for dust-panning later? You know how that pile of hair clippings looks sitting there? Maurice the Bastard was exactly as intelligent and useful as that little pile of hair clippings.

Maurice the Bastard did not understand what to do. Here was a person who asked us to perform the wrong tasks. If we were propulsion engineers, it's conceivable he would have asked us to design aircraft with three engines pointing forward and one pointing aft.

Unstable airplane designs on the brain, I stepped into the chiming elevator and let the doors slip closed behind me. The soft kiss of their rubber contact was followed by the engagement of the cable, and I felt myself rising, the lift a metaphor.

Now, I think it's fair to say that the migration up this business entity's ladder is a devolution through the different phyla, genera and families of primacy. We enter, neophytes, dewy and large-eyed like little rain-forest monkeys, bush babies. We climb through variegated septic layers of discovery and cynicism: marmoset, macaque, chimp, baboon, gorilla, orangutan, pontiff and so on. Lower orders of apes mimic the models of their forebears: the way we remember – *Monkey See, Monkey Do* – becomes a mantra, a behavioral mnemonic. And in this similarity, we are entirely into and of ourselves.

Only a great exogenous shock such as the call from Maurice the Bastard's boss pulls us out of our own slinking shells.

The elevator trundled upward, not exactly a Saturn rocket, and floors blipped by. I amused myself with a conceit, the absurd notion that the door would open and my own floor would beckon me, the elevator shape-shifted, morphed into merry-go-round. It wasn't so far as you think from the truth! At the time, it was as if we were whirling on a violent calliope: the horses had slipped their poles and snuck up behind us, nipping, tearing gobbets of meat from our shoulderblades, and the blood was spraying. Or was about to, anyway.

A microsecond of weightlessness as the cables and cogs stilled themselves, and the doors slid apart. Stepping forth, the trappings and symbols of authority overflooded me: Oh, the odor of rarified air! The shine of crystal, the matte caress of carpeting on my soles, walnut and cherrywood everywhere. Track lighting and muted, prescient quiet. Here was the wellspring of strategy! In these exact halls, these offices with their sentient, golden squatters, this *place*! The sun that circles this ptolemaic plot flooded in through exterior windows, lambent on the carpets at stimulating angles. I wondered whether I was properly attired. (I bought maybe $10,500 worth of suits, dress shirts and ties over the years, stuff to look good in. Suddenly we were *Business Casual*. I had no idea what in the hell to wear, but I was getting out my wallet.)

The secretary of the boss of Maurice the Bastard waved me in like a tarmac greeter at a major airport. I'd not have been more surprised if she had grasped little flashlights in each of her mitts, sported hearing-protection muffs on her dome. *Park your airplane here, ape.* She was very sweet, inquiring as to my coffee needs. The Boss of Maurice the Bastard had taken an unanticipated phone call; could she bring a pastry while I waited for his next availability?

"I'm fine," I said. To her offer of coffee, pastry, I bore false witness to my actual state of well-being. I smiled through a friendly moisture barrier enough to acknowledge her champagne mannerisms, her utter politeness and bracing enthusiasm. But I actually was *not* fine, was *far* from it, really, imagining this to be some sort of pending ass-kicking. *Oh where, oh where, had I stepped on my dong?*

I have to admit, at the time Maurice the Bastard's boss summoned me, I was at a low point. It was the second worst job I had ever had. (The worst was driving a L'il Joe ice-cream scooter. I heard the little recorded bell repeatedly play *Popeye the Sailor Man* and *Turkey in the Straw* until those ditties nested in my brain, and still nest there today. I had young children – five and six years old – demand of me, "Give us some free ice cream, you son of a bitch." I had teenagers try to trade me marijuana for Popsicles. I had to dodge real cars on the road, with the scooter's motor governed at 25 mph. I made $20.10 over the course of two summer days, working sun-up to sundown. I can still see the check. Working for Maurice the Bastard was maybe one-tenth of one percent better than that.)

I was sitting in a leather chair, diverting my near-panic with daydreams of Purgatory. Suddenly Maurice the Bastard's boss's secretary piped me in.

I entered the sacristy of his office, a Holy of Holies. Stitched in a sampler above the desk was a clever credo: *Beatings will continue until morale improves.* Mrs. Maurice the Bastard's Boss must have needlepointed it.

He sat, wreathed in a phlogiston of orangutan-ness, thick, hairy, broad. His eyes structured and restructured me, reevaluated my cut, the topography of me, my content. He bored holes into my head with his orange gaze, a search robot looking to validate his own prehensile judgment.

"You need a new assignment," he said, sans salutation. True. I had had enough of eating Maurice the Bastard's shit for a living. I wanted to tell his boss *Please don't follow me into the bathroom and listen to me sticking my finger down my throat in the stall* and explain that I was a bulemic shit-eater. Instead I just nodded.

"There's a new team," Maurice the Bastard's boss said. "I want you on it. Maurice is out. I want you to take care of it."

I nodded again as I heard my own voice report, "I'll take care of it."

"Good." He returned to his kingdom of paperwork. I assumed by this – the return of his cooing ministrations to his papers – that he meant for me to leave. So I rose out of the chair, out of his nest of

58

hardwood and tanned hides, retreated to the closed door, cracked it. "You'll need some help," he added, just before I slipped through the breach.

I revolved to face him, to barrage his orange hirsuteness with a tsunami of confidence. "I'll find help," I said. "I can handle it."

"You have all the resources of this office at your disposal." It was the longest sentence, I believe, the boss of Maurice the Bastard ever spoke to me.

"I'm grateful, sir," I sucked and swallowed.

Outside, the Ebullient One favored me with a genuine smirk. "Shall I update the distribution lists and organization charts?" she teased. "Order you a door plaque?"

"I think that would be jumping the gun," I said. But then, unable to contain the stain of my joy, I added, "Maybe later."

"Very good!"

She was like a self-contained glee club. The secretary of my new *Coach* rose with all the exuberance of a bathtub bubble, a gravity-defying sac of fetid vapor. She clasped her hands together and grinned like a deacon. "We'll see you later."

I stepped off into the hallway, punched a glowing button, enthroned myself again on the elevator. I reflected: When I came home at night, the first thing I did was kick the damned dog. If my kids were between me and the dog, they got the foot, too. I've kicked my wife a hundred times coming home from work. But tonight would be different. Free at last, free at last, thank God a-mighty, I'm free at last. *Lucy, I'm home!*

All the trespasses of Maurice the Bastard paraded through my skull. Scores of occurrences of accepting glory not rightly his, credit for work I or other upright-walking bipeds had slaved over. A mountain of offenses, not the least of which was the hiring of his screech-monkey secretary, thrust up into the light of day. The late nights, the weekends. The volcanism, the oratory, the bombast and demagoguery. His servility exhibited only for his peers and betters. What a blowhard! I began to consider a course of action, a tight little resolution for Maurice the Bastard.

As the lift dropped, so did I drop the blade on his Bastardness.

By the time the doors parted and I emerged downwind of the screech monkey, I already possessed a mental model of his recusal. I sped past her as she excreted nonsense into the phone, back to my lair, lifted my own phone from its Judas cradle. Summoned Matsuoka from Marketing, Sukovaty from Accounting. Called Bill Candy from Invoicing. "I'm calling in a favor," I said. "Sure," he said. Then I went down the hall to get Simms from Public Relations, a regular lemur of a fellow. "Simms," I said, "you're going to need a statement."

The four of us, me, Matsuoka, Sukovaty and Candy, a hulking quadrad of justice, embarked uphall to Maurice the Bastard's office. We arrived there like four dust-devils, reined in our mounts, tipped our brims at the screech monkey, who knew something life-altering was about to infest her cosmos of gossip. "Say," she commanded. "What's going on here?"

We pushed past her with extreme prejudice. She folded up, squealing the squeal of a throat-slit shoat the whole way. "Shut up, you twit," I heard Sukovaty say, but it was too late; the ruckus had alerted and enervated The Bastard.

He stood like cuckolded royalty in front of his hardwood, the desk between him and the window. Maurice the Bastard's arms were folded across his chest, the cuffs of his dress-shirt rolled up so the flesh of his forearms quivered in defiance. His eyes stared out from a pasty face, little holes through KKK sheets, daring one of us to speak.

"What's going on here?" he demanded, created in the image and spewing forth the exact diction and mannerisms and spew of his own cloying assistant. Still, even at that moment, Maurice the Bastard was simply this: a life support system for a hyperego.

"Well, I'll tell you," I said. The four of us formed a determined semicircle. "There's a new team."

"Yeah, and you ain't on it," said Bill Candy.

Maurice the Bastard, the nasty old baboon, could see he was trapped. To escape us at that moment would have rivaled the most violent prisonbreak.

"Do you remember from your history lessons the Thirty Years War?" I asked.

He just stared at me as if, for *business casual*, I had donned a straightjacket.

"No? It began in 1618 in Prague – doesn't strike a memory?"

"What in hell are you talking about?"

"I'm talking about good old Catholics and Protestants, and how they resolved issues of who's on the team and who ain't when things got too hot."

Sukovaty and Candy grinned. Matsuoka clacked his teeth, just once. It sounded like a rifle shot.

"One day," I said, "the one side got sick of the other side, invaded the House of Regents. Captured a couple of fellas with the wrong ideas, took 'em hostage."

Maurice the Bastard began to size up the insurrection that spread before him in a tableau. He stepped backward, pushed his fat ass up against hardwood, unfolded his arms, grasped the desktop at his flanks, accepted the *Bounty* rudder.

"Know what they did?" Candy asked.

Maurice the Bastard's head shook.

"They chucked 'em out the window!" I shouted.

And so did we, with Maurice the Bastard. Through his flailing arms and outraged protestations, the sour odor of fear flooding off of him, we four gripped him in the inescapable grip of equity and launched him through the glass. It happened slowly, so that we saw the form of Maurice the Bastard make contact with the pane, saw the glass improbably stretch, warp, fracture and wrap around him in a veil of shards, exploding outward with a deafening shriek – yet fast, so fast, that by the time the vacuum shockwave faded, the pressure of the HVAC-conditioned room rushing through the building's wound, he was already eight floors below at the locus of a rose pool spreading on cement.

In the act of throwing his framed accreditation certificate from the International Association of Bastards and Assholes (IABA) out through the window after him, I counted coup.

"Miss Screech Monkey," I called, "please call Maintenance. Get them up here to fix this window."

"Yes, sir," she whined, a new obsequiousness welling, dripping from every orifice of her. Matsuoka, Candy and Sukovaty congratulated me, acknowledged that I was the new Alpha Male on the block.

And I thought *Yeah yeah yeah, my wife and kids they love me and which one of you pricks 'll be there when they toss me head first out the window, huh?*

WE'LL LEAVE THE LIGHT ON

From the moment he spoke with the desk clerk, Revo knew there could be trouble.

"You got non-smoking rooms?"

"Buddy, I think you're mistaking us for one a them big-city motels," the clerk said. "We don't care what folks do in the rooms."

Revo opened his wallet, dropped a couple of twenties on the counter. It had been a long haul, from Crescent City to Kalama, northern California through Oregon and over the Washington line an hour ago. Dusk had dropped in at Salem, his wipers throwing fat rain through Portland. He'd been on the road for eleven hours — not as long as some stretches go — but with the rain and traffic, and drowsiness setting in, he'd had enough. After the third time he snapped awake at the wheel, he decided any roadside inn would do.

"You gotta credit card?" the clerk asked. "Need a damage deposit."

Revo looked around the motel's office. He stood on a worn-through rug. A single, shadeless lamp cast light across the burn-pocked desk. There was a National Hot Rod Association calendar on the wall behind the clerk.

"What am I gonna damage?"

The clerk offered a sneer. "Don't know, but that's the policy."

Revo offered his card, waited while the clerk made an imprint. The boy moved slowly, as if life along Interstate 5 were so boring any diversion, even a motel guest, must be savored.

"O.K., you're all set." The clerk turned to pull a key from a batch of them hanging from pegs, fumbled with its fob, read the number. "You're in lucky number three," he said. "There's only five rooms — it's the one in the middle."

"Thanks." Revo took the key and turned for the door.

He parked his rig in the lot aside the office. Then he rummaged for his small suitcase, which he had stowed behind the seat, locked the cab, climbed down with the case. He walked across the small lot. The five rooms were separate from the office, set off and tucked back against trees and a bluff, in a long, flat structure. He passed numbers one and two, stood at the door to number three. He sighed. Someday he'd be able to afford a sleeper rig. For now, unless he wanted to supplement coffee with amphetamines, it would be seedy motel after seedy motel.

He fumbled for the key in his pocket, thought of all these travelers' rests that sprout on the landscape like mushrooms across America and Canada. He'd driven the truck across more than half the states, and nearly all the provinces. He'd slept in a thousand of these dumps, it seemed. Some were better than others, but none of them was what he would have called pleasant. And the more he stood there, key in hand, the less confidence he had in this place. He looked around — there weren't any cars in front of the other rooms, no light behind curtains. All of the porchlamps were out, burnt up probably. A single sodium flood on a pole at the center of the lot, plus the inn's neon vacancy sign, cast the only light. The vacancy sign hummed.

He keyed the lock, twisted it, heard the tumblers roll and engage. Revo pushed the door open, stepped inside.

The room smelled unused, mildewy. He groped with his free hand for a light switch, found it. A lamp next to a twin-sized bed clicked on.

"Good grief," he said.

The room was tiny, maybe ten by twelve feet. Barely more than a mattress and worn coverlet, the bed at the center of the room sagged in the middle. There was a combination desk and bureau. An open door led, he assumed, to the toilet, sink and shower. He looked back at the window. An AC unit hung on the sill, half in, half out. It appeared as if it might tumble from the room any moment. On the desk were a black rotary-dial telephone, an ashtray and another lamp. The waste can next to the desk brimmed with dry refuse.

He stepped inside, set down his suitcase. The rug was patched in places with silver duct tape, threadbare in the high-traffic spots. There were ash burns on it, on the bedspread as well. Revo pursed his lips. There was no way he was getting into that bed unclothed. He imagined the sheets, decided he'd just lay on the top — but where the hell was the pillow?

Revo stepped again, heard floorboards creak. He picked up the suitcase, tossed it on the bed. Paused to take a look at the single ornamental feature of the room — a mean little print, framed in unfinished wood, over the bedstead. It was a riverscape — could have been any river anywhere. He chose to interpret it as a picture of a bend in the Columbia, which flowed outside his room two-hundred yards away across the Interstate.

He moved toward the bathroom. He'd been holding the urge to piss for fifty miles or more. All that coffee — it had little effect on his ability to stay awake, but it sure affected his bladder.

He toggled the light in the bathroom. A bare bulb like the one in the front office washed light over the dirty sink. He looked in the filmy mirror, listened to the faucet drip. A towel that at one time had been white was folded on top of the toilet tank. He lifted the lid to the toilet, relieved himself.

A moth flitted past his head to collide and re-collide with the bulb.

He flushed, buttoned his fly. Looked around at more of the bathroom. There was untended garbage in the wastebasket here as well, a beer can, an empty pint of tequila. Wadded up toilet paper. He turned to the shower closet, noted the streaked plastic curtain. Pulled it to one side and saw what he thought were the abdomen and back legs of a bug disappearing into the rusty drain. There was a half-melted bar of soap waiting on a shelf. A thick hair clung to it, half interred like some rude, wiry fossil.

Revo turned and discovered the pillow for the bed. It had been stuffed into the confines of a towel bracket. It came away in his hands like a release of gas. Motes of dust whirled in its wake, and they spun and gathered until he clicked off the bathroom light.

He remembered he should call Nancy. He should advise his wife, waiting back in Boise, of his progress. Pulling his wallet out to retrieve a calling card, he stepped back into the tiny room for the telephone. Threw the pillow over onto the bed. At the desk, he lifted the handset to his ear, but heard dead air. Revo clicked the cradle-pins, anticipated engagement of the line, a welcoming dial tone. But again he encountered silence. The line was dead. Then he noticed a note on a card resting next to the phone: "Our lines are out. Come use the phone in the front office. *–Mgmt.*"

He grabbed the room key and stepped to the front door, spun the lock knob and fished the security chain from its portal. He pushed the door open, breathed in breeze-borne river air, took a half step outside and peered in the direction of the office. The light inside was off.

"Shit," he said, looking around, wondering whether he should go over and find the clerk. Probably the boy had gone home — it was after eleven — although it had only been a few minutes since Revo had arrived. He heard vehicles swishing by on the Interstate, small cars and the diesel roar of trucks in overdrive. The floodlight cast a shadow behind him, in through the half-open doorway. The yellow vacancy sign cast a second, subservient shadow on the door, a weird double-exposure of conflicted light. Revo regretted, once again, that he'd yet to purchase a cellular phone. Nancy would be worried, and he wondered whether he should fire up the rig and drive to a payphone. On the other hand, she probably was already asleep.

He decided he would rise early and drive away at dawn. He would call her then. Revo returned inside the room. He locked the door behind him, re-engaged the chain. He lay down on the mattress. He could feel his clothes bunching up on him, a day's worth of road grime on his skin. He couldn't fathom navigating the filthy shower tonight, that bar of soap on his body, that wiry hair. Revo thought of the plastic shower curtain dragging across his wet calves, the cloying greasiness of it against his skin. He shuddered. He might take a shower in the morning when it was light. After some rest, it seemed at least marginally possible he might step, nude, into that slimy place. At least, then, he'd be able to see what he was dealing with.

Revo reached for the pillow, tucked it under him. Odors of heads that had preceded his rose from it like pulpy secrets. He reached for the bedside lamp, discovered it had no cord, that he would have to rise again to toggle the light switch next to the door. Just as well, he thought — he'd forgotten to set his travel alarm. There was no clock in the room, and no way to leave a wake-up call.

He lifted himself out of the sagging bed, picked up his suitcase, rummaged through his clothes for the clock. Found it and punched buttons on its face for five-thirty. He flipped the switch; darkness dropped like a compression brake. Through air like ink, he used each step back toward the bed to evaluate his nearness to the mattress and avoid stumbling. *There it is, there.* He lay down again and turned onto his back, closed his eyes, opened them again.

Revo's vision adjusted quickly. Light bled across the thin curtains of the window. From this angle, he could barely discern the vacancy sign, blurry through the drapes. Its wan light washed him in weak yellow.

Revo shut his eyes again. But the exhaustion that had so beset him on the road evaded him now. His hands rested on the bedspread. He could feel pills and grit on the fabric with his fingertips. His head began to revolve with unlinked thoughts. He recognized that he was generally anxious, over nothing really. Weather might make him late on tomorrow's run to Bellingham. Nancy probably was awake, waiting for him to check in. She would want to tell him about the latest bills, where they were going to come up short. Same shit, different day. And this room — *what was with this room?*

Traffic sounds from I-5 wafted through the AC unit's grate. Light from the pole and the vacancy sign leached through the drapes. The river print brooded over the bed. Disquietude began to creep onto him. Revo could feel his flesh pulsing, pushing beneath the skin. He no longer was even slightly drowsy. He turned onto one side to see whether he could find a more comfortable position. Just relax, he told himself. *Relax.* But it was not possible. He tossed one way and

65

another, changing sides, onto his back, onto his belly. Odors from the pillow engulfed him. He rotated again, spec-ulating about the room. He heard an intermittent *plink* from the bathroom door, the loose faucet. *Plink* — there it was again, and he saw the corroded fixture, the droplet fall slowly, forever, then plash on a greenish-blue stain that surrounded the drain hole like a moldy corona. He heard little clicks, bugs he thought, their feet skittering across the scraped linoleum in the bathroom. Their exoskeletons clacked against shot bedsprings under him.

The air around him morphed unexpectedly red — it was suddenly as if he were in a photographic darkroom. Through this minor confusion, he glanced at the curtains, saw the light of the vacancy sign had been overcome. A red *NO* glared there now. He imagined a blood ruby dominating the flow of light, the overtone of the room. But he hadn't heard any more cars arrive, no people get out, no slamming doors. And the office had been closed, the clerk gone, when he had looked outside.

His clothing clung to him. Despite the sweat, Revo grew cold from the inside. He sensed the first loss of underpinning, a slow unknotting of his thoughts. Revo's mind was in overdrive, *unhinging*. He sought self-solace, a calming applied to himself from within himself.

But it wasn't working, this sort of dark-night pep talk — he began conjecture: were there bloodstains under the carpet? He could imagine
"–*Mgmt.*" scouring the bathroom, wiping blood with tarnished towels from failing grout around the commode, the rotting caulk snaking the shower closet. He wondered whether the room had been painted over, spatters occluded with new color. He began to smell blood, other fluids. He heard sounds through the walls, the movement of rodents or bugs. Thumps and creaks emanated from the next units to either side, infrequently at first, but gaining moment and rhythm.

Revo reached for the alarm, sensed the thick air separate and clot as his hand passed through. Its resistance was like moving limbs through floodwater. He brought the clock close, read *2:03*.

He had to piss again. But like a child frightened by things that are surely there waiting in the dark, he feared rising from the bed, resisted the notion of walking through this place. *This is ridiculous*, his mind said. At the same instant it told him, *No, this is real.*

Revo knew a horrible thing had happened here. A murder or suicide. Or perhaps an abduction and rape. Some kind of experiment or sacrament involving the flow of blood, buckets of it. He struggled against the baldness of this impression, wanted to laugh in the darkness

66

at its absurdness. Wanted his laughter to drown the dripping of water, the clacking of insects. Like an animal in a snare, the harder he struggled, the more inexorably became his entanglement. A web of dark speculation spun itself around his mind. If he could summon the courage to rise from the bed, he could flee before the spider arrived — because *this* spider would be one horrifically large bad-assed arachnid. He imagined its giant mandible opening and closing.

Pinpricks of sour panic rose across him. "Jesus," he said, through a terror that was rising, and it was an honest call, not an outburst of cursing. "I'm outta here." From very deep, Revo summoned steel courage and threw off his fear. He rose like a bullet, grabbed the suitcase. *Where's that key, where's that key?* He scrabbled in the red dark. *There!* On the edge of the desk.

But leaping up in the dark had temporarily retarded his motor skills. He reached for the key, but unable to clasp with fingers that fled just in front of terror, he clawed the fob off the desk into the wastebasket. He bent and reached into the maw of the basket to fish for the key.

Something bit his finger — the sting poked him with startling, flat coolness. His hand shot out, body recoiling. *What the fuck?* It was like there was a wasp down there, the ice in his wounded finger rising like mercury, quickly, to heat and flow. He held it up in the dark, could see drops spilling from the fingertip. Maybe it was an old razor blade in there — he wondered how current was his tetanus vaccine.

He reached blindly for the desk lamp, found the chain with his free hand. Fumbled for the knob, jerked light into being. His finger was bleeding profusely, dripping down to his palm as he held it there. He resisted the urge to put it in his mouth, to lick blood away and begin the salving process.

Revo staggered to the bathroom, ripped toilet tissue from its coil. Wrapped the tissue around the wound in a make-shift bandage. He returned to the desk, to the wastebasket, peered into its contents as if he were expecting sharp teeth to snap and spray foam.

A syringe nested there, like a venomous baby bird, among discarded paper and rubber tubing.

Revo's guts lurched. *Drugs* — there must have been an overdose, *that's* what's with this room. And he could see it — a man with another man in his arms, the second man's head cradled and far away, nodding. The spike is still in his arm, has fed smack into him, but way too much. And the first man is crying *No, no* while the second man is saturated with the poison. The rubber tubes dangle unflexed, having released the heroin like a warm killing flood. The dying man's heart pops like a dropped egg.

Now Revo shares a needle. And the idea of this — that the same needle that had punctured the skin and pumped evil fuel into the dead man had piled into his own flesh — swelled before him like a fabulous chimera. AIDS. Hepatitis. Dried blood. White powder. Four horsemen harried forth the bloated specter of the dead junkie from the print, dragging river weed and balmy moisture (the weeping companion had dumped the body, still warm and smack-saturated, in the river) into the room.

"Oh Jesus God," Revo moaned. "Oh Jesus God."

Revo fled without his clock and suitcase. *Screw the damage deposit. Let them mark whatever they want on it.*

As he plowed out of the lot, gears of the big Kenworth grabbing, he wrought jerking compliance from that big clutch pedal and saw through the rear-view mirror the pulsing red of the NO superimposed on the vacancy sign.

As Revo sped away, toilet paper still bunched around his finger, the roar of his truck faded. Stillness fell on the roadside inn. The NO blinked out. The vacancy sign cast neon yellow on the half-open door to lucky number three.

The whole place bathed in the color of jaundice.

CLOWNS IN THE WOODS

Rolf Heiman Masterson is sleeping. In his sleep he is having a dream of magnetic clarity, which he will not remember, except for confusing snatches and disturbing motes, when he wakes.

Outside the landscape of the dream, his eyeballs are jerking under tightly closed lids. Kicking out, he disturbs a cat sleeping at the foot of the bedclothes. Rolf is sweating, lightly at first, but will awaken abruptly to sheets soaked in the shape of him, a pillow with a dot of purple blood, and moisture around his eyes. The cat stands on the comforter, stretches, loses footing as the man moves again, bunches and leaps silently off the bed in a clean, inky arc onto carpet below, and pads away through the master suite door into the dark hall. In its feline brain, it senses something amiss from above, hackles raising, and wants to flee downstairs.

The sweet pulse of adrenaline pushed Rolf Masterson up a game trail, fast. No longer was he making any attempt at stealth and he'd crashed through three hundred feet of pathway, much of it overgrown with ferns, salmon berry, nettles, and other Cascades flora. Ducking under fallen limbs that thwarted the trail at neck height, leaping over trunks, his rifle grasped loosely in his right hand, he slowed from time to time to look for blood on the leaves, dirt, stones.

The trail forked, one route rising, the other veering off toward the small creek that drained this ravine and fell, ultimately, into the Wind River. Which way? He drew up abruptly to survey, to choose, knowing he must do so quickly. His heart pumped like the muscle of an ox, rhythm in his ears. He drew arid, stabbing breaths.

There. He discerned another set of blood drips on the left fork. Further up, stained leaves, stag's blood over raindrops, and up more — a massive deep-red splash on a tamarack trunk fallen seasons ago across the trail.

Rubbing sweat running from forehead and temples with his orange cap, Rolf headed up the elevated path, fighting the draw of the earth, fire in his hamstrings, slipping on mud and fungus and loose stones, falling. Scrambling on all fours, his coat tight around him, he reached for his rifle, pushed up on his knees and rose again, hastening on.

Twelve strides later, Rolf was seven and a half feet higher in elevation, scanning ahead for another sign of the hemorrhaging deer, listening for the discord of the animal's flight through thick woods. Rolf Masterson paused, then stepped again, one step too many, heard a pop as his right foot slid on a moist, exposed root, ankle rolled up like a book shuts, and knew right away he'd broken the joint.

A dagger slashed into his calf, surging upward around his kneecap, hugged his femur all the way up until it stabbed into his buttock, sending him crashing forward onto the path, onto his left knee — driving that patella into a loose chunk of feldspar that may have been an inch round but felt like the impact of a doomed airliner — and rolling over onto his left side in the wet foliage, further over, onto his back. He lay there gasping, cursing the horns of pain that rose from his ankle in waves, growing instantly cold, lying in his sweat.

He closed his eyes and lay his head back into the plants, angry now, and took five deep breaths. He opened his eyes and stared straight upward through conifer branches at a low, gray ceiling threatening rainfall again. His stomach rolled, and he fought nausea, moving his tongue around a dry mouth and swallowing saliva. He looked around: the forest was not so packed here. He'd injured himself in a minor clearing; the woods grew thicker further up the trail, to the northwest, and down the path from which he had come, toward the crotch of the valley, where the stream wound twenty yards away. If he followed the stream back down the valley for a mile and a half, it disappeared into a culvert under a logging road. He'd left his truck there two hours and ten minutes ago at 6:15 in the morning and would meet his companion, Kevin, there at noon to break for lunch.

Thirty-five minutes prior, he'd fired two bullets from his 30-30 broadside into a trophy white-tail buck from seventy-five yards, five points on one side of its rack, four on the other. A massive, beautiful animal that was thrown to the ground with the second shot then, somehow, stood again, gathered, and leapt down the trail gushing blood from its wounds. He'd tracked the buck for ten minutes, further up the stream-path, before branching here and breaking his ankle.

Shit shit shit. Through the pain, and wrestling vomit, he realized the deer would likely bleed to death further up the trail and never be retrieved. Someone would find a pile of bones next season after coyotes tore the carcass to pieces tonight after nightfall. The worst transgression a hunter could commit — to not finish the fucking job.

Rolf groaned and fought tears of frustration. And moved just a little and the ankle throbbed anew, demons biting into sinew, a tattoo applied from the inside, right on the bone, its marrow broiling. He gasped, close his eyes again, lay still and waiting for the heavy seas to subside.

There's no way I'm walking out of here on this. Opening his eyes again, he steeled himself and slowly, with precise measure, lifted onto his left elbow. Compelled to keep his ankle still, he dragged himself fully onto that side, then rolled over as a cattle brand seared the flesh around his right foot. His objective was a fallen tree eight feet away that had rolled and come to rest at the base of another trunk. He'd use it for a seat so he could think, the fallen tree for his buttocks, the live trunk forming the back of the chair.

He crawled toward it on two elbows and one knee, trailing the useless limb, dragging the rifle by its sling, peripheral vision fading until the chair became his only focus, at the end of a tunnel, like peering through the lenses of his rifle scope backwards. Muddy, soaking outside and inside his layers of clothing, gloves sopping filthy with soil, Rolf dragged himself the final twelve inches and, summoning every remaining miter of resolve, vaulted up and around, his buttocks dropping onto the log, his spine slamming into the upright tree.

He wondered for a long time whether he would pass out from the exertion, from the pain, as he sat there rasping out great gouts of exhalation into the cold air. A few raindrops fell again, and he turned his face to them, then leaned forward, thinking for a foolish moment that he'd pull off his boot, two wool socks and one nylon sock, and take a look at his ankle. He imagined it must be bruised nearly black. But he knew that even if he could manage the torment of removing the tight boot and socks, then his ankle would puff up like an eggplant. If he waited a while for the pain to become somewhat routine, prepared himself mentally, actually cinched up his boot laces for better support, he might be able to limp back down to the truck — downhill, after all — and meet Kevin perhaps an hour late. At noon, Kevin would wonder at first where Rolf was, might even become slightly alarmed that he wasn't back at the prearranged time. But even if Rolf got halfway back, he could probably shout loud enough to be heard from the truck, even over the gurgle and splash of the stream sucking down into the culvert.

He waited a while. The ankle's throbbing continued but had grown dull, and the nausea had been supplanted by shivering. He decided to rise and take an exploratory step, try to put weight on the ankle, and see what happened.

Stiff everywhere, he carefully stood with all of his weight on his left foot and slowly shifted his center of gravity to the right, gradually increasing pressure on his right foot. At about five percent, pain welled up in him like a geyser; at ten percent a nuclear warhead went off at every point on the right side of his body. At twenty percent, a supernova filled his corner of the universe.

He slumped back to the tree trunk and slid down until his butt rode the log again. The ankle throbbed anew, and he knew at that moment he wasn't walking anywhere, not now, not an hour from now, not six hours from now when it was dark out and coyotes were slinking through the firs and undergrowth — probably not seven weeks from now if he couldn't...

What an idiot, he suddenly thought. He'd fire a rifle S-O-S, easy. Three shots into the air, a minute apart each. Kevin would hear the rounds, realize there was trouble, return to the truck then head up Rolf's route. Kevin and Rolf both knew this valley system from years of deer hunting; Kevin likely knew exactly where Rolf was. And Rolf had plenty of shells with him. An hour after the first S-O-S, he'd fire another triad and start shouting, allowing Kevin to home in on him. Kevin, a strong man, could provide a crutch for him to hobble out. It would take them most of the day, but they'd get out by dark, then drive down into Stevenson to a clinic, or if nothing was open by then, westward into Washougal or Camas.

Through the pain, Rolf actually began to feel reasonably upbeat. He reached for his rifle, clicked the safety off, and fired into the clouds. The blast filled the silent woods, then quickly died on the wet folds of the valley. Rolf pulled his coat sleeve up, noted the second hand sweep his watch for fifty-two seconds, pulled the bolt back and ejected the spent shell, shoved another bullet home, raised the stock, pointed at God, and fired again.

He ejected the second shell, engaged the third, without thinking set the butt of the rifle down on his right boot — resting exactly on the seven bones of his metatarsus at the juncture of shin and foot-top — hunched forward lazy to wait another sixty seconds by his watch, reached down and pulled the trigger. For every action there is an opposite reaction, and spitting a bullet out the muzzle of a modern rifle at two-thousand feet per second with a hundred and sixty-five grains of gunpowder means the ass end of the gun is going to move the opposite direction of the bullet with equal force until it meets something solid, which in this careless instant happened to be Rolf Masterson's badly broken ankle.

He passed out, falling onto the forest floor like a bag of loose shit.

Rolf's home Friday evening from a ball-busting week of sixty-five hours at work since 6 a.m. last Monday morning, a work-week from hell he thought would never end, that finally has ended. Bruised from deadlines, falling into bed exhausted and then lying awake, finally nodding off and dreaming all night for four straight nights, waking in damp sheets; in the mirror: black half-moons under eyes filled with grit, crow's feet. Three cigarettes and twenty ounces of crappy coffee on the fifteen-mile commute.

Teresa wants to go eat Mexican food, and rent a video afterward, snuggle on the couch, maybe hit the hot tub afterward.

They drive to Mi Amigo in Rolf's pickup, eat two baskets of chips and salsa fast, two sizzling plates of fajitas wrapped in flour tortillas faster, pay, and leave with medicine balls where their stomachs used to be.

Stopping at the video store, Teresa wants to rent some woman's movie — a comedy or a love drama or some epic three hours long on two tapes. Rolf wants a spy thriller, murder movie, maybe a cult classic. They separate in the store, wander around, reading synopses of a dozen or so of the seven-hundred tapes in the place. Rolf passes the science fiction rack and draws up short, staring at the cardboard jacket of one of the movies.

Teresa finds him there, staring.

Rolf's dad Walter would take him deer hunting in Skamania County, in southwest Washington state, from the time Rolf was seven or eight years old. Son of German immigrants, the old-country Mastersons having hunted the Black Forest for scores of years and generations, Walter was determined that little Rolf learn the process, ethics and pleasure of hunting and forest-lore at a young age.

Rolf and Walter would drive the forty-five miles from Vancouver, up the Columbia River Gorge past Beacon Rock, past Stevenson, in the rain — Walter sipping coffee, Rolf enjoying cocoa — in the warm nest of Walter's 1962 Chevrolet pickup cab. The truck carried a wood canopy on back, and the wipers pushed soggy road grit across the radii of hemispheres on the windshield when logging trucks, slow, ahead, threw torrents of spray into them.

Slowing at the Carson cutoff, Walter would signal a left turn and pull off the highway onto Wind River Road, which climbed out of the Gorge past Carson and Stabler, hugging the Wind River into Gifford Pinchot National Forest. They'd pass through the Wind River Game Management Unit and enter the Siouxon near Panther Creek, pull off of paved road and wind through gravel for another few miles, gaining elevation.

In some dense part of the wilderness, Walter would select a campsite protected from wind and off the road. He and Rolf would spend the first morning setting up camp and, if the weather cleared, maybe hike up into the hills to get a view of Mount Adams or Mount St. Helens.

That night after their campfire had died, Rolf would climb into a sleeping bag next to his father's, both athwart the head of the canopy, and listen to radio serials — The Green Hornet and The Shadow — on a transistor set Walter had rigged from the truck's battery. When Walter thought Rolf was asleep, he'd reach up and flip the toggle switch on the radio, lie back and long for his wife, Rolf's mother, who had passed away when Rolf was four and a half. Rolf usually wasn't really asleep by then; he'd listen to the tap of raindrops on the roof of the canopy, the meter of Walter's alarm clock, his father's breathing, and drift off in warmth, next to his dad.

The clock would wake them at 4:45, and Walter would rise in the cold to light lanterns and heat water on a propane stove. Rousing Rolf with a shake of the little boy's shoulders, he'd say, gently, "Wake up Rolfie, today we'll get one." Warm in the sleeping bag and cold outside, Rolf would pull wool pants over his thermal underwear, two sweatshirts, and a hunter-orange coat in the lantern's half-light. An hour later, after eating some pastries for breakfast, Walter and Rolf would pull orange ponchos over their coats and hike out of camp, up the road to search for likely hunting territory.

Now ten, Rolf was out for the first time carrying a rifle, a single-shot .22 with no optics.

"Remember, the most important part of this rifle is right here," Walter explained again as they walked, pointing out the safety lever.

"I know dad."

They hiked on, and a few moments later Walter paused in the road and looked intently into a break in the woods. Rolf wondered what his father looked for; all he could see was trees and moss and ferns, every shade of green and brown, some mushrooms and weird tree fungus here and there, dripping branches.

"This way," his father said, stepping off the roads on a game trail.

Rolf followed him up the path for a hundred steps or so before the way plateaued and the trees opened up completely at the edge of a small clearing, perhaps half an acre of meadow grass, with a few skunk cabbages at the low spot to their left, west. At the south and east edges, to their right, was an outcrop of volcanic rock. The hill continued to rise to the north.

"I'm going up there," Walter turned and whispered, motioning back up the hill with his gloved hand. "You sit over on top of those rocks... you'll be able to watch this clearing and I'll climb up a mile or so, wait a while, then come back down and push deer into here."

"O.K. dad," Rolf agreed.

"I'll be back here in two hours, and that will seem like a long time," Walter said, and Rolf nodded. "But I want you to stay here until I come back. On the rocks. Watch for deer — the whitetailed deer like I showed you only. Don't shoot at anything you aren't sure of."

"I won't."

They parted, and Rolf hiked over to the rocks. Climbing around the back of the formation, he saw easy natural stairs to the high point, ascended to a seat where he could survey the clearing, and watched his father grow smaller as the man hiked around the east side of the meadow and disappeared into the forest where the hill rose again.

Ten-year-old Rolf sat alone in the Cascades wilderness growing colder, his fingers and toes starting to numb. Making up games in his mind was good for about ten minutes. He looked around the clearing, willing a deer out of the woods. Nothing. Five more minutes. Fog rolled into the clearing for a while, then cleared. He listened to the sounds of the forest waking up — birds and chipmunks, and the unmistakable clatter of a woodpecker.

He fished in his pocket for a candy bar. Walter gave him two per hunt, for energy, in case he got lost. Within five minutes he'd eaten both of them, stuffed the wrappers back in his pockets with dull, unfeeling fingers. Clouds moved quickly from northwest to southeast above him and dissipated a bit to allow half-sunlight to fall on the northwest half of the clearing. Rolf figured he'd been sitting there a half an hour.

Thinking of nothing in particular, Rolf heard a short hum then a click from between his ears, all in the space of a millisecond, confusion and blackness for a moment while something flew up through his throat and neck out the top of his little-boy head and popped somewhere between him and his own zenith. He swooned, and a vision of a bright-red helium-filled party balloon, string carelessly let go, faded upward, upward.

Rolfie. Upward, a drop of blood, wine, recedes as it ascends to Heaven... *Rolfie...*

Rolfie! A single tear slips from his eye, as he gazes up into light, and the balloon becomes a ruby, and is eclipsed by brilliance...

Rolf twitched and then comprehended his father's shout: "Rolfie!" He started and his eyes cleared, and Walter was standing below him in the meadow, shouting up at him on the rocks. His father was smiling: the son had fallen asleep but it was time to hike back to camp and get lunch.

"Wake up, Rolfie," Walter directed.

"I'm OK," Rolf said sleepily. "I'm OK... I'm coming."

Rolf rose and climbed down the back stairs of the rock formation, joined his father and hiked back to their camp, ringing in his ears fading.

Kevin waited at the truck, his rifle still loaded, for forty-five minutes after noon before he started to get concerned about Rolf's tardiness back from the morning hunt. A big beefy fellow, he was hungrier than crap, lit another cigarette and scanned up onto the hillside, straining for indications of Rolf's egress – snapped limbs, footfalls in mud and pebbles — over the sound of the stream running under the road.

Looking at his watch, he vowed to himself that he'd wait fifteen more minutes, then head up the route he knew Rolf was most likely to have taken. Several hours ago, he'd heard two reports, followed by what he thought might have been a signal – either that a hunter had taken an animal or was in distress – but he couldn't tell from which direction the shots had emanated as their sound waves wound in and out of ravines and bounced off clouds, fading to echo and nothing. Nevertheless, he'd abandoned his blind, and returned to the truck, arriving from a hardy climb below the road an hour ago.

In the hour that had passed, he'd encountered two passing vehicles, a gold-colored Dodge pickup and a green Jeep, nodding at the hunters inside who were pressing on up towards Little Soda Springs. He'd leaned on the truck, elbows on the hood, sat in the passenger's seat for a while, walked around the truck and pissed, smoked four cigarettes, and repeatedly surveyed the face of the hill in front of him.

It was time, now, to go in and see whether something had happened to Rolf. Making up his mind, he strode into the woods and began the aggressive climb next to the valley stream, hiking hard and without regard for noise, for thirty minutes, staying on the game trail that hugged the stream. Hot, he stopped in the trail to leave his coat; he'd collect it on the way out. Pausing to drink water from a canteen, he looked around and, purely by coincidence, his eyes fell on spent brass, a shell. He walked over to it, bent and picked it up, a 30-30 shell. Rolf's.

He looked around, his breath heavy. Decision time. Rolf had clearly discharged his rifle. Which way had he gone? Looking up the trail for a boot print or deer tracks or any sign of recent passage... there! Kevin saw the unmistakable impression of Rolf's boot, further up the trail, where it continued to run parallel to the stream, over fallen logs and under limbs.

"Rolf!" he shouted into the silence, and waited for a response from the forest. A void, complete peace of sound in the woods.

He turned ninety degrees to his left and hailed again, "Rolf!" Nothing.

Following Rolf's bootprints, Kevin came to a branch in the game path. Shit, he thought, which way? Then he discerned the disarray of the game trail where Rolf had first fallen, and his focus rose from that spot upward and he caught a glimpse of hunter orange and moving slightly to the left, Rolf's profile, sitting on a fallen log with his back resting against a live Douglas fir. No more than twelve yards from him, Kevin marveled that he had detected Rolf there, hidden by trees and the rise from the main trail.

"Rolf," he called, and Rolf stared straight ahead, eyes wide. *What the hell?*

"Rolf, what the hell's going on?" Kevin shouted, ascending the slippery rise. Rolf didn't move, and Kevin was confused. Kevin stood there, finally, facing Rolf, who looked straight ahead, didn't move except for the rise and fall of respiration, didn't blink, just stared straight ahead, his eyes as exposed as the summit of a mountain.

"What's the deal, Rolf," Kevin asked. Rolf, a mannequin modeling outdoor wear, sat silently. Kevin, alarmed, reached forward and touched Rolf's shoulder.

Rolf exploded from his seat like a lit firework, yelling at the top of his lungs, *Funny People!*, scaring the shit out of Kevin, who recoiled as if he'd stuck his hand into a wasp's nest. *Funny People! Funny People!* screaming into the mid-day forest, baying like a hound, and falling to the ground.

Rolf moved from his collapse while Kevin watched, speechless, mouth agape.

"I hurt myself, Kevin," he groaned.

"What?" Kevin asked from another world.

"I hurt my ankle it's broke."

Rolf pushed himself up onto all fours, rolled onto one side and stared at his ankle. *Huh?*

"My ankle... I hurt it Kevin I broke it I fired distress shots."

Rolf, a grown thirty-four year old man with sideburns and a beard and a mustache and raised like a man to be like John Wayne, began to cry. Kevin was stunned by this unbelievable site, Rolf weeping, tears flowing down his ruddy face into his beard. This giant of control Kevin had known all of his mature life sobbing before him, total confusion written in his expression, beholding his painless ankle.

"Jesus Christ, Rolf," he offered. "Come on... it's OK. Let's go back to the truck."

"What happened?" Rolf asked looking up at Kevin through

tears, finally acknowledging him, eyes clearing, comprehension returned.

"I have no fucking idea, man," Kevin replied, ferociously alarmed. "What are you freaking out about?" His voice rising, interrogation insistent, a knifepoint.

Rolf rose onto his feet, answering "I don't know," on the way up. Bewildered, he tested his footing, the strength of his right foot, finding no anomaly. By now, he'd gotten a grip on himself but still hadn't banished his confusion. Still hadn't chased away the feeling of oddness, out of sorts, something not quite right; his mind was racing.

"I don't know, Kevin," he repeated, his voice fully his own.

I don't know as they returned down the trail, over logs, bleeding buck forgotten, under limbs, to Kevin's abandoned coat, to the truck. *I don't know* silent, back to camp. Looking every once in a while out the window unaware, up.

A small amount of blood drops out of Rolf's left ear at night in the canopy, a single minute sphere that drips undetected on the red and green plaid of the sleeping bag lining, smears a little on his earlobe and dries to crust.

His dream is far advanced for the product of a ten-year-old cortex, lumens pumping through him as neurons fire, colors reverse through a prism into profound white, arc-welder's flame, Deneb straight overhead and falling. In his dream, he reaches up to catch it and beholds God's face.

Rolf is sleepwalking for the first time in his life.

He walks down the stairs from the hall next to his room in perfect cadence, rounds the landing, and enters his and Teresa's kitchen. Across the stove island near the twin sinks, the matter of air begins to separate, multiplying and dividing into a proto-shape, an unfinished spherical disturbance, holographic. It's the middle of the night; even so, Rolf can see through it, but the sink and faucets and sponges beyond and through it are distorted, as if viewed through a whorling prism. Filtered light bends around it from an unknown source. He can see the declination of hemispheres on motes of dust orbiting near the intruder.

Is that what it is?

The object changes shape, morphs into geometric patterns, glyphs of three dimensions, then four, as it forms a tableau and he sees himself as a small boy in hunter orange sitting on a rock in a clearing, looking upward, smiling and laughing *it's God it's God it's God,* clapping his ten-year-old palms together. His little boy's giggle fills the kitchen and warm fluid of the memory of his father Walter flows over him, and light is flowing down on the boy, him; it bounces off the rocks and emerges from the object and draws him, sleeping, walking, closer to the pulsing construct.

And pure illumination: by diamond light he sees in the shape a vision of himself in the woods, broken, wounded, and little people are gathered around him as he sits, poking at him – his chest his arms his legs his neck — with sharp sticks *They're Clowns* and prodding his ankle with a bigger, sharper stick with fire leaping from its tip and he feels protons of light enter his ankle as he stands in the kitchen. They leap up his leg and down the other as a counterstrike flows from the top of his head down both arms and out his fingertips, down his torso into his guts meeting the upward stroke at his groin and flying forward back into the shape a jet of light from his hard penis, back to his booted ankle in the vision, and he is *HEALED*, matter and tissue in disarray unified and mended and WHOLE.

As he watches this mystery from his sleep, light further rises, fills Rolf's world as the sky falls on him, he hears a short hum then a click from between his ears, all in the space of a millisecond, confusion and blackness for a moment. Something flies up through his throat and neck out the top of his head and pops somewhere between him and his own zenith. He swoons, and envisions a cat leaping backward up the stairs of his home, twin red lights refracted in its lenses, merging as the cat recedes, a drop of blood the petal of a rose in obsidian years ago lipstick on his mother's mouth *oh,* one of Teresa's nipples, objects of red fire in the brilliant black sky…

…and awakes with new comprehension.

Leamon comes to the end of the world and makes a game of all the shades of gray that come to mind. There is no demarcation between the sea and sky. That boundary — hypothetical as worm holes — is occluded in mist. Let's see: there's flannel (not really a synonym for gray, as flannel could be any number of colors, Leamon thinks). Silver or platinum, although there is no lustrous edge to what he views. Gunmetal, steel, slate — all these names of mineral and metal. Lead, then. *Leaden.*

Leamon expects the end of the world to be a place where the ocean's sculpting power has gutted the shore. Where anticlines testify to the stresses of earth in sea-bashed cliffs. Some place like Cape Horn or the northernmost point of Svalbard's northernmost isle. A ledge separating Van Diemann's Land from the Southern Ocean. But this end of the world is none of these things, none of these places. Rather, it is simply a blank expanse. Without form, and void, with nothing moving upon its face, and it goes forever.

And where is this ocean Leamon beholds? Where is this world's end where he contemplates lead? Because Leamon is, at this very moment, nearly a hundred miles from any sea. He is, in fact, in Black Diamond, Washington, a suburb of a suburb of a suburb of Seattle. An old mining town tucked in the first folds of the Cascades Mountains. But there again he stands in a vigorous gust, a gale. That's the Beaufort, viewed in the failing light of the oil works at Prudhoe Bay. *Lead.*

The end of the world stretches out before him, matrixed over the wound of an open-pit coal mine. He has been here all night. Dawn is coming up. With it comes his hands, and he sees, as he expected, a dried discoloration in the webs of his fingers, in the places where he couldn't wipe it off. *You know what that is,* says a part of Leamon's head, that mounded part that is hard and protrudes just a bit.

Leamon believes that he must have been hit in the head with a thrown stone. He recalls walking through downtown Seattle one morning — he thought it was morning — through a group of people who were routinely unremarkable. Except that as he passed through them, he took a blow to the skull. He remembered gathering the back of his head together, thinking that the protective carapace of his melon had been stove in and he must, more than anything, hold his brains to keep them from dropping out onto cement. He had no thought that any of the unremarkable people had rained down upon him an act of aggression. Headstaggered, he moved across the sidewalk as slowly and lighter-than-air as a rudderless dirigible. He murmured to forms that enveloped him then vanished into the soup from which they had come. He found his truck parked on Seneca, somehow drove the thirty-or-so miles back to his and Violet's trailer, slept, and then woke with blood staining his pillowslip. He held a mirror up to a mirror and craned to peer around the corners of an infinite chain of reflection. The bloodflow seemed to have stanched itself. Scabcrust matted his hair.

A randomly hurled stone seemed the most sensible explanation. Or maybe a brick dropped by accident from a scaffold. Perhaps, then, this begins not with a spinning stone but, rather, with a stack of bricks collectively as heavy as a cathedral bell, but individually weighty as well, substantial, each in its own right. A stack of bricks shelved in an orderly manner some distance above the sidewalk, so that the dislodging of one brick from the stack might not be such an odd, unlikely, unimaginable occurrence. A chance slip or grazing from a layer above, enough to dislodge a brick and send it tumbling.

Leamon gave it very little additional thought. From time to time he would rub the mound that had gathered there after the skin re-knitted. He joked with his mates at the Coal Shack over half-empty glasses that it was a button he could push when he needed a little extra thinking power. There were damp days — ubiquitous as they are in Seattle and Black Diamond — where the button ached as if someone were pressing it vigorously into his skull.

And there were moments when it arced and sputtered, as if wired to an outlet.

Or it may have happened that Violet clouted him upon the head as he reclined in a chair. Too often, in her assessment, Leamon's eyes had wandered onto the delicious spaces of her rivals. He would be careful, intending to hide his interest and appear innocently circumspect, but alongside her husband Violet is abundantly cunning. She sees his unmitigated interest, the way his slavering dog mouth curls up at the ends in a prurient smirk. The way the pins of his pupils point at her rivals, as would a needle seeking magnetic north.

So then as Leamon rests, it's possible that Violet slips up behind. It just may be that she wields a fireplace poker. As a ball-bat is swung in a powerful arc of intent, she so swings the poker. There is a hair-muted thud, the poker clatters onto the floor of their doublewide, and Leamon's head slumps. When he wakes above the blood-soaked pillow Violet is almost gone.

Leamon's button would be an outstanding delight for a phrenologist. A mushroom-shaped cap rising there with a film-thin skein of scar tissue stretched over it, a bump reader would palpate this node with special desire. The core inside, flesh that has healed marble-hard — how could anyone resist fondling such a growth? Leamon himself can barely keep his fingertips from it. But there are days the skin above Leamon's node seems especially thin. When the boundary between the cicatrix and the heart of his unified wound is as insubstantial as the tiniest lamination. Those days, when the lump throbs, Leamon is put in mind of this: there is a second, possibly superior intelligence, housed therein. And it wants out.

And, of course, Violet has gone missing. There are reports, however reputable or disreputable, that she has been seen in Enumclaw. A town to the southeast straddling the highway to the Pass.

But back to the brick.

As it tumbles, there is a transmogrification. At the atomic level, protons and electrons go whirling off. The baked silicate crystals that once were mud and clay and now comprise the dislodged brick go unstable, their weight and structure unbinding and recombining through an alchemy not understood in this century. Eighty-two protons now coalesce inside each nucleus; an equal number of electrons frantically seek stable orbits around this, and the brick's substance collapses and reshapes itself into a twirling projectile made up of that dense element which has an atomic weight of 207.2. Only bismuth, neptunium, protactinium, radium, thorium and uranium are heavier. A bullet splits the Seattle sky and lodges there, Leamon's nut, an acorn of lead.

This is (or isn't) like the enormous woman who didn't know she was pregnant. She simply has a bellyache, then a baby rockets from her. So Leamon knew not what he carried, the bullet lodged there quietly, for a time.

Look, it was only the one time that Leamon fell to this temptation. It was with Janet, poor woman, widowed. Her husband Martin the tree-feller trunk-crushed. Leamon couldn't bear to see her so distraught, so his act was one simply of succor. Was this not, then, a generosity? But Black Diamond, by the very smallness of it, gave constant voice to gossip. Where he believed he had made Janet a gift of companionship, a nearly innocent thing, the town soon whispered of infidelity. And it was not long before the accusations reached Violet's ears, mangled in the translation so as to be perceived, by her, as her husband's act of wantonness. The bastard! She went about with scarlet cheeks and vengeance in her guts.

Yet she would not let on, and with the passage of time Leamon thought the town's babble had faded and disappeared, as the moon will set behind the cliffs of Black Diamond's open pits.

And all the while Violet plotting. In and out of bars and roadhouses on the highway to Enumclaw, giggling there for the scuff-booted boys who would be cowboys, laughing above tepid, amber pitchers, eager for the turn of her eye. They will do anything for her after she entertains them in the rainy parking lot. She bends on her knees and takes the man-children who have affected bow-leggedness, one by one, into her mouth, promising each as she spits out his semen that the first one to kill her husband can have her all the way. Having just shuddered mightily and staggered back against the muddy quarter-panels of their 4X4s, their decimal eyes peer out of shadow in the penumbra of their cowboy hats. They stare straight into space as they nod. *Anything.* That Violet — she's got more kinks in her tail than Leamon knows about.

One of the cowboys follows Leamon into Seattle, where he is working under a general contractor to pour concrete into a square hole that will soon be the basement for a massive, four-star hotel. Leamon parks his pick-up, backing into the spot, on Seneca Street's hill, careful to manually set the brake. The assassin parks discreetly, a few autos to the south, downhill. He is a long way from Enumclaw, this farm hand. In the pocket of his wool-lined denim jacket, a shiny .38. The boy's head thrums with hangover, his stomach impossibly tied. He has on his mind the secrets Violet has promised: an older, more mature lady will do what he wants done back on the self-stained sheets in his apartment. He's never fucked anybody, and for the first prospect to be another man's wife! Giddiness floods him, tangles with the upset in his bowels, and there is a moment where he believes he will push the door open and reject the stale void in his stomach. In this state he almost misses Leamon walking down the sidewalk behind him. There is movement in the rear-view mirror; he barely perceives it, but turns slowly to see his target proceeding at a steady gait toward the jobsite.

A layer sets down his mortar trowel, mops his brow and scans Elliott Bay. Ferries ply the waters of Puget Sound, leaving wakes of broiling, fluorescent green. As the 8:02 nears the terminal and its whistle blasts, he reaches down next to him for his thermos. A coffee refill and short break are what he needs. His glove brushes the stack of bricks and sends one, unnoticed, over.

83

Leamon's node pulses as he pummels her. "You should see what I did to the fucker she brought with her," he will brag, some hours later, before his wife and her lover have been discovered. He will be sitting on a high stool, the sort whose cushion vomits out stuffing where the vinyl has failed. Shot glasses arrayed empty at his wrists where he will have placed them, one after the other. Regimental, they will stand in a straight line, or as near straight as his befogged motor skills allow. He will spend some time at this, pondering what he has done through the filter of his node.

Later he will hear a tip that comes veiled through cigarette smoke and bourbon, a message on the wind, a warning: *Sheriff's looking for you. Don' know what you done, but you better git.* Leamon digs in his pockets for cash, dried blood barely discernible on his blue jeans. Crumpled bills litter the pockmarked counter, and he is gone into the night.

The youthful cowboy with Violet's paradise on his brain is startled into the morning with the ferry's second blast. He feels the weight of metal in his pocket. Leamon walks a few yards ahead, alongside scaffolding that seems to always be somewhere, around every corner, at each mid-block, whenever rare occasions take the cowboy into the maze of this enormous city. There is a group huddled at the corner, waiting for the pedestrian signal to change before they cross, and Leamon has just breeched their huddle. Now is the time, and the cowboy withdraws the weapon, levels it at Leamon's head perfectly lined up in the sights, his finger slowly pulling, the silver pistol reflecting the distilled light of a gray morning, the hammer clicking back and cylinder turning nearly one-sixth of a circuit, his hand steady and heart rushing with the prospect of Violet's legs flung wide and a third whistle blast while the brick rushes to earth, and as the revolver's pin pings into the back of the shell igniting gunpowder and a shockwave of sound mitigated by the ferry's long tone of arrival, the brick smashes into his forearm and the bullet is diverted not so far from center, but far enough. One of those odd incredible happenstances people read about.

For the lead lodges there aside Leamon's scalp, the .38 clattering to the sidewalk and quickly collected before anyone can detect it, and the would-be killer sees his quarry stagger away and mourns the fading prospect of screwing Leamon's wife tonight, this very night, *you son of a bitch*, how could you walk away with a head wound like that?

Yet Leamon does, as we know.

All is not lost for the cowboy. "You get this for trying," Violet says, and rocks his world. There is not even a mote of question that he will try again, that Leamon is alive yet dead at this moment. The second attempt is a foregone conclusion, a result without a plan or set of proceeding circumstances yet, true, but nevertheless, a known fact. While Violet seems to nurse her husband back to health, applying salve and bandages to what Leamon believes is a brick wound — *I walked into a brick wall that wasn't even built yet!* he teases her, self-effacing — unclear, really, whether this is true or something more has happened, something with more meaning and ultimate consequence. Something that will set in motion an irrevocable chain reaction, a stacking of events one upon the other, which Leamon is beginning to suspect heralds an end. The end of the world, maybe.

The hot button of his head sparkles like a heated diamond encased in meat. He fingers it, can't keep his hands off it tonight. It pulses in the way he imagines distant objects in the universe would, fantastic barely understood constructs and hypotheses he has heard about but not understood on the radio news. Scientists discovering this or that, astronomers gazing back into the origins of the universe. His hard node strikes him as this sort of thing, and what marvels sometimes emanate from it! If only he could tune in, find its frequency.

On the night he does, what it reveals is an agony. *Not a brick, nor a stone, you ass. A bullet.*

"Who?" he asks aloud, alone.

You know.

So he is on guard, and when they come Leamon is ready.

POLES APART

Our mediator guided the four of us through tight, poorly lit halls backstage. When we emerged into the hall there was a great round of ovation from those gathered, and spotlights tracked us to a long table with four glasses of water, four microphones and very nice name placards done up in a fancy font. Our host gestured that we should take our seats so that formal introductions could begin. He stepped to an oak lectern, switched on an electric lamp that overhovered it like a strange bird, and consulted his freshly lit notes.

"Thank you for coming." The audience – which must have numbered several hundreds – roared anew. The spotlights trained on the four panelists faded or, rather, swung to focus one unified beam on Dr. Ivan Jack, distinguished holder of the Bourne Chair in Applied Philology at the university. Dr. Jack closed his eyes and held up his hands, then clapped them five or six times to join the applause. Then he held them up to quiet the crowd, which shortly cooperated and calmed for his opening remarks.

"As part of our premier lecture series – which I must say you have all attended and supported so faithfully – we have again gathered four, shall I say, eminences, from their respective fields." There was sporadic applause and a few enthusiastic calls from the gallery. Dr. Jack continued.

"First, at your farthest left, from Bar-Ilan University in Ramat Gan, Israel, Rabbi Rev har-Shoshanim, an eminent scholar in…" and here our mediator's voice faded to me as I noticed that the ceiling, far above, was frescoed and gilt in the classic tradition. The walls to either side of the audience were curtained in colossal sheets of red, plaited velvet. I saw two exit lamps burning greenly at the back. Dr. Jack went on to introduce Col. Alphonse Verdugo-Gamboa, a ranking officer in the Bolivian military, then the single woman panelist, immediately to my right, Senator Janice Broth, the Republican from Wisconsin. I sat on the end, and was introduced last as the most recent recipient of the Petaluma Prize, writer of several novels and essays, etcetera. The spotlight had moved from panelist to panelist during the introductions. I nodded into it and smiled as Dr. Jack read my *vitae*.

Dr. Jack reminded the audience that each one of us would make initial remarks, then would field audience questions. "Shall we begin?"

Verdugo-Gamboa went first:

"The great Empyrean heavens expand exponentially – as some theorize." He cleared his throat, found the result unsatisfactory, and took a sip of his water from underneath a prodigiously Latin mustache.

"Ah, much better." A couple of chortles came from the front rows. He set down the glass. "As I was saying, distant, exotic objects pulse and quake in parallax, exactly as they should. The black vacuum of outer space turns out to be not-so empty as white-frocked savants in spotless laboratories discover 'dark matter'" – here he held up the first two fingers of each hand and cricked them twice, simulating quotation marks – "flowing in the manner of undulating, pleasant algorithms. Several comets scribe elliptically around our Solar System as precisely as Swiss timepieces. An ice-vapor cloud rises in the atmosphere if Io, one of the Jovian moons; the sun's rays are refracted into all of the visible and invisible colors of the prism. The atomic weight of Osmium remains, and will always remain, 190.23. Off the Icelandic coast, the planet sulfurously rejuvenates itself, from very deep, in a long, hot magmatic trench. All eighteen planets circling a star in the direction of Cassiopeia arrive at a perfect alignment for a millisecond, then sweep on in their arcs..." The Colonel went on in this manner for a while and I began to wonder what he was getting at. Before I could figure it out, I heard him conclude in a most odd way, saying, "In summary, I am most gratified to inform you that E still equals MC^2, and *that* is a very fine thing indeed."

There was a great tumult of hand clapping and feet-stamping. Dr. Jack indulged it for a moment, then asked politely for order. When most of the noise had subsided, he asked for audience members to please save their approbations for the end in order to most efficiently use the evening's time. Then he called on Rabbi har-Shoshanim.

The Rabbi said something in Hebrew, realized his gaffe, crossed his fingertips over his chest, and guffawed like a donkey. "Quite so," he said, in clearly audible and unmistakable English. "Let's see, what have I to share?" He looked up at the frescoes, perhaps for a clue from the God of Abraham. "Yes, well, I have it on good faith that the British Parliament convenes and makes a momentous decision whilst Big Ben chimes Greenwich Mean Time into history."

Several forgetful audience members broke into clapping, remembered Dr. Jack's gentle admonitions to the contrary, and refolded their hands in their laps.

"There are persons in many places – but most of all in Nippon – who sing karaoke better than the original," har-Shoshanim continued. "There also is word that several young pops stars are rejecting Britneyesque sensuality in order to concentrate on their music. My daughter herself yesterday drove her car safely home for the weekend from a summer camp near our home in Tel Aviv, where she is a counselor-in-training. And at this moment, an artist in Haifa illuminates a *kitubah* for a betrothed couple. A baseball player hits a grand slam home run on his son's birthday; in a ballpark down the road, a pitcher hurls a no-hitter on his daughter's. At the airport in Thessalonica, a young businessman rushes into the arms of his ancient grandmother. But most gratifying, word has just come to me – that is to say, I received a fax in my hotel room this morning – that the city council of Oostende, Belgium, has repealed a five-hundred-year-old city ordinance banning kissing in public."

The crowd, unable to discipline itself, showered approval on the Jewish cleric. He took a long draught of his water, and indicated that Senator Broth should take it from there.

"Oh, my," she said. She had left the waxy rose signature of her lower lip on her water glass. "Of course, yes, that was very nice." She assumed a senatorial stature – no stranger to public speaking and a Toastmaster's success story – and her voice boomed in a way I could only describe as positively *stentorian*, if that is possible for a woman:

"A white wolf on the Athabascan high plains suckles her speckled pups." The high volume of her voice rendered the microphone mostly superfluous. "Meantime, off the coast of *Terra Incognita*, mariners have discovered what may be an altogether new species – *Magnapinnidae* – of giant sea squid, proving that speciation still is the order of the day. Photosynthesis continues in a million varieties of plants. Our lemon-yellow sun ripens citrus fruit. Waves crash against the rocks at Tierra del Fuego. The palm civet, which used to be native to Singapore, is making a comeback just over the border in Malaysia. A representative of the coelacanth species – in its 400-millionth year – paddles through a warm ovoid of seawater. Somewhere someone is undergoing a successful organ transplant. Also in Japan, the *shinkansen* trains bullet passengers from city to city with the unmitigated authority of omnipotent rulers. In Istanbul, a *muezzin* strikes the most tonally perfect E^b ever to launch from human lips..." – at this, I could have sworn I saw the Rabbi's eyes narrow ever so slightly – "Ivory Soap floats, and is 99.9 percent pure. A boy pins a corsage on his prom date in Urbana, Illinois. A hen outside of Oaxaca clucks atop a well-laid egg. An Estonian boy admires the fat thorax of an iridescent bug."

She stopped so suddenly that it took moments for me to comprehend that it was my turn. All three other panelists and Dr. Jack looked at me in earnest. The Latin American colonel cleared his throat from below his pendulous mustache.

"In all of this I am the one thing not functioning properly," I said. Dr. Jack made a small, nervous sound and someone from the back of the house catcalled down the aisle. I searched for the heckler but couldn't see anything for the damned spotlight. "Believe you me," I said, "the Second Law of Thermodynamics – that everything runs out of energy and falls apart – is alive and well. The Girl from Ipanema staggers drunk toward home one night and is raped in a back alley. Everything you eat has a cancer in it that would knock a coelacanth off a shit-wagon, if one were ever on a shit-wagon, which makes no sense since it's a fish. All of this bit about speciation and species and so forth – here's a change in taxonomy for you – ten-thousand of them disappear every day. Extinction is forever, baby."

The boos started raining. Over them I could hear Dr. Jack calling my name – "Mr. Ames, Mr. Ames..." He wanted my attention, and he meant *right* now.

"Volcanoes bury villages. Talk about shit that runs like clocks, modern-day witch-hunts are conducted with pogrom-like competence and your liberties are savaged in the greasy process. Somewhere an automaton screws up my insurance policy again, or some misanthrope at a bank sends me an NSF slip. Come to think of it, that same misanthrope may be stuffing a thousand-times-Xerox'd copy of a form rejection slip into an envelope right now in response to the most recent story I simultaneously submitted to twelve we-don't pay, arrogant-as-all-hell, pipe-smoking ephemeris, elbow-patched college literary rag editors. Elvis has left the building."

The crowd went berserk. A head of rotten cabbage exploded just short of its mark on the hardwood stage in front of our table.

"You are driven by a *Sturm und Drang* of which you have no conception!" I shouted. "There is no hope." I laughed insanely. "Your sexual organs are rotting off." A tomato knocked the contents of my waterglass on me. "$E = MC^3$!"

Later, rigged into the back of an ambulance, I listened to the siren wail and watched them plug the soft, private space of my skin with long needles the color of quicksilver.

SPOOKY TREE

"There he is, kids."

They strain against their seat belts, craning to see out the rear window. "Spooky Tree!" they squeal, simultaneously, with delight. "Spooky Tree!"

The tree, or what's left of it, is an old oak in the center of a pasture. It's been topped so many times, and the bark fallen away, it looks like the hoary figure of a headless giant whose trunk might, at any moment, split and rise to walk the earth. Torso, neck, arms — all chopped off.

"Tell us how he got his name," my boy demands from the back. "Yeah, tell us," my daughter agrees.

"Someday," I promise. "When you're older."

More than a hundred years had passed and the valley looked very much the same. The sun still rose over a near ridge and cast light down on morning fog. The stand of trees to the north had grown up and the solitary oak in the center of the field was twice as large. No indication remained that a battle had taken place here except that the surrounding acreage was listed on the National Historic Register and, once in a while, developers nearby would find lead balls in the soil. Bones of soldiers rested in graves beneath the valley, forgotten.

Hiram and Mike sprinted through high grass toward the old oak that nestled their tree fort. Hiram was black, Mike was white. Because of this, they weren't supposed to play together. They did, though, and the fort they had built together beckoned. No other pair of boys Hiram or Mike knew had anything to compare with it.

The construct was reached by ascending a ladder of small crosspieces nailed directly to the oak's stout trunk. Mike climbed the ladder quickly; it was harder for Hiram, who weighed about thirty pounds more. But once they were up, inside, they both were equally at ease. After all, the fort was the most significant thing either of them had accomplished – their domain, over which they had total control. This was especially important to Hiram, whose daddy was always drunk-punching on his mama's face, who got hassled all the time by cops or truant officers for swiping smokes from Bandy's or skipping school. Hiram thought most of his teachers were pricks because they made no secret they thought he was unresponsive and slow. Sometimes Hiram was jealous of Mike, a kid who brought home great report cards to happy parents with no effort at all. Mike always seemed to have the upper hand on things that mattered. And he was the most fantastic smoker Hiram had met since he moved out from Charleston.

When the boys reached the top, the ground looked a lot further down than the fort had looked up in the tree. Articles that would be impossible for a boy of twelve to carry up the ladder could be transferred from ground to tree with a rope hanging from a small hatch in the fort's floor. They'd pulled diverse items up into their nest: two old chairs from a dinette, a length of mildewed carpet, a stolen boom box.

"Hey, here's the surprise I promised ya," Mike shouted. He reached in the pocket of his jeans and produced a pack of non-filter Camels.

"Lemme see 'em," Hiram demanded. "No filters!" You tryin' to kill me?"

"You pussy!" Mike laughed. "You gonna tell me you're not smoking with me, your best buddy, just cuzza no filters?"

"Uh-uh." Hiram liked to sneak smokes, and he was *not* a pussy.

The pair sat in opposite chairs and exchanged looks across a busted table. The pack of Camels sat open in front of them and Mike reached for the pack to withdraw two smokes. Rolling one to Hiram, he struck a match to his own, then held it out for Hiram to get a light.

They puffed deeply, inhaling. Hiram hadn't used to inhale because it gave him huge headaches, but he had learned to after Mike explained that only *pussies* didn't inhale. Mike had a number of cool smoking tricks, including smoke rings and inhaling through his nose. Hiram could almost blow rings but whenever he tried to inhale through his nose it hurt so much he'd usually just about puke from coughing so hard. "Pussy!" Mike would laugh.

"Look!" Hiram said, "I did it!" A perfect ring of smoke floated over to Mike, slowly turning out on itself.

"Not too shabby, Hi. That was as cool a ring as I ever seen."

"Well, now for my surprise," Hiram announced, reaching down below the table. He pulled his pants-leg back over his calve and withdrew a dirty magazine from his tube sock.

Mike grabbed the mag from Hiram's hands and immediately turned to the foldout. "Hmmm. Looks pretty neat." He thumbed through the rest of the magazine, tossed it back over to Hiram, who had already seen it. Hiram scooted over and added it to a stack of skin mags growing in the corner.

"Ya know, I think we should rip off some old mattresses or something for this place," Mike said. He secretly hoped that Hiram would soon agree to lift the ban on bringing girls to the fort.

"What the hell for?" Hiram misunderstood Mike's suggestion as an idea for a sleepover in the fort. Since he wasn't allowed to play with Mike, he couldn't imagine the reaction of his parents if he were to ask whether he could sleep out with "that white boy."

"T'bring up chicks, ya dipshit!" Mike answered, as if the intent was obvious.

"Yeah, buy ain't no chicks comin' up in our fort," Hiram vowed, closing the issue.

The Hiram remembered what he was going to show Mike, something truly amazing and un-pussy enough to impress him. "Hey, check this out what my cousin showed me." He crawled over to the hatch for the rope transporter, cleared it. Hauling up the rope was hard, since it was thick and long. "Gimme a hand, ya wimp," he demanded. Mike crawled over and started pulling too. In a few seconds, the entire coil lay at their knees. Hiram found the end and held it up in front of their faces. "This is how to make a hangman's noose," he announced.

Hiram began to work the thick rope in his hands, doubling the rope back on itself, wrapping the knot once, twice … thirteen times. Then he fed the loose end through the smaller loop and pulled taut, his arms outstretched. The knot was complete.

"Well, shit. That's the coolest thing I ever saw," Mike adjudged. "Show me how."

"Nope."

"Aw come on. Don't be a prick, Hi."

"I just did it in front of your face — can't you even see?"

"Just show me again. Come on."

"All right," Hiram capitulated. "Just don't show anybody else." He undid the noose and began again. "Now ya take the rope and make a loop, and when you done that, ya wrap it real tight thirteen times, because that's the unluckiest number. If ya don't wrap it thirteen times, the person ya hang will come back as a ghost and..."

"Oh bullshit, Hiram, you think I'm a pussy? Believin' in ghosts?"

"Don't matter whether you believe or not, that's just why there's thirteen loops — OK, then you take this loose end, feed it through the little hole and pull tight. Then when you put it on the person's neck, you take up the slack on this part here, see? It slides through the loops and the rope goes tight. And then you hang 'im."

"Who?"

"Anybody you wanna."

"OK, lemme try now."

"Here ya go," Hiram conceded, tossing the noose at Mike's eager hands. He undid the noose, made his loop, began to wrap it and was on the ninth twist when Hiram first sensed something odd. Mike finished the thirteenth loop, fed the loose end through and pulled taut. "First try," he bragged as Hiram caught another flash *kill him* from an unknown source.

"Hey. You OK, Hi?" You look like you just seen the ghost you was talkin' about."

"Yeah. I'm all right. I just felt kinda weird for a second, like someone was tryin' to talk at me but it wasn't you. It was here though..."

"Where?"

kill him

"In the fort." Hiram was tuned into something urgent, confusing.

"Whatever," Mike shrugged, pulling the loop around his own head. "Hey, look at this — it fits."

"Hold the knot and pull up on the rope," Hiram advised.

Kill him

Mike complied and fully received the noose. He stood, as best could be managed with the low ceiling, now proud at his achievement. "Whaddaya think?"

"Excellent."

Kill Him...

Hiram was stunned. It was too much for him to comprehend. He wanted badly to understand, but could only kneel agape.

It was the goddamned tree! He felt himself start to get dizzy, barely managed to croak, "Hey Mike... no shit, somethin's happening, somethin's wrong with me I think..."

KILL Him... like it had more to say.

"What's wrong, Hi. You look like crap. Let's get down OK? OK?"

KILL HIM before he KILLS YOU!

Hiram understood.

"What the fuck's wrong with you Hiram? Why you lookin' at me like that. What'd I say?"

But Hiram didn't answer. Instead, he exploded from the crouch and thrust his hundred and twenty pounds against Mike's smaller frame. Mike flew backwards into the wall, which failed, exploding outward with the sickening crunch of splintering wood, and the plywood burst like cracking eggshell followed by Mike, noose wrapped.

93

He arced out in a sort of whirlwind of wood chips and plywood glue and rope, and the rope uncoiled and grew long like a copperhead, then struck, and its fangs buried themselves in his neck. He dangled there, swinging.

It was a long time before Hiram descended. When he did, he stood in front of Mike, who had long stopped swinging. Hiram lit one of the Camels, looked at Mike's popped tongue, blue lips, eyes like marbles.

"Pussy," he spat. Tears coursed his cheeks.

"See kids, Spooky Tree comes after children who have misbehaved. You can be laying there in your beds at night, thinking you've gotten away with something, that maybe me and Mommy don't know about it."

I was just kidding them, watching them wide-eyed in the rear-view mirror. My boy six, my daughter ten. Some sense of humor.

"You might hear a little tap against the window, or some scratching outside, like a mouse trying to get in.

"Sure, Dad," my daughter pips. She's old enough to know bullshit when she hears it.

"Sure enough," I nod. "Step over to the window and see what it is. If you don't mind those slimy, rotten, woody limbs crashing through the glass and pulling you out, carrying you off to wherever haunted trees hang out..."

My wife will kick my ass if they tell her I've been teasing them like this. They already have trouble staying in their beds all night, always coming in our room in the early hours.

The day following the skirmish dawned like most others: gray dew and mist blanketed the valley's trough. The only difference, really, was the stench and the bodies. Birds and small animals started making their morning sounds, and shafts of sunlight filtered through lean spots in the fog. Dewdrops sparkled like little jewels. A pack of wild dogs rooted around some of the bodies, taking exploratory bites.

The footsoldier woke unharmed. His ears rang; he'd been knocked unconscious by the concussion generated when a Rebel shell exploded on the other side of a horse next to him. The horse had borne a sergeant. The footsoldier had been lucky, just sprayed with horse and sergeant guts when the shell hit. He knew it was just as likely that it could be *he* who could be in a state of anatomical disarray like that of his fellows. The falling of a shell had a cold sort of randomness to it.

He rose, aching, surveyed his surroundings. Every few yards lay another soldier wrapped around torn canvas strips, under cots, bedrolling. Broken muskets and swords. The horses were grazing over to his left; they had moved away from two that had been hit by errant fire.

As the silver fog cleared, he was better able to appreciate the full extent of the skirmish. *It must have been huge,* he thought. There were hundreds of corpses and pieces of abandoned artillery littering the valley floor. *Lasted for hours.* But he could only remember the first few minutes. He thought about this a moment, then sank to his knees and bowed, offered a prayer.

When he rose and re-examined his surroundings, he realized most of the corpses were dressed in blue. The North had lost this engagement. His stomach dropped at the realization; there might be Confederate troops patrolling the area right now.

"Best be getting' the hell outta here, I guess," he muttered to those fallen around him. He offered a mock salute. "Be seein' ya," he said, then turned for a copse of trees to the west, beyond a large, solitary oak. This direction took him away from where the Rebels had harried his regiment on the east.

As he neared the big tree, his fears of being discovered by a Southern patrol multiplied. Being black, he knew they would kill him, or at least torture him before sending him south.

He stepped over a gray-clad soldier, noticed a yellow glint in the morning halflight, a firefly of color in his peripheral vision. He looked again, square on.

A gold tooth shown from the soldier's mouth, and he weighed his fears of detection against the monetary possibilities. Finding that the potential for money won out, he stooped to excise the gold. The foot soldier drew his knife, cut into the gums adjacent to the prize. He peeled the gums back, revealing the root and jawbone. His fingers worked the tooth, wiggling it back and forth, but it wouldn't dislodge. He rose and stood over the corpse, slammed a rifle butt down onto the jaw, and the dead soldier watched him through stupid eyes. The tooth came loose; he bent to retrieve it, then held it in his hand, smiling. Then he heard a voice say, "Hey, what you doin' there, boy?"

The gold tooth dropped from the footsoldier's hand, spinning slowly, from a great height.

He started to turn.

"Turn slowly, I got rifles all over you. Raise your arms."

The footsoldier complied, turned, saw a dozen Confederate cavalry. He pissed himself.

Laughter broke out among the men. "Ha! He's pissed hisself!" The group roared. "Nigger, y'all smell awful this morning," spoke one, their captain, he presumed.

He was conscious that he had begun to sweat through his blue uniform. The fabric, of which he had once been so proud, was soaking through at the armpits, at the small of the back. A dark, circular stain had spread on the front of his trousers. Now, this morning, the uniform was a symbol of his own demise. Either way, he wasn't getting out of this one: He knew *they* would never let him go. And he knew *he* would never return to work the Southern farms. The wool clutched his skin like talons and its weight pulled him down in the grass, next to the dead soldier, the wreckage of its mouth. In rejoinder, the footsoldier's mind weighed the likelihood of escape against the cost he knew he must now forfeit for the terrible conduct he'd visited on the Rebel soldier's body. He glanced over and a fly lit, walking in the sticky pulp that had once been lips.

A shot wracked his body, spun him over and down. Lying on the ground, he realized he'd taken a wound in the shoulder. The Rebel patrol dismounted its horses, towered over him.

"Get up, dead man," their captain demanded. He struggled to rise, his back in agony, left arm dangling, half covered in mud. His breath came in gasps.

"Let's give you a ride on the captain's mount, huh?" They pulled him to his feet, threw a rope over a low-hanging limb. "Get on the horse," the captain commanded.

The black man was no longer afraid, only sad. He thought of making love to his wife, of holding his baby child, of the embrace of his mother when he was a small plantation boy. He thought of sun and springtime and honeycomb as he slid his foot in the stirrup, mounted the animal. He held his chin high and fully received the hastily tied noose, one wrapped a couple of times around a slip knot. The horse whickered; the sound comforted him. He whispered a Sweet Jesus prayer and felt the horse move under him.

They thought the black Union footsoldier was dead when they pulled him down. Truth is, he was probably close. But he moaned, so they brutalized him and desecrated his body like savages.

Then they began to dig graves for the fallen Confederates. But they let the Union soldiers lay out in the sun, and it shown down like justice, and a lone crow watched from the branches of the oak. The putrefaction rose in septic layers, and the crow stared out at it, and cawed a long reprimand.

"Mommy, we can't sleep," croak our little ones through dry throats. They have collaborated in their unease, come down the hall to disturb our sleep. There is strength in numbers. How one of them summoned the courage to rise from his or her bed, alone, out of the nest of covers, out from the sacristy of blankets pulled overhead, is a mystery.

"Why honey?" my wife inquires through half-sleep, of the eldest, our daughter. "What's wrong?"

"It's Spooky Tree," my son says.

"He's outside," agrees my daughter.

Their eyes are as large and wide as silver dollars.

NO WEAPON FORMED AGAINST ME SHALL PROSPER

Today —

Hey, you. I see you turn yo head away. Look at me sideways, cause you think I'm shouting at the air. See these hands — I weave my signals with them. Send signals ta the stars. Have a way a getting through. Like somepin sharp and pointy. Ice pick, yeah.

Kick it out. What I am: the hammer a God. Douchebag, I know you grip that steering wheel tight. I can see yo knuckles white through the winda. I bet you warm in there, motherfucker. Well this my co'ner. You just visitin'. You in my worl' now. That's right, drive-by. I'm in the side a yo eye. Always, when you turn, just over yo shoulder. Angel and debo'. You glance away, I come closer. Til I'm right there fo you know it. Like yo shada.

Lotsa sons a bitches drive by like you every day. Don' give a damn how col' it is on my co'ner. In my kingdom you freeze yo ass off, bitch. My fingertips are glass. They nails made a diamond. You know this is a col', col' land. My daddy give me this land, and his daddy fo him. We the kings and princes of this co'ner you driving by. You gonna cross through here, you gotta pay the toll. Open it up, open that winda up. Shove me some green, Mr. Clean. Pass me the cash, Mr. Stash. Bring it, don' sing it — show me the pill. Take yo cocksucking hands out round that wheel and dig deep. You pass my cor'er and I'm yo priest. Confess it. You wanna do good you best hook up here. Make the sign a the cross. Cross yo hands in a sign. Strap yo hands cross these engines.

When this land was young I stood on this here co'ner. I was standing here when these streets was gol'. When vapor rise and shows the worl' colors you ain't never seen, I watched it all. When the mountains throw themselves up all aroun' us I was here. When the river flow by I drank. When the rain soak me I spat back at the sky. I reach out and rip the face off the moon at night. I suck lemon yellow from the sun, suck that juice out. Squeezed in my fist. I'm a shark and a wolf and a rooster and a hornet wrapped inta one. Lectricity flow through these veins. High voltage. Lightnin's teeth gnawing at yo throat. And they try ta gimme medicine! Take it, they said. Fuck em, kill em all. We'll let God see who stays and who goes, who gonna walk on gol' streets. We'll see who the enforcer. God's hammer, right here, right now. Sting you with my power. They's no weapon you can make that will bring me down.

Everybody passes here, won' look me straight on. Crackheads, adulterers, sneak thieves, ho'mongers. Roll me for what little I got.

Stare straight ahead at the streets used ta be gol'. Filthy pigs, bastards' sons, cum-drenched sluts. They say man came outta soup, crawled on land, become a monkey. Troop a nasty apes. Don' know what made you. You better find out cause you spill from God's hands, but you runnin. Turn round, I'm telling ya. The whole thing's fallin down, everything broken and crashed apart. Yo eyes roll back in yo freak head, you look at me. See yo terror-face in the black a my eyes. Yo own empty self starin back. Look at yo blank face. Nothin. That what you afraid a?

You got Christmas presents in that car I bet. Hundreds and hundreds a dollars worth. They wrapped in papers, huh — I'll wrap you some, cross my land without askin, drive by my co'ner. I rip yo scabs off and stomp em. Suck the marra out yo bones. Listen ta me. I'm yo preacher, yo minister, yo rev'ren. You better come up front, get on yo knees, let yo tongue go loose, get that power a God in you. Testify. Let that flame burs' up outta you. Drive-by sinner, you gonna burn.

What is it with these fuckin seagulls anyway? Gull shit falling like rain. Got some right here, splat on my pack. You can't believe how hard it is ta wash off. Got run outta McDonald's toilet this morning. Jus' trying ta clean up. The king gotta be clean. Gotta wash off all a that dirt. That filth. Best thing about a icy wind is it blow the stink away from you. That's the only good thing. All of it.

Sometimes you come ta my church, the church of the Holy Resurrection Stink Seagull King's Streetco'ner, you see how I say my praises. Smash in yo headlights, kick in yo dohs. Tha's how I prophesy. Bash them windas right out all the way round the car. Tell it! Snap that antenna off and whip yo ass til you praise yo Maker. When the spirit descend upon me I bus' you up. Black yo eye and fuck you in the ass. I dance on top a yo hood. Crack off yo chrome dome. Get it on. I'm a bullet shoot from a red-hot gun. The bullet king, king a everything.

Pull over and come up. Bring yo sorry ass on up ta this holy altar. Get down on yo knees. Put all fo's on these here ol'-gol' streets. Humble yoself and swalla all a yo pride. I think it'd be a good idea. Fo pride cometh befo the fall. Amen an amen.

Open that doh'. Gimme a ride.

Tomorrow —

Believing against all the evidence arrayed against him, Kirby still thinks he may yet get a ride. He jerks in fits on a corner where the off-ramp leaps from Interstate 5 and drops an endless chain of vehicles into a shopping mall's parking lot. Kirby shadowboxes ghosts, the Interstate Bridge that crosses the river to Washington from Oregon looming behind him. He moves like the guts of a clock, in cogged spasms and pendulations. It's like bullets are going off inside. A rage-core in him comes apart from what he's made of, what he's become, and is unbound from a palmful of speed — really just caffeine pills — he got at a truck stop outside of Salem two days ago.

Kirby's shouts fracture the November air as they leave his bruised lips. They are hurled from the hanks of his beard. Outraged and broken, Kirby looks as if he expects one of the passing vehicles to run him down. And as if part of him wants this more than any single thing he can imagine. But another part of him wants to execute a fashion of proactive revenge on the warm drivers ensconced in their auto thrones, fat asses thrust into leather and velour, ear-held cell phones corrupting their fat cerebra. Kirby's gas-jet eyes are so wide one could easily witness this: they are truly spheres jerking in his skull. He waves his arms, calling down a righteousness only he perceives. His arms terminate in bare, brittle digits that splay from severed-finger gloves. Overhead, the scudding clouds drop low and filthy as the clothes he wears. Only a thin band of clear air hovers over the mountains, impossibly far away. Kirby's cheeks are as subdued as stains on the moon's disc as it gathers the last light of day and shines its brutal platinum.

In the same way revolution appears in a prosperous town, he sneaks in. Unperceived. The first kernel of cancer in healthy tissue. *Homo excreta* gone haywire. People don't appreciate their situation. They have no faith in the gift of fear.

Some drivers who pass have their windows rolled down a bit to expel cigarette smoke. They catch snatches of his half-human, half-holy megaphone screams. Imprecations rise rejected from the quicksilver core of him. They *hear suck the marra out yo bones — listen ta me — I'm yo preacher* or *the rain soak me I spat back at the sky — I reach out and rip...* Snatches of rage. They are only slightly uneasy, looking through him then glancing abruptly away if those filthy hands swing toward them in wild arcs. They refuse to bear witness to his devolution, turn up the volume on the CD player.

While Kirby's mouth spews as if by chance, his mind is focused with brilliant clarity. He is in Desert Storm. He is squatting in the bowels of a tank. In its iron guts he sights, lining up rag-heads in the cross-hairs. There is a thump and a universe-filling roar as the tank spits a projectile. Shells rocket from the turret as venom is spat from an adder's hissing hole. Entire civilizations are smashed, eradicated before him. Sand becomes glass. Great gouts of flame leap at the sky, and oily smoke blooms like a black, black rose. A viscous mist of petroleum.

100

Sgt. Kirby Batanian is an agent of destruction. God's Hammer. Overhead, the helicopters of Armageddon. This is the Valley of Fucking Megiddo! His tank-mates whoop as another segment of an Iraqi column evaporates before them. "Jihad *that*, bitch," one of the servicemen screams, and he's laughing, giggling like a seven-year-old girl whose odd, unwed uncle tickles under her armpits.

Even as Kirby's cortex is wrapped around the desert tableau, his unconscious attempts at communication with the globe slip from his tongue. It is exactly the same as one of those old analog tapes that reaches its conclusion, is rewound, and played again. We keep hearing, "The king gotta be clean." We keep being accused of whore-mongering, smoking crack, refusing to confess our sins. He keeps promising a righteous accounting's coming down. He's a bullet from a red-hot gun, Kirby yells. His cheeks collect, then spray, invective in spurts as would the muzzle of a Gatling gun. But we aren't listening, for pity's sake. We are not hearing this. This is not happening. Not now, not ever. We drive on, our sacks and packages rustling in the back seat. Shit up to our ears.

As if he alone built Babel's Tower, he is rendered impossible to understand.

Seagulls wheel and dive, lifted on fresh wings from the riverbank. The temperature falls enough that exhaust vapor now rises visibly from tailpipes. In the east, the full moon has just hoisted itself over the broad shoulders of the Cascades Range. In a few moments it, too, will be occluded in clouds. Kirby raves in its light, coyote man, ugly beyond comprehension, slipping sideways and down, spinning in a bipolar maelstrom. A vortex braids his mind with deft hands.

When will he stop shouting? When will he just stop? Doesn't he know we simply drive by? That our troubles carry us past him?

Get thee behind us, Crazy Man. Lift thy eyes back into thy head and examine thy own brain. Even so, Kirby rants and gesticulates, describing cuneiform and stick-patterns with his darting paws, impossible parallelograms, circles that defy all known physical laws and never meet. He shrieks equations, breath exhaled into clouds that rise with their own heat and join the low, gray atmosphere. This angry articulation alters nothing, no one, never, but speeds from him flung in sparks. *My daddy give me this land, and his daddy fo him.* He flings excrement and feathers. Surely there is no God who can find a way through this man's gate.

That is our judgment as we drive slowly by, stop and go, foot alternating between the accelerator and the brake, cursing the asshole in front of us.

Thus have we willingly entered chaos.

Tonight —

I'm sorry. Have I mentioned how ashamed I am? That I apologize for the mess I've made of things? I'll be good now. My father tried to school me up but after he was gone my momma couldn't contain me. I was too big. But people have really been so good to me. I forget that I have more than I can say grace over. Much to be thankful for. It's only my own foolishness that finds me here, hunkered down in the shadows, tonight. I'll only be a little while, enough to doze. Then I'll move on.

I remember when they found Dylan and Leona frozen together on the side of an alley dumpster in downtown Portland. They were the consistency of a free mass of stone. And they were the same shade of gray. His eyes were glass eggs; hers had no vision in them. Their final embrace was ceramic, formed and glazed not with heat but with bitter cold.

Cold creeps over me now.

I was once like you. I had Christmas. I had blue eyes and I knew who my daddy was. But people have been stepping on my shoes and taking what little money I got. Tonight I can't even get a cup of coffee at the Circle K. The air that is shot at me is like air that slides down a glacier. My Salvation Army jacket is merely an inadequate film. A second, wearing skin. Ice-breeze flows through it as if it isn't even there. Eating trash is all that keeps me moving, that keeps me thawed. But there's a down side to this — I stay just on the precipice of numbness. I can't slip over that threshold into sleep.

Even though lots of lights are still on, the stores have all closed. The security patrol will come around soon and give me the move-along. Then I'll wander across River Road, descend to the bank and wrap myself in shrubs. That one light over there reminds me of a bright, red balloon. When I look at it I want to release this string. Tilt my head back and watch my balloon rise, a drop of wine, a drop of blood. Until it's a red pinprick and then disappears.

Sometime soon —

Kirby will get into the longest car he's ever seen. It will pull up to his corner on a mid-afternoon in which the sky has fallen so fast and so hard that people refuse to look up. To the rear, the car will stretch impossibly back, trainlike. Its hood will be as flat and broad as a plain. The trailing wisps of deep cloud will be so close to Kirby's head that he will think the top of him is lost in cloudcover forever as the door pulls even with him. The car will be white, shiny, with chrome strips in

102

places he never knew chrome strips could cling, chrome so brilliant and priceless it may be platinum.

He will get in the car and it will feel like home. Scales will fall from him.

Inside, there wait two ministering spirits. By this I mean angels, one with masculine form, one feminine. The man will be driving, the woman in the back seat. They will invite Kirby into the front seat, passenger side.

"Gotta get you outta the cold," the driver will say, and his voice will sound like the booming of surf. "Come on in here."

Kirby will push his backpack through the door into the receiving arms of the woman in the back seat. Then he'll slide onto the seat, the smell of brushed leather rising. "Thanks," he'll say. "Colder than hell today."

There will be silence for a few moments, during which Kirby will inventory the features of the car. Buttons and knobs sprout from the burnished dash. Green numerals glow from hollow niches. The man's hands grip the steering wheel at two and ten o'clock. A digital clock says it's time.

"Which way you headed?" the woman will ask. Melody in her voice.

"Wherever you goin," Kirby says. "Outta here, that's all I know."

She will explain the two are headed north in their fabulous car. Kirby will squint and shrug, imagining the front of the car on the Washington bank of the river and the rear deck still in Oregon. Its Columbia-spanning chassis will carry him across, and north, he thinks, is as good as any direction now. On the Interstate Bridge he checks to see that, yes, the car proceeds and follows him; its extraordinary wheelbase makes him dizzy.

Finally, they cross into Washington. They see signs for Hazel Dell and Ridgefield. Woodland. Kelso. They remain still. Longview and Ocean Beaches. After Castle Rock they cross the Toutle River. Then they are in flat, green country.

Kirby will notice that the driver and back-seat rider retain light. For as they cross mid-state and pass Chehalis and Centralia, dusk will have fallen. Luminosity will emanate from his hosts well in excess of that to be expected from the dashboard lights.

Finally Kirby will break the silence.

"Where are you folks from?" he asks.

The driver exchanges a rear-view glance with the female in back.

"From not too nearby," she says. The driver laughs quietly.

"No, seriously," Kirby persists.

The driver's eyes remain on the freeway ahead as he begins to speak. Kirby anticipates an answer, but not what he hears.

"My dad's house is full," the driver says.

"Beg pardon?"

"My dad's *house*," the man says. "It's full. There's no place to sit, sleep. Barely room to stand. Tons of people there."

Kirby will experience a fleeting moment of confusion. He looks over his shoulder into the back to see whether they're having one over on him. But the woman looks as if she understand the driver, like there's nothing odd going on here. For a while there is only the hum of tires on asphalt, airstream slipping by out in the darkness. Kirby looks out and cannot see anything.

"But it's empty," she will finally say.

"Empty," the man repeats.

"Empty?" Kirby asks thickly.

"His house," she says, "our dad's... house."

Kirby, incredulous, will point at the man driving.

"He just said it was full."

The man and woman share a glance again. She nods.

"Not without you," the driver will say, and warmth and daybreak will saturate Kirby Batanian like a flood. As pre-dawn dissipates in morning, in the collection and rising of sunlight, so will the white car sweep north, and up.

And on that day, an indifferent wind will blow across the abandoned corner of Babel and touch nothing.

YOU ARE NOT A FISHERMAN

Suppose that a few years ago you made an important decision to become a fisherman. From a boatworks you bought a seaworthy purse seiner. You procured a marina berth at the mouth of a river. You investigated the intricacies of navigation, net-mending and knot-tying, running a fishing firm, hiring hands. You studied the ways of herring, halibut and salmon — their habits, the hydrodynamics of their hulls through water, the movements of schools, their seasonal migrations. You learned to read clouds and waveforms and the cries of gulls.

Suppose that there was a period there — say, between the second and third year — where you really began to feel like a fisherman. People in the seaport town at the mouth of the river warmed to you. They saw that you cared for your vessel and that you were fair with your hires. They smiled at you in the taverns, invited you to sit with them for a draught, introduced you to their daughters. They began to accept you as one of them.

Suppose though, that when all of this was going so well, something awful happened. Perhaps you made a slight miscalculation in judgment and lost at sea one of the town's favorite sons. Or maybe he was simply too headstrong and careless, full of his youth and immortality, and foolish. You weren't to blame; he was. It could be that it was "just one of those things" that happens. Like the sort of incident you might read about from time to time in the newspaper. No one is to blame.

You hired Ferron based on the recommendation of his father, who often drank with you after the seiners and trawlers and longliners and gillnetters were back in port and tied up. Ferron's father was a veteran seaman, but had no openings on his crew. One thing you have to admit is that you should have looked more carefully into the young man. Indeed, even the most cursory assessment of his family might have served you well. Hadn't you noticed how boastful Ferron's father was, how full of himself and his accomplishments? If that didn't tip you off, what about the way he would leer at women, or flash the contents of his wallet at odd times? Ferron's father peppered his conversations with exaggerations. His mouth ejaculated curses like black, restless notes on staves. Didn't that seem excessive or strangely manic? As the old saw goes: the fruit falls near its tree.

But you were so pleased to have your immediate problem solved. An undermanned purse seiner at the height of the catch means backbreaking work for everyone, and the take is necessarily suboptimized.   A full complement of crew might make the difference between black ink and red in your ledger.   And Ferron appeared strong and robust, with large hands and keen vision.   His uncle promised he was intelligent and cooperative.   How could you have known that an impulsive lash drove him, one that was impossible to mitigate?

So you put out to sea with him, and the others — you and seven young men — out past the boomers that break on the shoreline.   Past that chaotic, monstrous swirl of black undertow that harries seafarers traversing the mouths of rivers.   Over the crests and troughs of waves your boat knifed through ocean waters the color of slate.   You cruised to the vanishing point, that flat sea-gray line that defines horizon and boundary.   Salty wind washed you, and spray fountained from your bow.   The ocean saturated you — all of you — even though you were geared head-to-foot for heavy weather.   You and your crew pursed in net after pregnant net.   You pumped a wildly wriggling profusion of fish and their sparking scales from the nets into your hold.

You had named your vessel *Assurance*.

For a time you and Ferron became companions.   At the onset, before he complicated things, you sensed in your relationship something akin to what you imagined grows up between fathers and sons.   Having no heir yourself, you found at times that you would think of him in that way.   Pride would thump in your breast when he hustled on deck or successfully troubleshot the malfunctioning winch.   Or when he authoritatively weighed the anchor.   You assumed a protective role at the taverns — a benevolence you afforded your entire crew but that was especially available for Ferron.   Once when tempers flared you held the jagged fangs of a broken bottle-top against the throat of a fisherman who had looked askance at your charge.   The glass shards barely dimpled the man's skin before he was begging Ferron's pardon with a besotted whimper.

"I warned him not to disrespect my crew or my vessel," you explained, later, to Ferron's father.

You had thought this action — and others like it you took or were willing to take — would seal irrevocably your bond with your crew, and especially Ferron.   That in the act of championing them you would gain the full measure of their regard and that they would then follow you loyally and with absolute faith.   They would make *Assurance* the most productive vessel in port.

Which is why Ferron's betrayal was such a stark, bleak thing.

Over the course of a season he began to question your direction — in small matters initially, then larger.   The first instance you can

106

recall as clearly as if it happened only moments ago: he speculated in front of you and his crewmates whether you should have tied off a rig with a bowline rather than a half hitch. There was nothing more remarkable about it than that. He said, "I wonder whether a bowline would hold better." You said nothing at first, then, "No, this knot, I think." The other crew looked away and did not comment.

When you think back on it — to that first infidelity — you ought to have been more careful. You ought to have seen it coming. Ferron's arrogant father and haughty bloodlines, and all of that, for one. And the way the young man carried himself — he never spent a moment wallowing in self-doubt or anxiety. He was supremely self-confident.

Purse seiners work as follows: Crew members pay out a net off the aft deck as the vessel encircles a school. The weighted net drops to form a deep curtain around the fish. Then, the net's bottom is drawn closed, or "pursed." Trapped in the closed circle may be hundreds or thousands of fish. They are pumped into the vessel's hold for return to port.

Ferron began to call into question your capabilities as a helmsman. He encircled you with a net of dissatisfaction that disintegrated into contempt and unruliness. He drew taut its base.

You wonder whether there were times or places along the course of this devolution where you might have affected a stop to it. Instances where you could have "nipped it in the bud." But all this self-examination, this alternate history-building, these scenarios — all of this is hopeless. It happened as it happened, or so you have said.

It was late in the season, so there was a deep need to maximize every catch. Emotions ran high as the seas themselves. You might have skipped a step or tried to take a shortcut — the reason is not as important as the incident itself. Your miscalculation caused the cable from the pump crane to foul. The net — just rising from the water — shuddered. Smoke poured from the crane's actuators, the cable slipped, frayed, snapped with a bang. A sharp report followed as a blocker device ricocheted off the cabin wall behind you — it sounded like a box full of lead sinkers striking the ground after falling from a great height. The net settled limply back into the ocean. You turned around: the cabin wall was deeply cratered, the edges of this new blemish splintered, and your boom swinger specialist — a pockmarked boy of seventeen — stood transfixed in his yellow slicker, head half a foot from the site of impact. The blocker device rested on the deck at his feet. The rest of the crew stood gawping.

You hear about this again and again in town. Over the course of several nights the story is played back with new, nettlesome dimensions. There are inaccuracies, embellishments, absurdities added to the narrative. The descriptions of your actions, motivations, demeanor, countenance, your words themselves, become a bloated miscegenation of facts and pseudofacts. You wonder who is doing this, who is talking this way, who is fomenting this ridicule and rebellion. You go from crewmember to crewmember to see who has spoken, but you know it is Ferron all the while. The one on whom you bestowed the most favor gives you Judas lips. You are mocked in the inns.

For an unsure captain will be the death of us all.

Assurance is in heavy seas. The waves are high and sometimes bash violently against your vessel's hull. The percussive meter of the Wickman 5AX below decks is translated through the soles of your feet — you derive some confidence from its pulse. Your main powerplant is as reliable as the heart of an ox. It propels *Assurance* faithfully, and you have begun to appreciate faithfulness in a way you could not have comprehended weeks earlier.

You are not far enough out to deploy the nets. The sky has grown close and dark — it seems as if you could reach out with your hand and take into your grasp those weighty clouds. Wind comes in substantial gusts. Fat rain quickens, and gulls wheel overhead shrieking insanely. Ferron is performing an act of maintenance on the auxiliary forward engine Hytex box that runs deck machinery on the bow decks as well as the forward thruster. His toolbox is canted at an angle across the deck planking; he kneels next to it. There is a single crewmember in the wheelhouse. The others are below decks.

"Ferron!" You amplify your summons with palms cupped around your mouth. He looks up. You wave him to amidships. He sets the wrench he is using back into the toolbox, raises himself to unstable footing and staggers down the deck, gloved hands gripping hand-rails and cables all the way to you. *Assurance* has turned so that the two of you are leeward from the cabin. The crater from the errant blocker device still has not been repaired; you have been too busy catching fish and seething in the crosshairs of Ferron's lies. But neither of you look at the splinters. "Can you have a look at the net?" you ask. You wave over your shoulder, indicating the general direction of the vessel's stern. "Sure," he says, pointing aft to indicate you should lead him. As if he will follow you anywhere.

You arrive at the stern where the gunwale is at its lowest so the net may be easily paid out. The beam sea has developed a yaw and roll in the ship whose severity calls even the most meticulous bracing into question. It's like standing upon a wildly slipping faultline — with no harnesses or safety lines about you. "Just there," you say, pointing down and around the bottom of the net. Ferron, grasping with one glove at the low rail and reaching around with the other arm, bends over. You pick up a gaff hook. "I can't see anything," he says. "No there, around a bit," you say. He kneels lower and the sea hits. It's almost a foregone conclusion. The gaff flies in a great arc. The last roll pitches Ferron hard against the short bulkhead and he loses his memory.

He spins down, drinks in and breathes the salt. He plays the fiddle with herring, salmon, anemones, frosty eels.

You sound a deceptive alarm with a calm masque of near-hysteria, shouting, "Man overboard! Oh God, Ferron's gone over the side!"

The crew circles. You are disconsolate in your desolation. Night falls and *Assurance* heads for port with holds void except for the rotting, scaly stench of a few herring left from the last catch, and deceit in the scuppers.

Now you know that you are not a fisherman. Have never been. Never will be. But rather, you are what you always feared, but would not admit, not even in your blackest, abandoned moments.

Blood welling just under his bruise-hardening skin.

Gray oceans sweeping the vessel. Ferron pursed beneath them, part of their fathoms now.

Whirling in the maelstrom.

LAMENTATIONS

Our first encounter with worshippers constituted only a brief glimpse across the water valley. We were hunting great tawny cats, and had followed a pair through the forest, down the side of the valley. As we approached the stream at its base, we spied them from a promontory.

"Behold," one of our younger brothers whispered. "Are they worshippers?"

There had been rumors of them around the consecrated fire for many moon cycles. Some of the stories possessed substance — actual eyewitness accounts of sightings, as well as interactions. They came to be known as "worshippers," for by their actions we created an interpretation that they sought to plead with us, to perform acts of penitence, to raise the sphere of praise, to thus glorify our deity. In some instances, we birthed this understanding: their wish was to offer themselves up in propitiation. The number of accounts of them accelerated, as if they rose spuriously with forest vapors.

We saw the group some time later from a closer viewpoint. We were still secreted in foliage and silence. There were four, mostly hairless, all with coats of bright white. They wore strange, multicolored skins. Of confusing construct, they seemed to have fur only atop their heads or surrounding their faces. We marveled at their freakishness: "How they must glow in the darkness!" one of our uncles said later, laughing. We did not appreciate that he prophesied.

They appeared to be establishing an encampment. Their labors seemed purposeful as they cracked limbs and cleared duff from the soil floor. Without pausing to observe any sort of rite or pay homage, one squatted and struck a fire by smashing rocks together, the spark leaping into flame from dry moss. Neither did the impertinent firestarter make any attempt to properly vector the ensuing smoke, so that within minutes the valley was choked with it. Its fragrance wafted in an uncontrolled, unholy manner, and offended us. The garishness of it, the trespass! We watched stone-faced, and had to remind ourselves that this — the great gulf between their evil practices and ours — comprised the reasons for their presence here in the forest. They had come as seekers, and were well acquainted with their own depravity. Still, during the course of ensuing days we had to repeatedly bring into being an understanding among ourselves of this. So deep, alien and contrary to circularity were their offenses.

On the second day, we saw another of the worshippers put a boar to sleep. We had returned the night prior, chattering about their oddness and brazenness, their senseless violations. The fire and smoke

110

had been strange and nerve-jangling in themselves. But the erection of what appeared to be shelters directly in contact with the dirt of the forest, as well as the uncontrolled noise of their utterances — often shrieking and piling into the vocalizations of each other — were offenses too profound to be grasped in a single viewing. The worshippers were stunning in their disregard for righteousness. We made a debate of the enormity of this all evening around a properly sanctified fire, with the smoke carefully conveyed from us by the shape of the canopy above. The following morning a smaller group of us returned to the outcrop to ascertain their preparations. We supposed a detailed surveillance of their morning habits would tell us the time and manner in which they would make an approach of proper humility. A longer look, which we now intended to take, would help us author an accommodation for their worship.

We heard sticks and foliage snap in the forest, the movement down-valley of an animal. Then we spied the boar through breaks in the trees, tusking trunks and dragging its hindquarters on a path worn by the repeated passage of the forest's blessed creatures.

The boar snorted and stomped. It honked a squealed challenge to the camp, and we saw one of the worshippers emerge from its shelter. It carried a long, limb-like object, and seemed to balance this thing between its shoulder and extended arm. Suddenly the worshipper's head dropped, looking along the length of the object. Then a flame jumped from the end opposite the worshipper. There was a startling roar — the whole forest and valley shook with it.

The boar left off its squealing and fell over asleep. Then the worshipper and two of its companions retrieved it. We watched them drag the boar to their encampment, butcher the creature and hideously roast it above their immoral flames and putrid woodsmoke.

All of this we ourselves witnessed, the hideous depravity yet stunning ingenuity of these supplicants. At the same time we took great umbrage at their assumptive coarseness, at the blackened sin of them, we were pleased in the observation, knowing that the fabulous was confirmed. We were confident in their intent — to seek out gods and pay homage. To serve as penitents in the wilderness, which is, at the core of it, a right and honorable thing. They disgusted and fascinated us. We again and again had to remind ourselves that their moral putrefaction was the very reason for their appearance here: those who are holy and whole do not need gods. Conversely, gods are needed most by the wicked.

We spent that night debating whether we should make our presence known. There quickly resulted two minds. One, there was a part of us that believed we should remain silent and further observe the worshippers. Only by watching a little more could we properly discover how depraved was their behavior, over time, and thus develop a proper approach to their redemption. The second part of us believed our revelation to them should be imminent. The worshippers had exhibited ill-enough behavior already. We wondered whether to delay would irretrievably befoul the sanctity of our forest. Already we detected blemishes in the green foliage around us, in the forest's holy, spherical fabric. We needed observe no more.

"We are gods," the second part argued, "and must not be made to look upon sin for too long, lest it steal some of the deity from us."

This argument won the night. The essence of godhood is perfect, spherical holiness. At the core of perfect, spherical holiness is the absolute intolerance for unholiness. The worshippers should be acknowledged, confronted, and allowed to seek and receive forgiveness. Until then, the forest's wholeness and circularity was gravely at risk. The time had come to act, and with the pure courage of gods.

The following morning we gathered from our trees and caves. Our leader placed himself solemnly in our path in a holy and respectful fashion to ensure our readiness to confer salvation. He inspected the brilliance and keenness of our implements. He placed around our necks holy amulets and then placed one around his own. He led us in an invocation. A buoyant, restoring spirit filled us. Our labor would birth great blessing and righteousness. Our forest would overfill with wholly round sanctity. This was our great purpose that morning.

We stole down game paths before the sun. Mists whirled in low spots as we passed. The waking sounds of the forest bestowed blessings on us. The voluptuous fragrance of the air filled our hearts with belief. In the first vision of the sun's rays, soft and golden-green through the canopy, we saw victory and glory.

We strode to the edge of their encampment and assembled in a line of holy confidence. Our leader called them out: "Come here and be cleansed!"

His command circled the camp and hung in the air for many moments. We heard the sound of movement but none of the worshippers appeared. Our gazes moved slowly from each of the shelters to rest on the faces of each other, then migrated — as one godly inquiry — to the face of our leader.

"Come out and be made clean!" he shouted, more zealously, at the nearest shelter. We stood in a line with our implements of holiness. Another moment passed, and doubt crept into the folds and hidden places of our mission. Where were the worshippers? Why did they delay their own salvation? Their sins were egregious — to ignore the resolution we so freely offered might amount to a sin so monstrous as to be irredeemable! We shuffled our feet, shifted weight from ankle to ankle. Our leader's hair stood.

The next things that transpired happened so quickly that the order of details might be beyond our ability to properly reconstruct. There was a flash of fire and a huge, engulfing clap. Our leader was made to go to sleep. He lay down in the dirt. The worshippers emerged. They were unimaginably ugly — complete fiends in appearance, monsters, ogres from the pit. Their stench overpowered, as if their evil flowed licentiously from every raw orifice. I can still hear their horrifying vocalizations in dreams that torment me. They waved hairless, pale limbs around, mixing a great wind of madness. They brandished the fire-spitting sticks. We lifted our holy implements. We drew into the shape of a holy circle around our fallen leader. Our backs were to him, our fronts toward the direction from which the worshippers might attempt to touch him. We glanced over our shoulders and saw that sacred juice was draining from a terrifying maw in him. He had fallen so that his amulet lay at the core of this wound. His hole was bright and wet and vivid. The color we saw must have a different, more horrifying name than red.

Slowly, without making a flash or noise again, the worshippers quieted. No more of us went to sleep. Without removing our eyes from the worshippers, we stooped to gather our leader in our holy arms. We left the presence of the worshippers without conferring redemption, or even a small spherical blessing, upon them. Had we mis-authored their intentions? Where we had thought we would encounter the contrite, gentle, shattered hearts of penitents, we had instead suffered an utter, even violent, rejection.

We knew this was a vastly wrong thing, to put a god to sleep. The wound was a curious thing, something we had never before beheld. It was shaped conically, the point of the cone being at the front side of our leader's chest and intersecting the plane of his chest with a hole the diameter of a small stream stone. But the base of the cone, which was conterminous with the flat of our leader's broad back, was as wide as a clenched fist. The volume of this imaginary cone was empty space. Put another way, the agent of our leader's sleep — from which he would clearly not awake — had stolen a part of his sacred body. Either that or — and this is utterly black and horrible and noncircular, and young gods should not even be made aware of it — his godly meat had simply vanished.

In the flickering light of sanctified fire, we again debated. If their intentions were to make of themselves supplicants, their manner was mystifying and outrageous. We had made worship as an entirely holy and pleasant experience — in fact, it was the reason for creation itself. That they should express worship in such a corrupted form, so opposite the perfect original so as to render it anti-worship, was grievous. We pondered this as smoke was perfectly vectored away from our fur, and we groomed one another, and reached no conclusion in our divine debate.

But later, as we were parting hair with our female, an answer manifested itself. She had expressed some reservations about the holiness of the redemptive encounter we, even yet, still planned with the worshippers. She feared, even then, deep in what we would have described as her weaker heart, that there might yet be more of us put to sleep. We had vilified her for her waning zeal. Her convictions were weak, and unworthy of deity such as she should cloak herself in.

"Then," she suggested, "perhaps the worshippers prefer to be approached at night."

We stopped, having just retrieved a nit from her hair. We observed its struggle in our fingertips, felt the hard shell of it burst under pressure, placed it between our lips and savored its consecrated taste.

Yes, perhaps she was right — it could be that they wished to worship at night. The bleakness and enormity of their sin may be too much to expose in the direct light of day. They might believe their own trespass so great and non-spherical that to reveal it under the justice of the sun was simply untenable, too humiliating, unendurable. So that making such a public, open, lighted propitiation would be beyond any penitent's capacity. They were, after all, only worshippers.

And so this line of thinking grew in us and we became convinced, because of our female and her ministrations, that the answer indeed lay in offering them repatriation under and in the deep unspecified confession of darkness. Naturally — how would any guilty creature prefer to have its guilt laid bare? In broad white light, so that the hideousness and corpulence of it was utterly exposed? Or under cover of darkness? The choice is obvious, or so it became to us that night.

We ventured from the grooming session to persuade the others of the wisdom and righteousness and perfect circularity of this new course of action, a plan to yet save the worshippers before the sun rose again. We gathered us in the sacred sleeping name of our leader. We stumbled from our dens and vales and mists, into the wan light cast by the dying embers of our sanctified fire. We uttered an incantation then

114

fanned the embers into a small flame. In its flickering light, we made known what our female had revealed to us.

At first we scoffed — that we should pay any heed to the advice of a goddess!

"You have fallen prey to her ministrations!" our uncle teased.

But we quickly drew ourself to full height. We made our countenance persuasive, and as similar to that of the sphere as possible. We argued that the source of truth is immaterial, so long as it remains truth.

"Witness the sphere itself!" we implored. "It is utterly holy and purely true, whether it derives from the lips of god or goddess."

And this — the notion that perfect redemption may better be executed at night — was exact and precise truth. We asked us to further consider the evidence for our new belief: would our leader be sleeping even now, forever, had we sought at first to administered mercy to the worshippers in the darkness of night? If we had dropped our instruments of grace upon them in the blackness, would we, as well as the entire forest around us, have come so precipitously close to their corrupting cries and glances and the stench of their daytime practices? Were not all of these abominations that sought to twist and pervert and putrefy our sanctity and perfect circularity — were they not all perpetrated in the lush, broad light of day?

We spoke as the oracle and prophet of our own godhead, and in this way, won all portions of us over, all in our own turn. Then we discovered we had no more convincing to accomplish, that we — to a god — were convinced as well. Not only was the cover of night the proper time for a great redemptive work, but we should not tarry. Every moment that brought dawn closer jeopardized the salvation of the worshippers. They, at that moment, slumbered in their valley encampment unaware not just of the proximity of their own damnation, but of our role in conquering it on their behalf. We encouraged our brothers and uncles: "We must hasten!"

We fell upon them like sanctified, purifying harriers.

That they feared us cannot be argued. They made us understand they wished to be sacrifices, so we obliged them with our sharp implements. We still hang from a thong around our neck the head of the yellow-haired one.

We remember this one for he was especially plaintive. His sins had been egregious, he claimed. He bowed and trembled in our presence, rising from his slumber to at first proffer excuses but instead, finally admitting his own depravity, laying his head to one side to better our angle of holy dispatch. His hairless skin glowed in the darkness, as our uncle foretold.

We emerged with the worshipper's fair head slung through a clasp on our belt. Purified fluid washed from the holy place where his neck had been separated from the corrupt part of him — his reeking body and its flailing limbs. Our brothers and uncles visited an extreme distillation on the encampment, separating the flesh from the pod, so to speak, disinfecting our forest of their evil. We watched as the malignant spirits flowed from their carcasses, mixed in a single anti-spherical specter and flew off over the canopy. Then there was silence of an absolute sort, a purity that bloomed like a fabulous black orchid.

Alas, the ungrateful, misologistic worshippers! It is clear that one of them rejected our mercy. In the holy confusion, one must have grown too fearful of the awful prospect of purification, of complete circularity. The alien discarded the notion of self-sacrifice and fled to the comfort of that which was more familiar, and easier, for him — the life of the unfulfilled, godless, still-seeking worshipper. It reveals his folly, to exchange holiness for a softer, easier road.

For after a number of nights passed, he returned to the forest fortified with more worshippers. Then they exacted a terrible revenge, having grotesquely misunderstood our gift to his former compatriots — those whom we had dispatched in love. He put our uncles and brothers to sleep, and, after defiling them, all the goddesses, including our female.

Only I escaped through the agency of holy stealthiness, to tell this unholy story.

They slaughtered the gods, and now they have no hope. So they have nothing.

TABLEAUX OF MURDER

Paul Rheese has sent a private car to pick me up. I'm to write a piece for a genre magazine on his life as a mystery writer, but everyone, including Rheese, understands that I am to collect material for a tribute, an obituary. Rheese's health is failing. It is rumored that he is cursed with numerous cancers, cysts, boils — that he is using a walker to get around his own mansion and seldom, if ever, venturing outside onto the grounds. I am also made to understand by his agent that this interview is rare indeed and, by inference, a privilege for which I should show the appropriate gratitude. To whom — Rheese himself or the agent — I'm not sure.

The car's there precisely on time, picks me up in Culver City. The Hispanic driver's a rental, I can see when he shows me his I.D.: Guilliaume Muñoz, Transportation Services, Inc. A rented chauffeur, which means Rheese has divested himself of most or all of his longtime staff. He knows he's going to die soon. Muñoz is holding the back door of the vehicle, a long, black Town Car, open for me. "Be seated, miss, *por favor*,' he says. "*Gracias,*" uttered, as I step into the vehicle and settle there on the leather.

Later the car winds through Beverly Hills. As we, Muñoz and I, enter Hollywood and start to climb higher, I can look back through the wide rear window and view the entire Los Angeles basin laid out. It's a sunny April day; I can see all the way to the San Gabriels to the east, down to the hump of Rancho Palos Verdes in the south. Palm trees, lifted up above everything, lean ever so slightly three or four degrees to face the sun's ecliptic. Soon Muñoz has driven me to an iron gate at the base of a long driveway. He says, "We're here, miss," and the gate opens, he cranks the wheel and we run up through a tunnel of eucalyptus and madrone, jacaranda, plum trees — ivy as groundcover to the sides. Despite the sunny day, it seems dark because of the overstory, but the driveway is clean black asphalt.

As we near the front of the mansion, Muñoz points out some excavation going on near gardens to one side — a tractor with a large dirt-bucket, some men. "Señor Rheese, he making some new buildings," the driver says, not directly to me, but to the air. His statement has touches of disbelief and chastisement in it: Muñoz knows Rheese's life draws to a conclusion, yet the famous author continues, even so near to his own demise, to spend money. I think to myself that Muñoz's statement reflects a struggling Hispanic driver who wouldn't appreciate this sort of conspicuous consumption; he would rather husband resources near the end. It would never occur to him to do otherwise. "Maybe he's crazy," I offer. *"Muy loco,"* Muñoz grins, spinning his forefinger around his right temple, and pulls up at a brick portico.

As the car stops, I open the door and step out, forgetting that my own egress is the concern of Muñoz. I see, too late, this frustrates the driver. *"Pardone,"* I say, meekly. But he's smiling, a man of grace. *"Da nada,"* he chuckles, *"Da nada, senorita."* The sun is high and the courtyard in front of the portico is clear of the cloying trees from the driveway. This places us below a bright, blue bowl, and I can smell wisteria and hyacinth, and an undercurrent of freshly exposed soil from the excavation. The workers there must be on break; I can't hear any of their machinery or the tractor. I look at my watch to ensure we are punctual: 12:55.

"You are ready to meet Señor Rheese now, *sí?"* Muñoz asks.

"Sí." I am looking around the still courtyard and luxuriating in the radiated, captured heat from the surrounding brickwork.

"Let me assist you, then, *por favor,"* Muñoz says, affably, and extends his arm, indicating that I should take it and we should ascend the stairs leading through the portico together. We do so, then stand before a large wooden door. Muñoz presses the call, which I can hear as faint as a baby peacock's *aaaarr* inside, from somewhere deep and far off.

After a moment, the door opens inward and another man appears. My appointment with Rheese is scheduled for an hour and a half, commencing at one o'clock. The door-opening man acknowledges Muñoz, extends his hands to me and the exchange is made as carefully and choreographed as a baton passed between a relay runner finishing and one starting her race. "Mr. Rheese will be with you in a moment, and Mr. Muñoz will wait with the car in the courtyard," the manservant says. I nod acknowledgment, and he seats me in an anteroom that is a tall, classic library. There are two overstuffed chairs here, a cherrywood table between them, and the shelves loom two stories over all of this. Light filters through one high multipaned window, but it's not the bright, mid-day light of the courtyard — the kind of light that suggests justice — but a subdued, wintry light filtered through branches — a halflight that signals abduction or loss. I fantasize the absurd for an instant: The trees from the drive must have moved up near the house to listen to my interview.

A few moments pass in the dim library and the subject of my interview tarries. I decide to rise and inspect the spines of some of these books — there must be several hundred titles in this room! I wonder whether this great writer has read all of them or whether, like many of us, he simply has an affinity, an addiction, to the shape and feel and

118

notion of the books, the objects, themselves. Whether, like many of us, he has the admirable intention to one day read them all. I step over to the shelf nearest my chair and discern the books are arranged alphabetically, by author regardless of topic or form: Hemingway, Herodotus, Homer, Hubble, Huxley... I reach out and retrieve a hardbound copy of Hesse's "*Siddhartha*," admire the clean, exact cut of its pages, run my finger up the cloth spine. I blow softly on the gilt top edge and watch eddies and currents of dust spiral away. As I am about to open the book, about to learn in which typefont this beautiful *objet d'art* is set, a salutation is exhaled from across the room.

"Miss Satriani, welcome."

I turn and see that he is an ogre. Just in beholding him, I witness that the rumored cancers have devastated his body. Open, on his face, sores. Bits of extremities simply missing, digits truncated under gauze. His left eye is hooded, filmed with a cataract and, in fact, the entire left side of him hangs flaccid, clearly the result of a recent stroke that must have gone unreported. He stoops over an aluminum walker, with his manservant behind him for support. I must be agape, because soon he says, "Don't let an old, sick man frighten you." He lifts one bandaged claw from the walker and gestures toward one of the seats. I make to place the Hesse volume back on its shelf, into its slot, but he stops me: "You're in the H's," he states. "What do you have there?"

"Hermann Hesse," I answer. "'*Siddhartha.*'"

"Oh yes, 'Siddhartha,' well... please don't replace it, Miss Satriani. Rather, I hope you will accept it as a gift, a souvenir of our visit this afternoon."

I want to decline the gift, but am silent instead as he approaches. I'm suddenly alarmed by the notion that he will want a handshake, that he will clasp my soft, clear skin, my bright nails, with those fetid, leprous half-fingers. This thought, the thought of his sick skin, is almost overwhelming. I hope I am not visibly shaken and I hope, *Oh God I hope,* that he does not extend his hand for a quick clasp between fellow writers. So relief washes me when, rather than approaching me for the loathsome shake, he falls into one of the chairs like a rubber bag of meat soup.

"Welcome to my home," he says," gesturing around him with his bandages. "I hope I haven't kept you waiting?"

"No, sir," I reply.

"Oh, please... there are no sirs here," he chuckles, and it comes out like the sound of a cicada and evolves into well over a minute of rough hacking, a cough that is an oracle of pending decay. He recovers and smiles through brown teeth that drop down and jut up out of gums nearly white. "Welcome," he says. "Oh, dear, I am repeating myself... so, then, let's get under way, shall we?"

"Yes," is all I am able to manage.

"We are writing an obituary, yes?" he asks. The directness of his question is astounding.

"Your agent, sir... I mean Mr. Rheese..."

"Call me Paul," he interrupts.

"OK, Paul, sir... I mean, Paul... your agent was careful to characterize this as a tribute feature to one of the great mystery writers of our time."

"Yes."

I pause and the silence weighs me down like a lead sinker. "So that's what I'm here to do."

"Then let's do it," he laughs, and I notice a small well of saliva overfills a pocket of his lips and spills, strings onto his collar. He notices, swipes at the mess with a handkerchief. "You have to forgive some of my — how shall I characterize it?" He looks at the ceiling, smiles when the phrase comes to him, looks directly at me again. "My lack of some very basic controls!"

I decide the best course is candor. "You're obviously very ill, Paul."

"Yes."

"Dying."

"Yes. Yes, I am."

"That will be an enormous loss for everyone who admires your work."

"But such a relief for me!" Again, he is laughing at his own wit, and his mirth devolves into great racking convulsions for another moment. When he finally recovers, he sends his manservant for refreshments, and says, to me, "Why don't we begin the interview?"

"OK, let's see..." I consult my notes, retrieve a hand-held tape recorder from my bag. Looking up at him, I ask permission to record his comments, since some interview subjects don't like this.

"Of course," he says.

"Great, then, um... uh... people who like your work say they like it for its realism. Has that been a goal of your work, Paul — realism?"

"Well, you know, they say a writer should write about what he or she knows, right?"

"Yes, that's true — that's one of the basics."

"And a writer should never try to create an experience from a vacuum, yes?"

"No, I mean, yes... well, your statement is correct."

"I tried to make anything I wrote, ever, realistic — I never tried to fake or force anything."

I think of a scene from his novel "*The Supervisor*," where the past of a former felon who's reformed and has a new job and a new life is discovered by his boss. The former felon revisits his felonious, former life just long enough to murder the supervisor hideously.

"How about in '*The Supervisor*,'" I ask. "I mean, that scene where Whelk murders his boss is so realistic, some people say there's no way that scene could have been written by anyone who hadn't eyewitnessed the act. That's quite a compliment, isn't it?"

"Well, yes, it's quite a compliment unless it's an accusation!" Rheese responds.

"May I use that?"

"Use what?"

"What you just said, the part about it being a compliment unless it's an accusation. It's perfect."

"Perfect," Rheese seems momentarily confused.

"For the piece I'm writing."

"Oh, yes." What I'm doing re-dawns on him. "Yes, the obit! Of course you may use it."

The refreshments arrive, iced tea with slices of lemon, and small cakes, petit-fours.

I start again. "I'm thinking of calling the piece '*Tableaux of Murder*.' What do you think?"

"Hmmm," he says. "First, let me congratulate you on a stunning phrase — tableaux of murder. I simply will have to work it in to my next novel, with your permission and the proper acknowledgment, of course. But then, unfortunately, we all know there most likely will be no next novel, so perhaps you *will* be so good as to use it in your piece, yes? As the title."

"Provisionally, at least, let's agree on that."

"Agreed."

"So, here's a question: Where have you gotten all your ideas for your stories – I mean, you have thirty-some-odd novels — where do the storylines come from?"

"Most I would say, from dreams."

"You must be a very troubled sleeper!"

"Well," he grinned, "yes, but I'm troubled when awake as well, so what's the difference?"

"Tell me about '*The Indigent*,'" I ask. "*The Indigent*" is his most recent novel, unavailable yet in paperback. It's about a homeless psychopath obsessed with the killing of fellow indigent persons, a

121

troubled woman who feels that with each murder she performs a service of mercy, a sort of fascistic euthanasia. "Or rather, I'm interested in the final murder scene in '*The Indigent*.'" I see that Rheese is instantly troubled.

"I don't know where that idea came from," he says.

"It was so realistic I couldn't sleep the clock around," I say.

"I'm not sure why — I mean, not sure what would distinguish it from the scores of other murder scenes in my books." At this point, I hear the tractor start up outside, the crew is going back to work on the new outbuilding after a long lunchbreak.

"It may have been one of those scenes from a dream," he says. "On the other hand, it may have been real — it maybe really happened."

The hair on the back of my neck raises for a second. "Surely, Paul, you didn't intend this interview as an opportunity to confess to a murder?"

The final murder in "*The Indigent*" is the undoing of the mercy killer herself. She is stalked by a wealthy entertainer, abducted and taken somewhere in the Hollywood Hills, raped, strangled, buried in a garden. She is never discovered, and her absence is never noted, and it's a perfect crime and an allegory for society's need for someone or something — some group — of unfortunates, who can be ignored, who are valueless. Who can be killed and erased without consequence.

"She was wistful, I think," he says. "That is, when she finally appreciated her position, she didn't panic, didn't struggle. She accepted it with what I thought was a hell of a lot of grace."

"You mean the last scene of '*The Indigent*' is true," I ask, much more than alarmed. "You did that?"

But he backtracks: "I'm not sure... it's so confusing. I remember wanting to know, after all my writing, how it felt — from both ends really, that is, from both perspectives. To be the murderer and the murderee, so to speak. I'm just not sure whether I actually did murder someone or whether it was a very vivid dream."

I can't believe what I'm hearing, but then I conclude he is engaging me in an elaborate hoax, he's just teasing me, he's affecting this great confusion for the benefit of my piece. "Of course, I'm just teasing you," he says, and I bathe in fresh naïve cheer. "Nevertheless, let me take you on a tour of the house. I'd like to show you where it might have happened."

I'll play along, I think, pleased that I have his number. I am a co-conspirator in his afternoon game, and it will make an interesting part of the magazine piece. I'm so pleased, because a construct like this — a *ruse!* — makes such interesting copy, and was so unanticipated. I'll

122

have to remember to thank Rheese's agent for this pleasant surprise. My editors will love it!

He rises with the help of the manservant, who has stayed in the room after delivering the refreshments, and the three of us depart the library. Down a brief hall to a door we go, and Rheese says, "We'll go downstairs first." The manservant opens the door and where I'm expecting stairs and wondering how Rheese will negotiate them, it's a lift that's inside. We gather in the small space, me closer than I would ever normally concede to Rheese and his sweet dying scent, and then the doors are sliding apart again and we emerge into a study with divans and lamps and a frieze of angels on one wall.

We gather in front of the first sofa, and Rheese points at it. "There," he states.

"What?"

"That's where I raped her."

The manservant betrays no reaction, and I am silent as well. I follow Rheese's gesture to the fabric of the couch, a rich velvetish burgundy, the sort of fabric that would never reveal a stain of any kind — whether blood or sex-juice.

"I tied her feet there, and there," Rheese points to the sofa legs, "and ran the rope underneath, back around here," he gestures again around the back of the couch, "and tied her hands with the same rope."

He expects me to speak. "In your dream, right? Or for real?"

"Like I say, I don't remember for sure."

He points again at the velvet cushions. "Try it," he says, "Have a seat."

Oh God, this is going to be so good in my piece! I think, and I sit on the couch without a second's hesitation. "Where's the rope?" I ask coquettishly. In fact, I'm starting to enjoy Rheese's game in a *physical* way, somewhere deep in my stomach. The muscles between my legs contract and clench, then relax in warmth. Rheese looms over me, even with his walker. He appears suddenly ghoulish, interested, prurient. His one bright eye flashes and he manages to aspirate, as a labored wheeze, "Don't tempt me..." These three words are filled with threat and promise, and then we both remember we are at the locus of Rheese's game for the benefit of my piece, his obituary — *tribute*, rather — and we laugh as I rise from the cloth the color of blood. "By the time I was finished, she was unconscious," he claims as we move through the study toward a door. "Let me show you where I killed her."

The three of us exit the study and enter a guestroom, at least I suppose that's what it is. There's a veiled, encurtained bed here with a giant cedar hope chest at its foot. The bed is as large as a small boat, with an oversized, stuffed mattress and huge, billowy pillows. We arrive at its starboard side and again he points.

"I laid her there and strangled her."

Without prompting I lie on the bed, reach my hands up above my head like a lounging feline and caress the fabric of the pillow shams. Writhe a little and grind my pelvis into the mattress. With my eyes, I invite Rheese to place his bandaged hands around my throat, to finally allow him to touch me. As he does so, reaching across the aluminum walker and downward, the odor of his failing flesh rises, and it smells of honeycomb and jasmine, and hyacinth and cocoa. I close my eyes and sense the feeble grip of his fingers, and wonder how much strength he has lost since the night he fucked her and killed her with his bare hands, *these* hands, in this very house.

I open my eyes because I hear the sound of him quietly crying, and sense the boundary of his pitiful confusion. I rise up on one side, roll off the mattress in dismount. He is staring at the floor. The room darkens, and I cannot discern why, and wonder whether it is the passing shade of his guilt, whether he is confessing after all, whether this is no game at all. Sweat breaks out in my armpits and the small of my back and on my scalp.

The manservant steps forward with a fresh handkerchief; Rheese makes no sign that he recognizes this kindness, just slumps above his walker. The manservant daubs at his eyes as Rheese is finally able to collect himself. "I'm sorry," he says. "I get so involved with my writing, with my characters. Every writer must do that, you know."

"Yes," I murmur, out of arms' reach.

I check my watch, note that almost two hours have passed. I cannot recall having asked some of my most important questions, nor do I recall the click of my 45-minute tape as it reached its conclusion and needed flipping. I'll have to hope I took some notes and can generally recall our conversation and experience together.

Next thing I know I hear the door ringing again, from the inside, of course, this time. The sound that struck me as the purling of a peacock has grown large in the interior of the mansion: AAAAARR. "Shall we all go see what that's all about?" Rheese asks. I am relieved that he will not, instead, send the manservant to leave us alone here, in this room, together with the specter of Rheese's contrition, or at least its very vague, very unclear possibility.

The three of us ascend in the elevator, proceed slowly down the front hall. The manservant opens the door and brilliant light spills in, warmth all over me. It's overwhelming to the extent that it takes me a moment to appreciate what's going on here. One of the workmen, one

124

of the excavators is standing in the doorway gesturing back to the work site, crossing himself, gibbering in Spanish. I hear the words from what seems like a distance. They sound like *muerte* and *cuerpo* and *cadáver*, but I'm simply standing there, half in and half out of the door. Then Señor Muñoz has me in the back of the Town Car and I can't remember saying goodbye to Rheese or the manservant, simply spilling out of the Town Car back at my flat in Culver City and stumbling upstairs with my keys, and then turning the lock, and a hot shower.

Paul Rheese died before the district attorney could file charges. The excavators had disturbed the shallow grave of a young female, aged eighteen to twenty-five years, nude of course, and in an advanced stage of decomposition. Even so, forensics confirmed she had been raped and strangled.

I listened to my tape and its record of what Rheese had said and during its initial 45 minutes. I examined my own body afterward. I read what the bastard had written on the inside cover of *"Siddhartha."*

I turned the tribute piece over to another freelancer. I knew I had much more than a magazine piece on Rheese's life. I had a whole book, a reference work of near miss, of escape.

Instead of an obit, I would write an epic on the random miracle of survival.

CUMBERLAND PLATEAU

Our doorbell rang one afternoon in early spring and Georgia called into the living room, "Honey, it's Red." I was watching the NCAA tournament on TV. Tennessee, so far, was kicking the snot out of St. Johns, but as a Vanderbilt alum, this was not an occasion for happiness. Any enemy of the Tennessee Volunteers was a friend of mine. "OK," I hollered, meaning *invite him in*. St. Johns was making a run late in the second half and I hoped it might set off a rally. I figured Red might like to join me for a few beers, an upset.

"Honey?" she called. A St. Johns forward stole the ball, raced down court alone, dunked the ball, and I could hear the crowd going nuts on the tube as Tennessee's coach called a time out. Then I heard my wife over the volume, again: *"Christopher!"* Georgia *means* it when she uses my full name. So I set my beer aside, stubbed out a smoke, went to the entryway.

Georgia was standing there with Red, our tall neighbor, who filled the frame like one of the college boys on the tube. But the similarity in appearance ended with height. Instead of gym shorts or tank tops, Red was in a flannel shirt, utility jeans, hiking boots and a fleece vest.

"Chris," he said.

"Afternoon Red," I acknowledged. "You watchin' the ballgame?"

"Who's on?" *I guessed not.*

"St. Johns and Tennessee." Whatever Red wanted, I was strongly hinting that my afternoon plans were no more complex than to see this ball game to its final horn.

"Oh."

"You wanna watch?" I asked. Red was from Florida; I didn't figure he'd much care about any game unless it involved Florida, Florida State or Miami.

"Naw," he said. Then he explained his presence at our door by offering: "I was wondering whether you'd like to go hiking."

Red had referred to his hikes periodically over the past few months, how he enjoyed them, how they kept him in shape, how he thought I might come along with him sometime. Wishing to be properly neighborly, I had indicated interest in the hikes — or the notion of hiking with Red — where there wasn't any, really. Apparently, I had feigned enthusiasm too often with the wrong man, because here was Red, in my doorway, like a thin collecting creditor.

"Uhh," I said, balancing neighborliness with the draw of the game's final quarter, and trying not to be painfully honest, but tactful. "Uhh."

Georgia, goddamn her, offered this kind endorsement for Red's proposal: "Wouldn't hurt to get your butt up off the couch." She was halfway kidding, halfway serious, of course. I rolled my eyes, which elicited a guffaw from Red, said, "Oh *thanks*, sweetheart," or something like that. "I just *love* your support — isn't she wonderful?" This last comment, to Red, an appeal for him to side with me, an appeal to the conspiracy of men. I'd forgotten, for a moment, it was he who wanted to rob me of the final quarter of the basketball game.

Instead, he dramatized a stolen glance at my buttocks, feigned wide-eyed fear, and uttered in perfect deadpan: "It is growing rathuh large, suh."

Georgia started giggling, and I had to laugh too. Red was a humorous fellow, and in no more than a second I found myself attracted to his company and in mind of forsaking the ball game. Red had been a good neighbor, particularly friendly when me and Georgia had upgraded into the neighborhood a year ago after I'd been promoted to a management job with NASA after fifteen years. He and Missy had been among the first neighbors to visit. Red had one of those universal faces everyone has met before, memorable and familiar, I thought during the introductions a year ago.

"I reckon' yer right," I agreed. "Now where are my hiking boots, woman?"

Red and I hiked up past the cul-de-sac where we lived onto the face of a hill that had been given the place name Sugar Tree Point and bristled with Huntsville's tallest radio tower. It was a typical northern Alabama mid-March and we all were weary of the shades of brown. Brown fields, brown hillsides, brown streets — even the sky, although fundamentally gray, seemed in places, at times, to be tinted with brown, a characteristic of the winter months in the South. I'd never been up on Sugar Tree Point, but the trail was well-defined, probably by humans during spring, summer and fall, but by deer for the past three months. Last autumn's fallen leaves, soggy shades of brown, of course, still covered the ground everywhere. The bare sticks of deciduous trees — only a few weeks from their first buds — pointed at the brownish-gray sky.

The trail wound steeply up the face of a hillside that formed a preliminary foothill of the Cumberland Plateau, the last southern lumbar of Appalachia before North America slides like sweat into the Gulf of Mexico. Red was in shape and practically bounded up the trail, which in places rose at a grade that necessitated falling forward onto all fours and crawling. Too, in spots, the trail was saturated with water and had turned muddy. So it was a rough climb for me, out of shape, with a pair of substantial buttocks and a gut in front to match, with a pack-a-day habit (that's *both* a pack of cigarettes and, often, a six-pack of beer). I was wheezing and blustering, soaked through my armpits and the liner of my Commodores ballcap, heart racing and blood roaring. So Red must have thought I'd simply succumbed to temporary exhaustion when we rounded a rare stand of green jack pine and I slipped onto my knees and stared.

In front of us, impossibly, on the side of a hill thousands of yards from any road, I saw the rusted-out shell of an automobile. It rested there with trees growing right up around it, so close that the presence of the car here could not be solved with logic. How could it have come to be here, aside from a helicopter drop? The trunk was popped, rubber tires gone. It was beached on its raw wheels, canted maybe thirty-five degrees nose down. Kudzu grew out the glassless back window, as it grows everywhere in Alabama, with authority. The rear driver's side door was ajar, and a network of bullet holes moved up the rusted steel. All the chrome was gone, or rusted as brown as the rest of the hulk. Taillights, gone; license tags, gone; mirrors, upholstery, headlamps, gone.

The car's presence would have been mystery enough, but this riddle — how it came to be here, an anomaly in the woods, rusted, bullet-ridden — was secondary in my mind at that moment, gasping on my knees halfway up the side of Sugar Tree Point.

Because I *knew* this automobile.

I was flat busted after my freshman year at Vanderbilt, which would have been, let's see — the summer of 1973. It happened because I was studying for finals and holding a job in the Student Union cafeteria, and I couldn't do both very well. So with a couple of weeks to go, I quit the job.

My folks had me on a sort of allowance. That is to say, they gave me a certain amount for spending every quarter, and from that stipend I was to parse out expenses — clothes, bus tickets for the ride from Nashville to Anniston, Alabama — that sort of thing. Basically, anything beyond the tuition and books, if I remember correctly. I was allowed to spend some of it on fun things, too. But I blew all the money on beer parties and pot mostly — got so that I enjoyed my new independence so much I had to get the job at the Student Union to keep up.

128

After finals, which went all right, I was fixing to get the two-hundred miles home by hitchhiking. It wasn't the best solution, but I'd advertised for a ride south for a couple of weeks on the bulletin boards, hoping I'd make it lucky and hook up with some cute girls from my part of the country. Or ugly girls even; I just wanted to get home for summer, especially before stock car season got into full swing out at the Speedway. And having no money and no prospects in Nashville, and with Mom and Pop expecting me "sometime in June," I figured that my thumb was probably the best, and last, resource I possessed.

I got a quick ride from one of my roommate's sister's roommates south on Interstate 65 from the campus to Brentwood. We shared an afternoon joint on the highway, and she started to look kind of foxy sitting in the driver's seat with her hair blowing, a brief halter top, nice thighs emerging from summer shorts. But she dropped me off at a truck stop without me scoring anything but her telephone number. There, after some supper, I made a cardboard sign that read HUNTSVILLE BIRMINGHAM ANNISTON — the first two indicated a general southerly migration, the last a hope to get lucky with the early '70s equivalent of a direct flight. As twilight assembled, I wrestled my backpack into position, carried the sign and my thumb to the on-ramp, pointed both of them in the general direction of Alabama, and waited.

Even though it wasn't summer yet, the asphalt had absorbed plenty of the day's heat. It radiated through the soles of my sneakers. The onset of the deep humidity that characterized this part of the world was a couple of weeks away yet. Even so, the air was damp and I inhaled moisture, smelled the warm damp as fireflies glowed briefly and went out over at the edges of the parking lot. Between the rush of vehicles passing on the highway, I could hear the white noise of cicadas.

Not long, five minutes, a few trucks and cars, maybe, and then a car slowed on approach and pulled to the shoulder a few yards after it passed me. I tucked my sign under my arm and jogged up to the passenger door.

The driver reached across and levered the doorlatch, pushed the heavy door outward, open. "Hey, thanks, man," I said.

"No problem," the man answered. "You can put those in the back seat," he said, indicating my pack and the sign. A ginny odor flushed with burnt tobacco emerged from the open door. "C'mon in."

I complied, slipped into the seat, pulled the door shut with a meaty chunk. The smell of ingested alcohol and tobacco was even more acute — the man had been driving without benefit of open window for some time, I'd judged. Maybe hadn't even cracked the wing window. Even so, a ride was a ride.

129

"How far you goin?" I asked.

"'Ontsvull,'" he murmured through what was clearly an acute inebriation. Huntsville. "Name's Theron," he said, offering his hand, lurching away from the shoulder.

"Fred," I lied, offering him a false name. "Thanks for stoppin.'"

"Yer very welcome," he replied, gaining speed on the on-ramp. I noticed in the headlamps ahead the white stripe on my side of the road move way over to the right, then swerve back until it was under where I was sitting, then oscillate again. I looked over at the man, Theron, who had both hands off the wheel. He was fumbling with a pack of Lucky Strikes, steering by applying pressure at the wheel's four o'clock and eight o'clock positions with his knees. Theron was obviously in no shape to be stunt driving, though I'll be damned if he wasn't able to get that smoke lit.

"Wanna smoke?" he asked.

"Sure," I agreed, and he tossed the pack over to me. I looked for a seat belt, but there wasn't one. So I lit the smoke, cracked the wing window to a vacuum rush of air, and hoped for angelic protection. Not that I believed in that kind of thing.

Theron drove for a while, weaving some but mostly keeping generally between the white line and the yellow lines, squinting into oncoming headlights, and we smoked without conversation. Then he drifted too far into the opposite lane, and snatched the wheel to the right simultaneously with the blaring of an oncoming horn. He swerved back into our southbound lane, giggled and coughed. The coughed evolved into a hack, and I saw some of the matter of his lungs ejected in the analog light from the dashboard. I looked over at the speedometer; the needle bounced around 75, and I thought, *Enough is enough.*

"Hey Theron, man," I said.

"Hmmm?"

"Theron."

"Yeah."

"Dude, I think you're too fucked up to drive."

He thought about this for a moment. Long enough that I wondered whether he was fixing to pull a pistol out and cap me, maybe, or whether he'd dissolve into tears, or whether his eyes would shrink to red slits and he'd look over at me and lick air with a cottonmouth tongue and say, "I'll show you what fucked up is, *Fred*," and then drive the car purposefully into an oncoming tractor rig, laughing like Legion all the way.

Instead he said, "Why ya think I pick't you up?"

Relieved, I offered to drive.

"Yeah," he agreed. "Tha's great, yeah." He slowed the car, pulled onto the shoulder again. I opened the door and breathed fresh Tennessee night air and as I walked around the car I could see a radio tower in the distance to the east, maybe two or three miles off in the flats. Its beacon lights were flashing into the night, warning airplanes away and pumping electronic wattage into antennae all over central Tennessee. I wondered whether it was a rock and roll station, a country and western, an old-time gospel hour. Made a note to turn on Theron's radio in the car.

We got back in, and I rolled the window down on the driver's side, turned the ignition, felt the starter spark and the motor catch and rise. It was an old Dodge sedan, with a three-on-the-tree gear shift, so I engaged the clutch and popped it, grinding the first time, but Theron didn't seem to notice or mind. He was already lolling in the passenger seat like a drunk scarecrow. And glancing at him as I pulled out onto the highway and accelerated, that was exactly what he seemed like — a tall, thin scarecrow. Gaunt as chicken broth, gangly, rough looking, pock-marked. Older than me, but probably not by as much as he looked. Maybe between five and ten years. That's the best look I got at him, or all I remember anyway.

He pulled a bottle out of glovebox, took a hit. Offered it to me.

I took the pint, held it up. Potter's gin, rotgut, pukebag stuff, cheap. I swallowed hard a couple of times, big belts, felt the liquor slap the sides of my esophagus and burn down to my stomach, where it sat and glowed like a coalfire. "Thanks," I said, passing the bottle back to him. He took another hit, placed the pint back in its cradle. He mentioned he had been in Vietnam, had been a soldier.

"I was lucky," I said, "deferred for college."

"What kinda college?"

"Engineering."

"You muss be smart."

"Yeah."

The two of us were silent again for some time, then I noticed he was fishing around in his pants pocket for something, then pulled out a plastic bag of marijuana.

"You get high?" he asked.

"Yeah."

Theron started rolling a joint, but couldn't coordinate his fingers quite right, so made several starts. After a while he got it though, and we passed the doobie back and forth past cutoffs to Shelbyville, Mount Pleasant, Lewisburg. As the marijuana had its effect, light of oncoming traffic turned gentle, and a red-amber necklace of taillamps laid in front

131

of us down the turnpike. I glanced over and it seemed Theron was dozing, so I thought I'd try the radio — see whether I could find some good rock and roll — and as I reached down to toggle the set on, he spoke lucidly, as clear as a full moon over frost.

"I killed a man, you know," he said.

It creeped me out a little, I mean, the hair on the back of my neck stood up for a second, until I remembered he'd said he'd been in Vietnam.

"That's tough, man." I said. "I'm sorry you had to do that."

He was quiet for another while, and I saw a sign for Pulaski and Fayetteville and figured we were maybe twenty miles from the state line. Then he elaborated.

"It was in Nashville," he said, then added, "Yesterday."

I kept both hands on the wheel and the high from the dope was turning bad. I looked straight ahead and wondered whether this Theron character would stick a knife into my ribs. My stomach churned, sitting there on the upholstery of his old Dodge sedan. But when I finally summoned the courage to look over at him, to barely glance in my periphery to behold that silver blade of mercury that must surely be poised there, I saw that Theron the Devil Himself was passed out, lying all the way against the passenger door in a blackout.

"Sweet Jesus," I whispered.

I crossed the state line into Alabama at about 11 p.m. and the surface of the highway instantly deteriorated. I drove another ten miles south on 65 then headed east on State Route 72 to Huntsville. Theron snored and snuffed the whole time, barely changing position. We entered Huntsville from the northwest and I started looking for a good place to stop, a place with a lot of light, an all-night diner or something. It was getting close on midnight, and unfamiliar with Huntsville, I couldn't find anything open on the main thoroughfares. Suddenly I was headed up a grade out of the city on Route 431, up to Monte Sano Mountain, and I thought *What the hell?* and drove up in there, stopped at the park just as Central Daylight Time crossed over into morning.

I shut the Dodge's motor down and wondered what to do. Theron had said he was headed for Huntsville, and here we were.

"Theron," I said. "Theron," louder this time. I reached over and nudged his shoulder. Birthed a thought of abandonment, quelled it. "Theron!" I shook him and he moaned and batted my hand away, slumped again into unconsciousness.

That made up my mind for me, and I realized the reason I hadn't found a well-lighted place for Theron to let *me* off was that I was going to let *him* off. He was home; he'd be fine.

I got out of the car, walked around to the passenger's side and pulled it open. Leveraged Theron's inert form onto a bench there next to the parking lot, laid him out like in his own pine box. Thought for a second, lifted him up — all maybe hundred and forty pounds of him — and fished his wallet out. Rolled him for eight bucks and the bag of dope he had in his front pocket. What was left of his pack of Lucky Strikes, too.

I got back in the Dodge and pulled away, the pulse of fireflies hovering as snapping lights over Theron's body. Pulled out of the Monte Sano Park parking lot and headed over the ridge from Huntsville into Northeastern Alabama, down to Owens Crossroads, across Lake Guntersville, the bass-fishing capital of the free world, through Gadsden. I was in Anniston by two-thirty in the morning, loaded on Theron's pot, dry-throated from the Lucky Strikes, the Potter's bottle tossed out, an explosion of red shards in the taillights somewhere between Boaz and Attalla.

I abandoned the car at Mercy Park, about twelve blocks from Mom and Pop's house. Rummaging through the contents of the glovebox, I'd found Theron's hardware, a needle, spoon, a box of matches. A bag of white powder. I left this, his kit, in the box. I'd never tried smack and didn't plan to. Then I hiked through our neighborhood in the small hours of a cool June morning, disturbing only dogs with my staggering passage. Let myself in through the always unlocked kitchen door and passed out on the sofa.

The Dodge sedan remained at the park for a few days, then a couple of weeks, and I'd pass it sitting there to see whether anyone claimed it. I'd worry a little that Theron might somehow show up in Anniston with a murderer's heart and intent. But I never saw him again, and the car disappeared from the park sometime after the Fourth of July maybe, I can't really remember. I stopped looking over my shoulder for Theron in August or so and had written the whole thing off by the time my sophomore year started back in Nashville.

Back in Huntsville, twenty years later, Theron's rusted-out Dodge sedan lay dead before me at an angle that suggested, insisted vertigo.

Chris.

Huh?

Chris, you OK?

I stared at the car from my knees. A fight went on in my head:

"This *is* Theron's car," whispered one part of me, the part that had never released the fear of his revenge.

133

"This *could* be *anyone's* car," whispered the logical part, the NASA engineer. "It's just like Theron's."

"This is Theron's car and therefore Theron is *near*."

"Theron was a crapped-out scarecrow junky."

"So what, Theron was a *murderer*, or claimed to be," Fear whispered, or perhaps it was the voice of Guilt. "In fact, Theron was the Devil Himself."

"Theron was a weak, crazy, blasted useless doper, probably long since overdosed."

"Chris," Red spoke to me across a universe of confusion. "CHRIS!"

Who cares how the fucking car got here in the first place!

"What?"

"What? You're on your knees in the mud staring at a busted up car, that's what!"

"Sorry, it just... it just surprised me to see it here... in the woods... like this."

"Yeah," Red said, "it is strange. It's been here a long time, long as I've been hikin' up here."

"Let's go," I said, resolved to leave the place, repress that silly two-decades-old dread again. I didn't want to look at the car anymore.

"OK," he said, and we resumed the hike. A half hour later we crested Sugar Tree Point, stopped at the base of the radio tower to appreciate the view, eat sandwiches Missy had packed, sip some fruit juice. At this particular spot, five-hundred feet above the rest of northern Alabama, one could look northwest over the city of Huntsville and its attendant geography: Redstone Arsenal with its distant rocket gantries, the Tennessee River bridged at Whitesburg to the south. Turning around to the east, one could survey the rolling country of northeastern Alabama, Owens Crossroads, New Hope, Lake Guntersville, or southeast toward my hometown of Anniston, Fort McClellan, the Talladega just beyond the horizon of brown gloom. Looking north, a rise to Monte Sano.

My eyes tracked the rise of the tower from base, up, until it reached into the gray. I could hear wind thrumming through the crosses of steel, across the cables that stabilized it. I could see its beacon pulsing on top, warning away low-flying aircraft. I wondered why Red had invited me along. I wondered why he had, in fact, been insistent over the course of the past year that I take up hiking with him. Why he had looked somewhat familiar in a gaunt, scarecrowish sort of way, when me and Georgia moved into the neighborhood.

134

I felt utterly open, exposed here at the summit, the tower pointing straight up like an energy rod. I waited for one of the cables to snap and break, for the tower to lean over and in the leaning, gain momentum and speed and purpose. Its fall would be spectacular.

GRANDPA'S ORCHARD

Someone other than Oliver's Grandma would get off the train. He didn't know this, but he was about to find out.

Oliver had been waiting in the Tacoma terminal. When he had grown tired of sitting, he stepped outside onto the platform. The morning was clear and across the tracks a long freight overlander slowed to a stop. There was an enormous squeal from its wheels, a weighty steel friction that put him in mind of the bones where his head and body joined. The cervical parts of the spine; he thought he remembered someone having described them in those terms. He looked north at the curve in the tracks and regretted again his decision to come in the pickup rather than the auto. His grandmother was old and small; she would have trouble climbing into the cab.

But there was no more time to worry, and he was here, waiting. A small boy stepped across the painted yellow line on the platform. A security officer asked him to step back in the same way the guard would have scolded a dog for shitting in an inappropriate place. Adults who seemed to be in charge of the boy collected him abruptly, confining him again. It was quiet once more, as the slowing train across the way had squeaked to a rest. The air smelled of the nearby harbor. Oliver thought, for a moment, that he could hear the whispers of many voices. But it was just a light wind.

Which car was it she had said? Was it 1430 or 1340? This was Train 14 from Bellingham via Seattle, so it must have been 1430. But were there thirty cars? He thought about this for a while as the sun rose and its light fell from higher above. He couldn't recall ever having seen a passenger train with that many cars. Could he have misheard her? He reconstructed the short telephone conversation. There was a lot about Grandpa being "at it" again. Her tongue was acid, the sort that could lick off grape-skin. She wanted Oliver to collect her at the rail station (since her sight was too poor to operate an auto anymore) then drive back to the orchard with her to see for himself. "He out a his mind," she had said. That much Oliver remembered. But what had she said about the car number? Perhaps she had said 1413, but it had been garbled over the phone. Oliver had hoped to be waiting at the correct car door when she emerged. That is what she would be expecting, and it might put her in a sour mood if her expectations went unmet in such a matter as this.

Again, those voices, like the sound of a breeze flowing through many leaves.

Then, a whistle blast from down the tracks. Its cry seemed to spill like brilliant plasma from a single halogen eye that had appeared

136

from thinning air. Oliver's cervical parts rocked in their sockets as he turned to behold Grandma's conveyance. It moved in his direction like a chrome worm.

At the border, Sergeant Stebbins passed hours playing games on a laptop computer. At times, the guard was so intent on the screen that a battalion of enemy saboteurs might have marched — one by one, in single file, for an hour or two — around the gate. There had been much hubbub surrounding the agency's decision to cut back its annual budget, thereby reducing the number of guards at each frontier crossing from two to one. But, in secret, Sgt. Stebbins was quite happy with the new arrangement. He could play computer games all day. He could look at filthy magazines. If he liked, he could step outside the guard kiosk and piss on the agency's seal, which affixed itself waist-high to the kiosk like a stamp of absurdity. At this crossing, border traffic was so rare as to be an event, and all Sgt. Stebbins had to do was show up on time and pass the hours until his relief arrived. Five or six autos might come through in the interval — mostly mountain-family people visiting cousins across the line, one way or the other.

Sgt. Stebbins conquered another electronic level in his game, so he decided to look at a magazine for a while. He scooted the laptop aside and extracted the magazine from under the tiny counter. She was hot on the cover. He unzipped his fly.

After a moment, though, movement and noise to his side caused him to look up. Down the road, a large delivery truck struggled uphill in his direction. Its motor churned and its tires clutched at the gravel surface. Sgt. Stebbins hid the magazine. He zipped his fly. The truck pulled up to the guard station and stopped with a mighty back-fart of exhaust. Its windows were fogged and its panels road-gritted. The driver clutched out through neutral to park, and set the brake. All of these mechanisms clicked and scraped beneath the chassis. As Sgt. Stebbins stepped out of the kiosk with a clipboard, the truck's door cracked. Sgt. Stebbins sniffed the air; it stunk. He saw that flies buzzed around the aluminum seams of the volume behind the cab. The door opened fully and a woman climbed down.

"Hold er right there," Sgt. Stebbins said.

The woman turned around. *Sheesh*, Sgt. Stebbins thought, *don' she look like hell?*

"What er you wantin me to hold?" she said. It looked like she suffered the filmy onset of cataracts across her eyes. Her nose had the tip of a fishhook and one side seemed mashed in by an unseen pressure. Also, her hair was unkempt and stringy.

"Jus step down an hold on," Sgt. Stebbins said. "I gotta ask you a few questions about yer cargo there," — he gestured at the fuggy container — "and yer intent in-country."

She stepped toward him. "Wha's the fee?" she asked.

"The fee?" he repeated. He decided he would play ignoramus for a few minutes to see what he could wheedle. "Don' know bout no fee. I jus gotta write down here on this slip" — he indicated the clipboard in his hand — "the nature a yer commerce an such."

She seemed to consider this, but he couldn't be sure whether she was scheming or daydreaming. Then she brightened, and said, "I was tole to give you some money, an that would do." She stood with her hands on her hips and pushed out her chest. Sgt. Stebbins saw that she had remarkable titties. "But I got more'n that fer you." She dropped to her knees and reached for his fly. That zipper got a mind of its own, it seemed — up and down, up and down. Second time today.

After a moment, Sgt. Stebbins staggered backward, cross-eyed, against the kiosk. She spat in the dust and wiped her chin.

"I jus be on my way," she said. "You write whatever you need to on that paper."

"Godspeed, darlin," Sgt. Stebbins moaned.

The truck's motor kindled, then roared like Apocalypse. Sgt. Stebbins lifted the gate. The truck lumbered across the border. The cloud of stench and flies passed with it, and Sgt. Stebbins sat back down in his chair with his member softening. What had that smell been? Meat gone bad? Although a light breeze soughed through the fir needles, there was no answer from the quiet forest around him. Soon he was back in the kiosk dutifully making an entry on the paper clipped in the board. It would have to be validated when she returned to cross back into her own country. Then he went back to the laptop for a fresh game.

At Grandpa's orchard, there was a bright buzz on the wind. The language of the trees was fresh and tinged with optimism. A harvest and a planting! Oh, the joy of the cycle. Sow and reap, reap and sow. Utterances in the rows of trees stacked themselves one atop the other; verbs and nouns and past participles joined in chains of clauses and wrapped themselves around the orchard.

"What fresh Babel is this?" Grandpa asked aloud. He stepped through the screen door and on to his weathered porch. The orchards started at the edge of the yard and stretched toward a bluff. The clouds lay low in that direction, but if he walked down the porch stairs to his left and rounded the corner of the house, he would see clear sky and the sun. The sum effect of this was that his tree-stands were lit against the flannel clouds. The trees and their fruits shimmered and danced as if with internal glow. The fruits seemed to smile and sing.

"My beautiful babies," Grandpa cooed. A light breeze seemed to sigh then lift, and he heard bountiful words on it, phrases that might be lines of poetry or sensual promises. As he smiled upon his trees from his place on the porch, their leaves shivered like those of aspens, so that the entirety of his acreage appeared to shudder ecstatically. The mouths on the fruit broke into colossal, clown grins. Joy pulsed from the orchard as if from a single organism in passionate throes.

Oh, Grandpa, he heard. *Oh, Oh, Oh!*

Bright opinions and enthusiastic dialogue flared here and there in the rows. It tumbled in waveforms downwind to Grandpa. Like a swell that forms, grows, crests and subsides, a consensus moved from one end of the orchard to the other. Ripples of counsel spread from epicenters, and these articulations formed a sing-song accretion of flushed cheeks, scrunching noses, brows raising alternately, wiggling ears, tongues whose tips rolled into little round O's, flashing seed-teeth, blinking eyes with merry glints at their pin pupils — the fruit were joyous indeed!

"Soon, babes," Grandpa promised. "Soon!"

Even as it slowed, the train pushed a bow-wave of displaced air in front of it. Oliver took an involuntary step backward when the gust passed around him. Cars moved slowly past, reluctant to stop, all that enormous energy that had been carrying the train forward now inefficiently retarded and confined. And after all that worry, no numbers painted on the cars! He looked up and down the platform. The train's brakes shrieked. He felt something in his neck lift, give, separate and — perhaps — reconfigure itself. Doors opened up and down the line. People popped out like little perambulating candies.

Three or four cars toward the end of the train from where Oliver stood, a door emitted someone other than Grandma. From the distance, though, he could not yet tell this. All he saw was the diminutive shape, familiar stoop, her oversized hand-bag, and heard her tart lips call his name: "Oliver! Oliver, where are you, boy?" Her head turned like a bird's. One of the station attendants moved to help her, but setting down her purse, she lifted her cane like a ball-bat and aimed a swat in his direction. She missed. But the promise of blows rained from this minuscule — but, clearly, cantankerous — old woman sent the porter backpedaling.

"Get my grandson," she cawed. The porter looked up and down the platform with much consternation, then shouted," Who dis biddy grandboy, eh? Come git dis crazy bitch out my station!"

For a moment, Oliver wondered whether he should simply turn and flee. Zip back out through the turnstile, hop in the pickup, and push that pedal through the floor. But no, Grandma was here, now, and that's why he'd come. To accompany her all the way back to the orchard and see what was the trouble.

"Right here," he called. The porter pointed in Oliver's direction. "There yo grandboy," he said. "Why don you go try an gib he head a beatin?"

"Don' you think I ain gonna," Grandma snapped. Meantime, Oliver had nearly reached the two and Grandma turned to him. Oliver stopped up short.

"Wha's wrong with you, Oliver?" she demanded.

But it wasn't Grandma. Or it was, but wasn't — Oliver couldn't be sure. The shape and voice and mannerisms were all familiar, and her face somewhat so. Yet the look of her was different, transformed. Older in spots, younger in others, with slightly altered architecture. Nothing that could be detected from further than fifteen or twenty feet off, but up close strangely unfamiliar.

"Wha's wrong?" she repeated.

"Grandma," Oliver said. He paused to shake off the dissonance and collect himself. "Nothin wrong. I fine. I jus happy to see you lookin so well."

"Crap," she spat. "I look like shit."

"Listen to yo gramma, boy," said the porter. "She know wha she talkin bout, neah's I can tell."

"Shut up, you," Grandma snapped. She turned to Oliver. "Get my han-bag fo this hose ass put his big unwilly paws on it an break sumpin."

Oliver did. They left the porter cussing on the platform, back through the turnstiles, across the lot to Oliver's pickup. He lifted her into the passenger's seat. She seemed to weigh as much as a desiccated bone. As he settled her into the seat, her head bobbled from side to side like a doll's, then snapped into alertness.

"Wait till you see wha that ol fool done now," she said.

Oliver got in, started the pickup, pulled out of the lot, and pointed them toward the highway.

Diamond couldn't get the taste of the border guard's jizz off her tongue no matter how many times she rinsed. She lifted her thermos, took a pull, and swished lukewarm coffee around the cavern of her mouth once again. She rolled down the window and spat into the airstream. Still the taste of that nasty man's spunk. Even so, she reasoned: *the price a riches.* This haul oughtta set her up for months. Lots a valuable product in back, *yeah.* The orchard farmer promised a pretty penny, *uh-huh.*

Through dim eyes, she consulted again a paper that had been folded, unfolded and refolded many times. It had come from out of a computer up north, and a man in a bar had sold it to her. On it were directions to the orchard farmer's place up against the hills. According to the words that were printed there, she was just a couple of miles away.

The truck bounced along the road. A few miles back the surface had evolved from gravel to asphalt (just after the border), then back to gravel that had become increasingly uneven and pitted. When the gravel gave way to mud, all the bouncing had started to make her feel woozy in the stomach. Especially when she could hear the parts in back shifting, and sense the movement from right to left and forward to back of the whole mass. She imagined all of that gluey matter slapping moistly together, adhering one moment here, one moment there, separating in oily glissandos, slipping through and around itself. The truck's center of gravity would lurch, and so would her guts. And every once in a while the funk from the back would somehow — in defiance of the airstream — waft forward. Diamond would swallow, get the taste of that spooey again, and fight a gag going into overdrive.

Even so, across the rough roads and through the forests and down out of the hills she persevered. She came out of a valley into a bright pasture with bob-wire fencing strung from moss-covered wood posts on either side. The road leveled. And even through her filmy irises she saw a stand of trees in the distance that seemed configured. As she neared, their rows and columns made themselves apparent in that geometrically pleasing way they will when one encounters an orchard or a large assemblage of tombstones over a graveyard or a phalanx of soldiers standing exactly in precision. That is, rows appear, dissipate and reassemble as the observer moves through angles of perspective. Diamond found this visual algorithm altogether pleasant and soporific.

She saw Grandpa's gate and, past it, Grandpa's house and porch. Beyond, the orchard pulsed and smoldered. When Diamond's eyesight had been better, she had once seen the Northern Lights up near Kelowna — *aurora borealis*, the drunken man who was with her that night had

141

called it. They had watched for a few moments from the back seat of his Oldsmobile, then returned to the business at hand. Diamond had forgotten that boozed-up fumbler's name, but she never had put away from her mind those shimmering solar-blown and — in an odd, warm way, humbling — celestial curtains. The orchards beyond Grandpa's house were like that now. Beautiful and compelling, calling her with the most gorgeous voice she had ever heard. *Oh, Diamond. Oh, oh, oh. Come be with us!* Those lips, those teeth, those tongues. That exquisite fruit.

Diamond's truck lurched through the gate. She laid on the horn. Its blast caused a second and a half's worth of silence from the orchard. The only sound was the truck's motor in low gear. Then a noise like the cheering of a large crowd overfilled the valley. All of the trees and their branches, all the fruit that dangled from them, all the quivering leaves, seemed to turn, gasp, and babble in her direction. She geared down and rolled to a stop. She watched the old man step down from his porch and cross the small yard. Rich brown mud sloshed his rubber boots. He had a beard the color of pale, yellow eggshell, and a leather hat cast a shadow on the features of his face. Diamond cranked down the window.

"You got my product?" the old man asked. His voice sounded like the honking of Canada geese.

"Don' know what you order ol man, but it sure do stank," Diamond said.

Grandpa giggled. "The orchard like stinky stuff," he said. "Make it grow and grow. Real big and strong. You'll see, pretty gal."

"Where you want to unload, gramps?"

Grandpa turned around in a circle, and then pointed at a place at the edge of the yard, where the nearest trees lifted their fruit from the ground.

"Let's make a pile right over yonder," he said. "By them trees."

Diamond followed the imaginary line his finger made. She squinted at the orchard. "What kinda trees you growin, gramps?"

This made the old man giggle. Silly gal, couldn't she see for herself?

"Them're melon trees," he said. "You know, cabesa bushes. The Espaniards comin roun here for harvest call em *árbol del pista*. Come have a look."

The old man took Diamond by the arm and escorted her to the edge of the yard. As she drew close, Diamond saw, through the scum stretched across her pupils, that the tree-fruits were, indeed, heads. In various stages of ripeness, of course, but the most mature of the fruit were fully formed, adult-sized human heads. They hung from branches pregnant with their weight. Their mouths formed circles of surprise. Who was this delightful creature accompanying their Grandpa? Their eyes blinked. Inhalations and exhalations caused their nostrils to flare. She smelled *yummy*. But there was a better smell coming from her truck. *Mmmmm.*

Diamond stood without speaking. She had never seen anything so strange before. And, for some reason, they struck her as beautiful. The heads were more beautiful than flowers. Even the little, unripe heads, whose eyes seemed as stitched shut as hems, whose nostrils seemed barely to be decimal points. She stepped closer until one of the unformed heads dangled from a branch at eye level. She marveled at the thin skin of the closed eyelids, minuscule capillaries just below forming a tiny red and blue network. *Look at those tiny veins*, she thought. *How lovely!* She reached with her forefinger extended to touch it.

"Go ahead," Grandpa said. "Take it. Eat."

"I mustn'," Diamond said.

"Surely, it O.K."

So Diamond plucked the fruit and drew it to her mouth with two hands. Her teeth closed over the tiny skull. The fruit cracked in her fingers with a newborn's sigh. It broke at the fontanel and divided, and rich, red juices rushed down her wrists. The shards of the underskin were not quite hard, and below that was a gray, milky pulp that had the consistency of the bread pudding she remembered from childhood Christmases — it would come from the oven warm and sweet — and the nectar of this small fruit washed her in fantastic oscillations that drove the taste of the border guard from her mouth forever and ever.

Grandpa came up behind her with a shovel and finished her off with a swing of the blade.

When Grandma and Oliver arrived at the orchard they saw Grandpa clearing out the back of a large truck. By shoveling out the big truck's container, he was making a pile of something over by the edge of the yard.

"Look at that fool," Grandma said. "Out in the sun workin like one a them young buckies."

"Grandma, he jus doin his chores," Oliver said. "Wha's wrong with that?"

"Don' you sass me, Oliver. I ain too ol to slap you a good one."

Oliver fell silent, and Grandpa, hearing their approach at last, left off his shoveling. He took off his hat, wiped his brow, put the hat on again, and leaned on the shovel's handle. Oliver pulled to a stop and Grandma hopped out of the pickup like a bobwhite.

"How do?" Grandpa called cheerfully. "Look at the mess I got here!" His hand swept in an arc that indicated the truck, the pile, the orchard, the whole valley.

"Quiet you ol goat," Grandma hissed. A fly buzzed around her cheek and she swatted at it. "What you got there?"

"Oh," said Grandpa, "the usual. Parts from up north. This nice lady come an drop em off."

"Where she get to, then?" Grandma asked.

Grandpa giggled his goose laugh. "She join right in with em, heh heh!"

Grandma commenced a massive scolding. In it were phrases like, "...wha'd you think, her people ain a come lookin...," and "...you'll bring ruin down on us all..." — those sorts of whiny protestations. Oliver just shook his head and looked at the flyblown pile of parts — arms, legs, torsos, a neck, a foot or hand here and there (one still had a nice gold ring on the finger and painted nails). Some unrecognizable components, as well. The bones of Oliver's neck ached, and Grandpa and Grandma's arguing wasn't helping matters.

"The both a you..." he shouted. "The both a you quiet down! My head is splitting!" But this only made his grandparents chuckle, and resume arguing all the more vociferously. It also caused the heads in the trees to draw in great gales of breath and start guffawing — acres of mouths laughing, spraying nectar and spittle as if Oliver's complaint was the funniest thing they had ever, collectively, heard.

"Look," Grandpa said. "I gotta fertilize, ain I?"

Grandma refused to answer.

"Well, ain I? I paid good money for this." He gestured at the pile.

Grandma turned her back on her husband and looked at Oliver. "See?" she asked. "You see him? He impossible! Help me gather him up. We goin to the hospital."

Then Grandpa put a new head on Grandma. It happened so fast that Oliver just stood there with his mouth agape. One minute she was braying like a donkey — *See* this and *hospital* that, *blah blah blah* in that old bitch-biddy voice that had so offended the train porter. One minute her yapping, next minute her old head on the pile, Grandpa busy at one of the branches, and the next minute a new head on her, nice and quiet. "Respectful, like," Grandpa pronounced. "I like a woman that way."

Oliver nodded in agreement, went around the back of the house to the tool shed for a second shovel, and helped Grandpa finish emptying Diamond's truck. Grandma and her new head went inside to make

144

something cool to drink. A little bud of a head poked out of the branch-tip where, until a few moments before, Grandma's new head had grown. Her old head lay on the pile and flies lit upon it. The eyes lost their luster in the heat of the full, fat sun. The men spread the parts throughout the orchard. This must have pleased the fruit a great deal, because they sang and celebrated all night. Oliver couldn't sleep, and although his headache got no worse, it didn't subside either. His head just hummed all through, and the cervical parts of his spine scraped like a branches against one another on a stormy night. He could hear the scrapings resonate in his skull.

After a while, government people from the agency that guarded the border came to the orchard. They asked whether Grandpa had seen a large truck and container that might have come through a couple of weeks prior? Because there was an entry on a clipboard recording this truck's entry, but not its return. Since the border was nearby, it seemed reasonable that Grandpa might have seen it, or its driver.

"She was a woman with the beginnings of cataracts," said one of them, a man with oil-slick hair, a black suit, and dark sunglasses wrapping his face.

"No," Grandpa said. "I seen nothing nor no-one of that sort." Oliver shook his head, too. As did Grandma, from her chair on the porch.

The government men asked whether they might have a look around. Grandpa agreed. Their attention drawn for a moment to the quaking leaves and hanging fruits — and what seemed oddly like a crowd of voices — the men turned toward the orchard. But as soon as the two men put their backs to Grandpa and Oliver, Grandpa and Oliver put the shovels to them. They used those nosy government men to fertilize more of the orchard.

Still Oliver's headache persisted. One day — it must have been a month or six weeks after Grandpa baited Diamond into a first bite of that immature fruit — it came to Oliver's mind that in order to rid himself of his neck-ache he might try a new head himself. After all, Grandma seemed to be doing fine. She was, in fact, quite pleasant and appeared to be happy enough. And besides, thought Oliver, I have always disliked my head anyway. For one, it's ugly. Secondly, it feels like it's stuffed too damned full. There is too much whirling around in that crammed space, and no room for it. And, of course, there was the creaking, cracking, frazzing neck and its cervical parts.

Even so, it was a difficult thing to ask Grandpa. It wasn't that Oliver was frightened. He supposed it might sting for a moment when

145

the one head was exchanged for another. He thought he could ask Grandma about that. No — it wasn't the specter of pain. It was just that, well, even though it constantly hurt and was packed with spinning thoughts and eddies of nervous impulse and electric zappings and all sorts of confusing… uh… well… *shit*, even for all of that, it was still *his* head, and a man's head is his own. He ought not to go losing it lightly.

Finally, he summoned the courage to seek Grandpa's counsel. They were walking between rows in the orchard. Grandpa had his shovel for turning the soil next to roots so that fresh air would stay in contact with some of the fertilizer. All the fruit was fat and pink and bright-eyed now, as harvest time was very near. The pair — grandfather and grandson — paused at a particularly fine specimen of *árbol del pista*.

"Lookie here," Grandpa said. He stuck out his old bony finger, touching the trunk, and let a centipede crawl aboard. "Lookit this little bugger."

Oliver looked. Fierce needles of tension stabbed at his neck. They were like glass daggers. "He a cute little fella, ain he?" he said.

"Cute, maybe, yeah," said Grandpa, "but I tell you what. This here cute little fella gonna infect the whole orchard if we ain careful. This cute little fella like to bore right into the fruit, and you don' wanna see nothin like that."

Oliver nodded. Grandpa crushed the centipede between his fingers and wiped the goo on his trousers leg.

"Grandpa," Oliver said.

"Yes, boy?"

"Grandpa, I been thinkin. I been thinkin bout a new head. Mine hurts."

"Everybody head gonna hurt once in a while."

"Not all a damn time, though, yeah?"

"Typically not." Grandpa shook his head. "Not as a rule."

Oliver's ears started to bang with a noise like he recalled from a baseball game he had attended once in Seattle. It was the sound of thousands of voices. The sound of a stadium roaring at a well-hit ball. Through the noise he heard individual voices echoing what Grandpa had just said: "Typically not," cried one; "Not as a rule," shouted another. The wave of voices waxed, crested, and waned a little. When it was quieter, Oliver spoke again:

"I been thinkin bout exchangin my head." He turned to Grandpa to gage the old man's reaction. But there was none — Grandpa might as well have been sleeping with his eyes open. "What would you recommend, Grandpa? I mean, which tree gives the best fruit?"

146

And again Oliver heard the fruit begin to cry out, individually and in unison, so that he couldn't be sure whether it was melon tree fruit or Grandpa who said, "...well, this here tree good as any..." and simultaneously "...not as a rule..." layered over "...surely its O.K...." shot through with "...seen nothing nor no-one of that sort..." and one lonely, frantic cry of "...behind you, watch it..." *Oh, Oliver! Oh, Oh, Oh!* A cacophony of desperate alarm.

He turned and saw that Grandpa had raised the shovel. Its blade glinted in the sun. The screams of *árbol de pista* fruit grew frantic, a huge wail and dreadnought of wind that occulted even the pins that drove from one side of his neck to the other. Oliver's head was an unmitigated, savaged bulb of pain, true. But it was his. The only one he would ever have.

Oliver snatched the shovel from the old man's arms. *Ha! ha! ha!* Oliver put a new head on Grandpa! Just as slick as you fucking please!

"Raise your shovel to me!" Oliver shouted. "Jus you go ahead an try!"

But Grandpa would not do it again. No — he was a changed man, and followed Oliver back to the house. Grandma set out some iced tea on the porch rail. They sat in chairs and watched the sun grow large and more orange as it slipped toward the horizon. On the rail, another centipede folded, unfolded and refolded itself, slowly traversing their line of sight. Oliver watched his orchard.

Voices blowing on a harvest breeze:

Good night.

THE HUMMOCK KING

My father was digging a hole for a fencepost and struck something. It was a skeleton. The shovelblade had bitten a gouge in the skull. The bones were wrapped in a purple cloth slick with the oils of earth. I thought the cloth looked like a folded-up saddle blanket. I told my father so. The heat of the sun was hard on us and the flies were bothersome. He told me to get my brother Andrew and clear a space in the root cellar. Our mother usually laid up parsnips, onions and taters and stored them there, so we would have to eat a lot of them for supper that night if none were to go to waste. We'd put the bones in the root cellar and decide what to do.

I left to obey. I assumed the post-hole digging was over for the day. Andrew was in the barn combing out his horse. He didn't believe me at first, but I threatened to go get our father and Andrew knew if he was wrong he'd get a strapping. We brought a dozen cartons of parsnips, onions and taters to our mother. She made a mash of them for supper. While we sat around the table we wondered about our purple-blanketed bone man. I don't know why we thought the skeleton was a man's, but we did.

"Maybe he was a nigger, got lynched," my father said.

"Around here?" My mother spooned up more potatoes.

"Been known to happen."

There was a period of silence, for it was a rare thing to challenge our father at supper. His fork clicked his plate and teeth repeatedly, in a cycle. Then he pushed his chair back. Andrew offered his own theory.

"Maybe he was a robber. Could have been lynched, but by townfolk tired of his thievin' ways."

Our father nodded; this made reasonable sense. A nigger or a highwayman — it made little difference to him. Could have been a nigger thief, too, both things at once. No one asked my opinion.

I lay in my cot that night turning this problem over in my mind. There was a good chance, I thought, that the bone-man was some kind of royalty. His purple wrapping, for one, led me down this path of logic. Our farm nestled in fields at the edge of hummocks. He could have been the ruler of those hummocks a hundred or two-hundred years ago. I decided this was a fact and not just an idea. With a smile on my mouth and the tiny chirps of crickets in my ears, I fell asleep.

Then in the middle of the night the hummock king got out of the cellar and came up alongside my bed. His hard fingertips gently stroked my forehead and he tucked my hair behind my ears. He woke me with promises.

148

I rose in my nightgown and went with him down the hall. We usurped my father's authority. We put him in the hole from which we had taken the hummock king. Then we dug a hole next to it for my mother, and another for Andrew. We rode my brother's horse into the hummocks, and the air was damp and close. The stars arranged themselves in patterns I had never before seen. The hummock king explained this was in honor of my coronation.

His throne was an oak bole at the edge of a muskeg swamp. It was a strange place for a swamp, up in the hummocks. His royal bedchamber was a bed of sphagnum surrounded by long, thick-bladed grass and cattails. Giant skunk cabbages ringed the chamber, and mangroves lifted their branches high and veiled us in club moss. We tied my brother's horse to a tree. The hummock king laid me back on the bed, lifted my nightgown, and made me his queen. Afterward, I held his cold skull against my breast and kissed his spade-wound. Above, in the branches, the round eyes of opossums bore witness. His bone-nectar swam into me and made the start of a prince. He whispered that he was a thousand years old, or two-thousand.

The next morning my brother's horse had sunk into a bog. The reins went straight down from the tree-trunk into the slime. Fat, black beetles climbed up and down the reins all day.

People from town came looking for my father. We watched from the hummocks as they milled about the farm. They found the dirt mounds and stepped quickly away from their contents. Even from the distance, we could see them clasping their hands over their mouths. The hummock king giggled and laid his arm about my shoulders. "My little queen," he said, an endearment he had begun to use frequently.

The townspeople organized themselves and came looking for me. They couldn't have known that I was the hummock queen now. Finding only three dirt mounds, they would have assumed there had been an abduction. They probably thought some niggers or robbers had come along and taken me off. I laughed at this thought. When I shared this humor with my bone-husband, he sang. His voice was sweet and dry and ancient. Then the townspeople came into the swamps. We put them in the bog with my brother's horse.

Pretty soon it came time for me to have our hummock prince. I lay down on the sphagnum bed and my bone-husband commanded his son to come forth. When the boy came out, we saw that he was half bone-man and half person. There were places on him where the bones came through and cast their own light, and other places where his skin was bright and pink. He was beautiful and perfect! We cleaned the birth fluids from him with clumps of moss and wrapped him in my hummock king's royal purple cloth. No sooner had my bone-son come into the world than the hummock king had me under him again.

There followed several seasons. Before I knew it, there were our lovely children everywhere, hummock princes and hummock princesses. All of them were half-bone and half-people persons. We warned them often to stay away from the edges of the muskeg. Most of them did, although we lost two or three in the bog. Each time, it made me sad for a moment until I remembered that there were so many, many children, and that their bone-father and I could make more any time we wished.

Then something terrible happened. A brown bear sow, protecting her cubs I suppose, ended the reign of the hummock king. My bone-husband had been harvesting skunk cabbages and stumbled accidentally into her den. He would certainly have meant no harm to the cubs, but the sow would have assumed otherwise, being a bear. One of our hummock princes, who accompanied his father at the time, said the sow reared up and bashed off the hummock king's skull with one mighty swipe of her paw. Our hummock prince said his father's skull rolled into the undergrowth like a ball. The rest of him clattered into a pile, and our hummock prince ran from the angry bear.

I wondered whether the hummock king could make himself rise again, as he had done from my family's root cellar. I went to sleep on the sphagnum bed that night believing that he would do so. That I would wake to his touch and kindhearted promises once more. That the half-bone, half-person child in my womb would, too, squall in its father's arms as had its royal bone-siblings. But instead of his tender ministrations, I was wakened by the sour sounds of argument. Our two eldest hummock princes clashed over succession — the eldest and first, who had the birthright, and the next in line. They had never gotten on with one another.

Having been raised to respect their mother, my two bone-sons sought my decision. Both promised they would abide by it. It was true: the eldest was the proper heir. But his younger bone-brother was wiser. I had observed all of my children carefully; there was no getting around this fact. I told them to wait for my decision. Then I went off into the swamp to contemplate this puzzle and arrive at a conclusion. While I was walking and thinking I had visions of my bone-husband. I had memories of the afternoon we discovered him, my father and I. This put me in mind of my mother and brother, and our farm. I found myself weeping because all of it had passed on.

I came to a creek that ran slowly at the base of a ravine. There was a large boulder to one side of it; this I used to sit upon and think.

150

There also was a felled pine tree. Its trunk lay across the creek before me, and I sat on the boulder and looked at the tree. The water burbled at my feet, beyond the hems of my nightgown. The sound made me look down. A small leaf slid by on the water and disappeared. When I looked up, a great gray wolf sat on the log. I asked him what to do.

The wolf showed his fangs and let his tongue loll over one side of his muzzle. His eyes sparked and I heard a thunderclap. While he summoned weather, I lifted my gown and birthed the last half-bone, half-person child. It was a tiny girl. She was as delicate as a waterskipper. Minuscule veins were visible under the paper-thin skin of her eyelids, and her small nostrils were like spores. Where her bones shown through they glittered as if flecked with precious metals. The sweet smell of honey rose from her, and the wolf's nose twitched. He sniffed the air and made his neck long in our direction. Lightning flashed and he exacted his price. When he had finished, soft bones and all, he spoke. His muzzle dripped my daughter's blood as he bestowed the hummock kingdom on the younger of the two bone-princes.

"He is the wiser," the wolf said.

"Yes."

"The older is headstrong, but not as bright."

I shook my head and dismissed him. He trotted away with a full belly. I was sad about my last bone-daughter. But then I thought of her coming out of the wolf as shit and being eaten by birds. How she then would be carried into the sky on their wings. This seemed to make her loss an easier thing. This, plus the fact that I had resolved — with the wolf's help — my dilemma, made my spirits rise. A final pulse of thunder rolled above and the weather moved up the valley and away. I went back to our muskeg and announced my decision. I gave the wiser bone-son his father's royal purple cloth.

It so displeased my eldest hummock prince that he fled with several of his supporters. While my new hummock king moved over me that night and I returned the gaze of opossums, I heard sounds in the swamp beyond the circle of weak light my new husband's bones cast. While the hummock king busied himself at the source of royal souls, his brother prepared for a betrayal.

Soon there were bone-princes clashing to my left and right, in front of me and behind me. What a terrific noise they made! And then there were wolves among us. Running and leaping, they sunk their long fangs into the flesh and bones of my children. My eldest son was in league with them!

The great wolf from the stream leapt onto my bone-husband's throat and tore it away. His blood spurted and soon overran the sphagnum bed. I fled while the wolf gobbled him up, then I slid into the bog and waited. In order to breathe, I kept my nose barely above the scum on its surface. Fat, black beetles walked across my face. I thought I could feel the bones of my brother's horse against my bare feet. I imagined the bone-fingers of the townspeople grasping at my ankles. I looked up and saw that the stars had once again collected themselves into new constellations.

When the light came up in the morning it was quiet. All the hummock-children were gone. The brothers who had vied to be my new bone-husband both were piles of bones held barely together with drying sinew. Flies feasted on the last of this. There were many dead wolves as well, and I stepped around their carcasses all day as I dragged these dead and passed-on things into the bog. I wept as I did so. I recalled with an ache my days as a girl on our farm. I sobbed for the loss of simple, happy times. I longed for my mother's embrace, for even a stern word of direction from my father's lips.

When my tears cleared the great wolf was waiting. His grin was large and filled with intent.

"Who shall be the hummock king now?" he asked. His tail wagged once as he unsheathed himself. Where his wolf penis should have been there hung a knife-blade.

"You and only you, forever," I said.

FLEXOR

The first thing the ocular specialist did when he saw Kevin's cut-up eye was shook his head and said, simply, "No."

Kevin heard this as if he were listening with another boy's cotton-stuffed ears. The specialist squinted at the surface of Kevin's eye through an ophthalmoscope. Its halogen felt like a scalpel when it crossed those scratches. The invasive light and the stainless steel tool prying his lids apart had Kevin clenching his teeth nearly to the crack-point. His nails dug at the flesh of his own palms. His guts roiled and heaved. When he had the presence to recall it, there was the violent memory of the attack itself. Then the sedative they'd delivered to the base of his optic nerve with an enormous hypodermic. Now this head-shaking specialist.

The receptionist had turned the color of a wordless page of paper when Kevin stumbled in from the parking lot. "The d-doctor will want to see y-you right away," she stuttered. He clamped his eyelid shut, but tears and blood still dripped. He saw with his good eye that his T-shirt was stained bright red on his chest, over his heart.

He had to wait half an hour for the specialist. The emergency-room doctor kept saying they needed to call a parent. "Mom's at bowling," Kevin said. He didn't have the number at the lanes. They lay him on a thin, tall bed with a paper sheet, rigged him up with painkiller, and waited.

Later, he thought he heard the specialist say, "That cut's as wide as a drainage ditch. This poor kid has the Grand Canyon running across his eyeball."

"What'd he say did it?" a nurse asked.

"A cat," the emergency-room doctor said.

The specialist took his own eye away from the ophthalmoscope. "A cat?"

"That wasn't no cat," Kevin mumbled. "I thought it was a cat, but that wasn't a cat like I ever saw."

Afterward, when his mother had finally gotten home and they had reached her, he sat in the waiting room with adhesive eye-patches on both eyes. The specialist had said that if he wanted to save his damaged eye, he would have to wear patches on both to slow eye movements. The injured eye had to rest, the doctor explained. Kevin might have the patch off the good eye in a week or so, after the healing process had a while to take hold.

Kevin could hear other people in the waiting room moving around and talking. He heard, from time to time, the automatic doors whoosh open. He heard the big tropical tank with the fake ceramic castles and the exotic, slow-moving, stupid fish bubble and aspirate. He heard old magazine pages flip. Somewhere between the darkness and the painkillers, he thought he heard a purr that started small but grew and morphed into low guttural, back-of-the-throat words.

"No, I'm not finished with you yet," that cat-growl said.

Kevin had watched the cat in the sycamore tree drop onto unsuspecting prey for weeks. It was a mid-sized all-black housecat, and it spent whole afternoons stretched its full, languorous length in the fork of two limbs that overhung the sidewalk in front of Kevin's mom's house, waiting for something or someone to go under. When something or someone approached, it gathered, arched its inky back, then simply dropped. If the victim were small – a squirrel, a bird, or a tiny dog, for example – it would make a startled sound and attempt to flee. The dogs usually got away, but he watched the cat kill and carry back up into the branches at least ten, maybe fifteen, squirrels, titmice, chipmunks, nuthatches, vireos – you name it – over the course of weeks.

Rain or shine, didn't matter. That cat was on the hunt. Hot afternoon, cold morning, the cat was always there.

And after a while it seemed that the cat grew to prefer larger prey. Bigger dogs, other cats, a rabbit. Young Zach and Trista Dunleavy, the seven-year-old twins from a house up the street, rode bicycles down the sidewalk one day and the cat just dove – timing barely late – landing on the concrete between the two as they whizzed by. But not too late to startle Trista into running her bike onto Kevin's mom's picket fence, scraping her knees and ankles so blood oozed slowly from the abrasions. She flopped on the sidewalk with her skinny legs spread, arms akimbo, and shrieked bloody murder.

"Bad kitty!" she had sobbed. From the living room window Kevin had watched the cat slink away to the base of the sycamore, then zip up its trunk like a little inky rocket.

Out of the house and down the steps he had come to help Trista to her feet, wary eyes peeled on that branch where the leaves provided just enough darkness for its eyes to flame and pulse iridescently. Once they locked on Kevin he couldn't look away – even from twelve or fifteen feet he could make out their details. He forgot for a moment about Trista. The eyes held him transfixed: green-gold, all-iris and jewel-like, with that vertical pupil shaped like a knife-blade but bottomless black. The mesmerizing eyes of a predator. And then sound almost too low and flat to be heard – one he should not have been able to hear over Trista's wailing – but which he heard nevertheless: that clotted, throat-full-of-blood, mewling of a killer whose stomach wants filling.

That voice that keeps saying, over and over in his claw-filled dreams and when he wakes sweaty, when he lets his mind wander, when he tries to focus, when he watches from his window, when he tries to read his books or do his homework before bedtime.

That voice that keeps purring, "No, I'm not finished with you yet."

When Kevin's parents got divorced, he and his mom moved into an apartment across town. Most mornings Kevin's mom would let him go out and start her car, a '69 Buick with a robust V-8 under the hood that roared into ignition on the first turn, every time. It was one of Kevin's favorite things to do. It made him feel older than his twelve or thirteen years, mature, a boy – no, a young man – on the cusp of all that the teenage years have to offer.

One morning he turned the key and heard the engine thump and cough. He tried it again – it caught and flared, then died. Once more, and he heard, muffled through the dash and translated foggily through the steering column, pieces of mechanism flying apart and hitting the driveway. He stared at the dash, then at the key in his fingertips. From the corner of his eye he saw through the window his mom approach, hands held up, mouth open in a startled O. He heard through the window, "What's happening, what are you doing to my car?"

He got out. They opened the hood.

There were pieces of cat everywhere. The fiberglass blades of the cooling fan were snapped off. Bits of fur and flesh clogged the flywheels. Cat's blood drained and pooled in the manifolds. Belts now at rest clenched its tail. Kevin's mom's palms flew to her mouth. Kevin threw up. A neighbor's cat had crawled up through the engine compartment onto the cooling block sometime during the chilly night to warm itself. It had taken its last catnap.

They went back into the apartment. Kevin cried while he changed his clothes. His mom went back out with gardening gloves on and a shovel. She put the cat's broken body into a plastic garbage bag. She asked Kevin to take it to the dumpster.

The horrible package seemed to grow heavier as he carried it. He recalled seeing the cat – a dainty little black tom – padding around the apartments. He didn't know where its owner lived. He had killed it, and he didn't know whom to tell. He didn't know where or to whom he should confess his crime.

But it wasn't his fault! Who would ever have guessed that a cat would crawl up there? Were people supposed to check under the hood every time they decided to drive somewhere? It was just an unfortunate accident. Still, the dead cat's face had been twisted into an accusatory grimace, thrown there against the air filter. Those eyes wide but dim, mouth jacked wide and fanged, pearly pink tongue out and limp. One ear laid back against its misshapen skull, the other ear who knows where but no longer attached.

Kevin grunted as he lifted the dumpster's lid, hefted the bag over its lip, dropped it in with the garbage, flies and stink. He let the metal lid bang back down with no effort to muffle the noise. It resounded like a cannon shot. With perhaps some smaller, daintier, more feline sound underlying it – the suggestion or shadow of a small, weak meow that he perceived for just an instant, but dismissed without it really even registering.

He went to school and told his story. His buddies thought it was cool. And although he didn't – not really – he played along.

"Teach a damned cat to mess with me," he said.

Could he be mistaken? Was that a different cat? Kevin sat in his mom's rocker listening to KISS Alive II through headphones. Watching through the living room window, he had just seen the cat drop out onto another squirrel. The cat swiped at it a few times, then bit its head. The squirrel went limp. Then the cat collected the rodent and headed back up the tree. It seemed bigger, Kevin thought, as the guitars from *Calling Dr. Love* died, the record popped in its grooves a little, and the band started the next cut, *Christine Sixteen*.

How could it be a different cat? What new cat would do that same thing, come hang out in a tree and drop onto its prey like that?

Kevin removed the headphones and went for the front door. Down the steps and out the front gate to stand with hands on hips and gaze into that hellish face. Same cat, all right. For some reason, it had just appeared larger.

The cat seemed uninterested and unperturbed by Kevin's presence. It gripped the squirrel and tore at it, cracking bones with sickening snaps Kevin could plainly hear. Just inside the penumbra of shade, he could see the cat's mouth open the squirrel up. Neat as you please, like a surgeon with the sharpest scalpel you could imagine, the cat pulled the skin back with one claw and gnawed hard from the side of the carcass.

Kevin saw something drop. He looked at his feet. The squirrel's tiny foreleg rested there on the concrete, shaped like a tiny

156

backward N. Kevin looked back up. The cat had paused in its meal and glared at him. "Don't worry," Kevin said slowly. "I ain't gonna touch it." The cat bared its fangs and hissed. The noise put Kevin in mind of the cicadas that shrieked and buzzed in trees all night in the humid summertime. Kevin took one cautious step back, then another.

"Man," he said under his breath, "you are one mean bastard cat."

Another piece of the squirrel dropped, a rear haunch that dotted the sidewalk with blood when it hit. Substantially meaty, Kevin thought, and decided to go back into the house before the cat got a notion to come down to retrieve it.

Inside, he sat back in the chair. KISS came tinny out of the earphones at his feet. He was no longer interested in the music anyway. He was thinking of something his cousin – an boy four years older than Kevin – had told him when they were moving from the apartment into the new house, this house, a couple of years after the cat-under-the-hood accident. For some reason Kevin couldn't remember, the incident had come up. His cousin had told a cat story of his own.

"Aw that's nothing. When I was your age we had about a million cats running all over the damned neighborhood. We used to get these coon traps and put a little Meow Mix in there. Catch them cats every time. There were so many of them cats we just did the neighborhood a little favor. We'd get us a Boy Scout knife and slit that cat's belly from the chest to the nuts, then let it run around meowing with guts and intestines and shit hanging out. After a while, it'd just lay down and go to sleep."

Kevin had looked at his cousin as if the older boy were a serial killer, or at least one in the making.

"Kevin, I'm just kidding," his cousin said, and laughed. "God, you'll believe anything."

"That ain't funny," Kevin had said.

When the cat tried to drop onto his mom, Kevin decided enough was enough. She came into the house after retrieving mail from the box. Her normally orderly hair was in disarray, and she trembled as she asked him about the cat.

"I don't know where he's from," Kevin said, "but he's been out there for weeks. You should have seen what he did to the Dunleavy twins."

"I'm going to call Animal Control," his mom said. "That cat is huge. It tried to attack me – just came flying through the air. Crazy as all get out."

Kevin thought about this. "Might as well call, but I ain't sure it'll do any good. There's something funky about that cat. First of all, it's the meanest cat I ever heard of, and it's... getting, uh... well, bigger."

His mother looked at him askance.

"You know," he said. "Like, it was a little guy when I first seen him. The next time, I could swear he was bigger, and the next, and the next."

His mother paused to consider this. "That's just plain weird," she said. "Are you sure?"

Kevin held his arms up, palms open wide, and shrugged. His mom got out the phone book.

But when Animal Control came to have a look, the cat wasn't in the tree. "Let us know if he comes back," they said.

"Right," said Kevin. "OK," said his mother. She had to go to her bowling league; if she didn't leave soon, she'd be late.

At that moment, Kevin decided to take matters into his own hands. Animal Control was not going to solve this problem. His mother was not going to do it, and she shouldn't have to. He thought, I'm the man in this house now. It's up to me. It's my responsibility.

As soon as it grew dark outside he went into the garage to get a flashlight and his Louisville Slugger. He went out to the sycamore and trained the light upward. The cat's eye's caught the light, reflecting every color in the spectrum, although the colors were strange and twisted. Colors like you would see in Hell, Kevin thought. He moved the light back and forth across the cat. It was bigger than ever, there was no doubt about it. He wasn't just imagining things – this cat was growing.

"Come on, kitty," he called.

The cat hissed like a dragon.

"Why don't you come on and take a little jump. Right into my strike zone. Come on, fella."

The cat bunched in the light. It opened its mouth. Its throat seemed like an open hole in space. The cat howled as if a demon lived inside and controlled it, a startling caterwaul that sparked and leapt from its forked tongue. Its hair stood up from the cap of its skull to the root of its tail. Then it collected its weight on its haunches.

Kevin had just a second to wonder what to do with the flashlight.

The cat leapt.

158

It came at him puma-sized, grew in Kevin's face at fabulous, fascinating speed. He dropped the light, raised the bat in one hand. He tried to get his other hand on the grip and swing. But it was too late.

His eye exploded in agony. He heard the bat clatter woodenly on the sidewalk. In the silence that followed he heard his name whispered. Or not whispered. Purred.

Other people in the waiting room moved around and talked. The automatic doors whooshed and the fish tank bubbled. He heard magazine pages flip. Because the eye patches occluded his vision, he had only his mind's eye at work. But across the backs of his eyelids burned an image of the inescapable notion of cat's claws. That is, their purpose and mechanics and the genius and utility of their razor-sharp design. He had learned how they work in Biology. But now he could appreciate like none of his classmates how each of a cat's claws is attached to the last bone of each toe. How each waits like a dagger in a sheath, within a layer of modified skin, under a hard protein cuticle. How when it comes time to take those daggers out, muscles in the cat's legs contract. How this pulls the flexor tendon taut under each claw.

The claw comes out like a hook or a sickle and does its work.

Then it goes back in.

Simple enough. Stunningly simple. And beautiful.

"No, I'm not finished with you yet," the demon cat said.

After a couple of weeks the ocular specialist said the one eye patch could come off. He examined the damaged eye, appraising his work.

"Your son may yet get full use out of this eye," he said to Kevin's mom, as if Kevin weren't there in the room. "He may not. Time will tell. He needs to keep it protected, keep the patches on the one for a few more weeks still."

Kevin grew nauseated on the way home. Twilight was falling, and in that flat half-light everything they passed in the car seemed to leap at him with no warning, to just appear suddenly from nowhere.

"The doctor said you would have trouble with depth perception," Kevin's mom said. "Just looking at things with the one eye, and all."

Stop signs, street lights, people strolling through the neighborhood, fire plugs, juniper bushes, the curb, the mailbox... everything seemed to appear right on top of him. From behind a veil of gray flannel into his close-up world in a flash.

A picket fence, a giant sycamore tree. Right there, suddenly, in Kevin's face.

They got out of the car. Kevin looked up.

The limbs sagged under the weight of the cat, larger still, as large as a lion, but jet black, as black as a tunnel with no other side. Never, no matter how long you walked, would you ever – having entered that awful maw once – come out the other end.

The maw roared.

"Come here, boy!"

THE SPOKESMAN

When the power dies, Brandon Verity is the guy you see on television or hear on the radio. The mouthpiece for the power company. Lines down? No problem — "We have crews working around the clock and we're estimating power back on in ninety-five percent of our coverage area within the next three hours. Hang in there with us, and we appreciate your patience."

"Mr. Verity, is there anything customers can do to help?"

"Well Jim, our crews have the matter well in hand. What people *can* do is walk around their homes — please, with a flashlight! — and unplug appliances, switch lights to the off position... that sort of thing. There's nothing so hard on a newly restored electrical network as a surge in requirements. That's what happens when we come back on line and everything's still switched on."

"Thank you, that was Brandon Verity, with Pacific Northwest Power & Light, and we'll get back to weather in a moment — and we've all just been socked by this windstorm — but first a commercial word from KYRX, your morning AM traffic and weather station..."

Verity is used to calls in the night. The phone rings, it's one or two a.m., no big deal. That's the life of a press officer for the region's major electrical utility. He sleeps nights alone on a bed sagging in the shape of only him — there is no vocation harder on marriage, or for even starting a relationship, than public relations. The calls at all hours, the petty rudenesses of reporters, going to bed on a stormy night and knowing the first call could come at any time.

So when Verity's phone cut the stillness of early morning on June 13th, just after midnight, he thought nothing more of it than to reach out and stop the ringing. Through that murky place between sleep and wakefulness, he assumed it was either a report from the power company's switchboard — which mobilized everyone during power losses — or a member of the media, calling about an outage. He knew his home number, as well as that of his cellular phone and two pagers, was on the news desks of every media outlet within the surrounding three-county region. It was as likely either way — a company operator or Jim Jessup down at KYRX, the number one AM commuter station in this market. He knocked the handset from its cradle, scrabbled around for it in the darkness, found it. He held it to his head.

"Verity." His voice sounded like oiled gravel.

161

"This is a USWest operator, and we have a collect call for you from the state penitentiary at Walla Walla. Will you accept the charges?"

Verity stared at the red digital display of his clock. 12:01 it washed, ponding in the area around his bed-stand, spreading in a blood pool onto the sheets near his pillow. He reached to click on the lamp, and the features of his room resolved themselves in the commodity of light.

"What?" He swung his legs out from under the bedcovers.

"A collect call, sir. From the state penitentiary at Walla Walla. Will you accept the charges?"

"No." Verity knew no one in the State Pen. It must be a wrong number. "No, I will not accept the charges. Tell the person he must have the wrong number."

The line clicked dead with no acknowledgment from the operator.

How annoying — a good night's sleep was rare enough, especially during storm seasons. He snapped off the lamp, laid back on his pillow, and spun scenarios in his head. A wrong number, a prank call — could even be some journalist having a good laugh, although he thought that was pretty unlikely. Nested in the warm bed, he slipped back into a lonely, dreamless sleep. At the moment he slipped from consciousness, the clock returned to blink *12:00 ... 12:00 ... 12:00 ... 12:00 ...*

Between August 8th and 11th, storms from the west smashed the three-county region in a series of waves. No one could remember a set of summer storms as violent. There were more than fifteen-hundred lightning strikes a day, one lifeguard hit (what the hell was he thinking, on top of a county-park tower in the squall?), two golfers fried — one in the moment of his backswing, the other grasping the flag on the seventh green at Royal Oaks.

Brandon Verity spent as much time on television, tossing sound bites, as he had all year up to that point. His voice was as familiar to commuters as those voices of the radio personalities who invited him to speak. And everywhere in the area, people talked in the main about the weather — not in the way folks simply *do* — but because the weather was legitimate news. *It's August, for crying out loud,* they whined. This was the time of year when people could properly expect the sun's cooperation, when office and church picnics could be scheduled without fear of downpour. It should, by all the laws of seasons, be hot and dry.

Instead, thunderheads had gathered like hoary anvils on the 7th, sky monsters brooding, towering over them to select victims. All hell had broken loose on the 8th, from a sky the color of dark-green slate. Rain fell in sheets blown sideways, drops transformed into vandalous hail from time to time. These assaults carried power lines to the ground, sparks flying, live arcs whipping from cable to cable. Ceramic insulators blew apart and threw glassy shrapnel onto the streets below. Transformers exploded as supernovae and the downed lines whipped serpent-like. An apprentice utility worker, unused to the rhythms and laws of electricity, got fried in a cherry picker.

It was the spate of media calls that resulted from the apprentice's carelessness that brought on Verity's first bout of sleep deprivation that summer. Although the unfortunate green-pea clung to life, the prognosis was "real crappy," as one of the doctors had put it to Verity in private. At a spontaneous news conference on the hospital steps, Verity translated this grim prognosis succinctly for the cameras and microphones: "We are not commenting on the condition of this public servant until we have talked with members of his family. Thank you."

Assignment editors and print reporters pestered him all afternoon at his desk at the power company, on his cell phone and beeper all the way home. When he arrived at the house, he discovered his own home was without power. He tossed his briefcase into a chair, went into the kitchen, and opened the refrigerator for a beer. He drew a bottle out — *still cold, good,* he thought — and twisted the cap. He took a few pleasant swigs before he started returning calls. One of the messages, the third from the beginning, was a notice from the hospital that the apprentice had died, with his family at bedside.

Verity revised his statement to include words like, "Our hearts go out to..." and, "Every man and woman at Pacific Northwest Power & Light grieves with..." He included a review of the finer points of the company's apprenticeship program, and its special emphasis on safety. He thought, as he wrote, how people — even the most *ignorant* people, although he couldn't say this publicly — are smart enough to understand you want to make damned sure a 180-volt wire is not hot before you wrap your green-pea fingers around it. The beer tasted good, and he returned all the calls in the order they were left. He finished in time to meet all their deadlines. The sky dimmed. He lit candles and located a flashlight.

His television was dead, so he couldn't wait up to review the late news. Nor would he be able to see how the stations had covered the apprentice's electrocution. He indulged a moment of absurd, black

163

humor — behind the anchor the graphic would read *"Electrocution '99,"* instead of "Election."

Verity decided to turn in early. The storm showed no sign of abating, and he was certain he'd receive early-hours calls to update the morning's commuters on how many customers were out of power, when restoration could be expected, and so forth. He got into bed after setting the flashlight on the bed-stand and started to read a novel by candlelight. His mind wasn't in it, though. After he realized he'd scanned the same page three times and still had no idea what he'd just read, he snuffed the candle.

Only sporadic flashes of sheet lightning mitigated the darkness. He counted between flashes and thunderclaps, and over the course of a few minutes noted the storm-cell was moving closer. With no air conditioner, the night was moist and close. He thought of the dead apprentice, the power surging through him. The poor green-pea had risen this morning like everyone else, probably marveling at the power of nature but a little put out that he'd surely have to work overtime... then, *smack*, 180 volts. Unabridged, raw power, and that's all she wrote.

Verity tossed his covers over the edge of the bed. He fluffed his pillow. The storm moved closer. He turned onto his stomach and the storm moved directly overhead. He buried his head under the pillow as lightning struck very close and a thunderclap shook the windows. He peaked out from under the pillow, and lightning flashed again. He saw the burned apprentice in his open closet. The man held up stumps.

Blackness again as the hair on the back of Verity's neck rampaged.

Whuh?

Lightning struck again, and there was nothing.

Verity's phone jangled. He must have dozed for only moments. His head was heavy as a cannonball, his eyes gritty. "Shit." He reached for the lamp, but knocked over the candle instead, then recalled the power was out. He lifted the handset.

"Verity."

"Hello, this is USWest. We have a collect call for this number from the Washington state penitentiary in Walla Walla. Will you accept the charges?"

Verity noticed that his clock was *on*: 12:03, it read. He reached to pull the lamp cord, felt the string in his fingertips, pulled, heard the click — but no light. *Huh?*

"Sir? Are you there?"

"Yes, I'm here."

"Will you accept the charges?"

"No, I won't accept the charges. And this is the second time this summer they've called. Make sure they know they have a wrong number, O.K.?"

A click followed, then the vacuous dead hum of dial tone. He dozed again. Then the calls started — early, as he had predicted — and nearly two-hundred thousand more customers were without electrical power. Verity knew the day ahead would be interminable. He saw he'd lost power again during the night, but that it had then been restored, at least in his neighborhood, for now. His clock blinked that bloody 12:00 again and again. He rolled onto his side, consulted his wristwatch, set it correctly at 5:41, and rose to a lukewarm shower — all to no avail. By the time he emerged from the shower, the power had again gone out. He dried and dressed in pre-dawn halflight.

Verity consulted the morning paper. The banner headline was, of course, about the storm. And there he was, accurately quoted several paragraphs into the piece. The front-page picture was a color photograph of the empty cherry picker. The article noted that at press time, power still was out for nearly 300,000 residents. That had been before last night's round. Now the number was closer to half a million, and the wind and rain outside were not letting up.

No coffee, no toast, things in the refrigerator getting warm, freezer defrosting. He'd need to find time today to clean out the spoiling food. But that could wait. For now he needed to get to the office and check in. Working from home was doable in a pinch and after hours, but he'd feel a lot better behind his desk, the resources of Pacific Northwest Power & Light arrayed around him.

He flipped over the paper for news that had not made it above the fold. There, next to the contents box, his eye washed a headline: Lerris pays in chair for '89 spree

Dateline, WALLA WALLA, Wash. The story described the execution, at 12:01 this morning, of Edward Marcus Lerris, for the 1989 handgun deaths of two bank tellers, a security guard, and a bystander in the bank's parking lot. All of Lerris's appeals had run out, and the Governor's office had not called with clemency. Witnesses included relatives of the victims, Lerris's attorney and a few individuals from the media.

There were details of the execution itself, which had been carried out in the penitentiary's death row complex, and a review of perspectives gathered from death-penalty pundits both pro and con. There was a summary of the coroner's remarks, which placed time of death at 12:03 a.m. Pacific Daylight Time. There was the detail that this was the second Washington execution in less then two months, the state having pumped voltage through rapist/killer Charles Martin Coombs last June 13th. Verity noted the use of all three of Coombs and Lerris's names: *These criminals, they always use three names in the newspaper.*

"Sorry, Edward Marcus, looks like you and our apprentice have something in common." Verity had long been a cynic. He knew it, and blamed it on working with reporters.

He left for work.

The storms persisted another two days. Power came back on at his house. He was able to clean the smelly food from his refrigerator and freezer. He slept in short, clipped batches. The inquiries settled down.

In the dream, that *lonely* part of Verity's life is over — or perhaps, it never *was* lonely, and he always had her here with him. That is to say, he has a wife, and she is curling up with him in his bed like a cat. They have just finished a long, slow, delicious episode of lovemaking. He has turned over to sleep. She is behind him, and she reaches across his torso to pull him closer.

The odor of cooking meat. The skin of her arm as it reaches around liquefied and scabrous. The stench of her embrace.

He blanches, gags. What happened to his beautiful companion? Only moments before, she took him in with sweet gasps and an urgent, fundamental scent. The skin of her forearm — it feels like half-dry cement.

He turns on the pillow, beholds the dream-hag. Her face has gone skeletal, the bone foundation jutting up through sopping putrefaction. Skin is hanging off of this... this skull, this witch's face. The eyes are like milky spheres, occluded in cataracts. The orifice of her mouth, bedecked with the remains of tooth crowns, exhales a burnt odor as she whispers through a charred voicebox, "It hurts, Brandon. It hurts. Oh God, how it hurts..."

The power has gone off. The phone on Brandon Verity's bed-stand rips a hole in the fabric of the night. It jars him from a dream he cannot remember with any clarity at all, but which has managed to render him utterly terrified in his sleep.

My wife is his first thought. *Where is my wife?* He stares up into the black, at a ceiling he still believes is there. *It hurts, Brandon, it hurts,* he hears, barely aspirated, from across the pillow. Or maybe further, from over there — the closet. *Oh God, how it hurts.* The phone

166

goes off again. He inadvertently knocks it from its place next to the lamp.

"Hello?" It comes from the floor, the handset. He is afraid to reach down, afraid of his dream-wife's reach, that she will reach with her sopping, rotted arm from under the bed and pull him below, under the mattress in a sticky grotto of burnt, charred electrocution death. "Hello? Is anyone there?"

Verity remembers he is the company spokesman for Pacific Northwest Power & Light, that this is likely one of two sorts of calls. It's either the switchboard or a reporter. Either way, he'd better summon some professional demeanor and quick. He reaches for the handset. He brings it to his ear.

"Hello. This is Verity."

"This is a USWest operator, and we have a collect call for you from the state penitentiary at Walla Walla. Will you accept the charges?"

Again? He can't believe it. He'll accept the charges, see whom this fool is who persists in disturbing his sleep.

"Sir?"

"Uh-hum?"

"Sir, will you accept the charges?"

"Yes. Yes, I will."

"Hold for a moment please." The voice on the line pauses, then continues. "Go ahead." Verity isn't sure whether the voice means he should say something or whether the operator is beckoning the caller on board the phone call, whether this is her signal to him that the charges have been accepted and he may begin speaking. There is a short click, then a hum. It is a signal that the operator, having concluded her business, has left the line.

Verity and the caller are alone.

There is a silence that at first makes Verity curious, then slightly perturbed. "Hello?" There is only silence. "I said, hello?" It's quiet and his room is black. Then he gasps, nearly swallows his tongue as the bedside alarm clock blinks on at 12:02. The sudden light is like a flash of red electricity that stays with him, burning into his corneas and he hears for the first time the voice of his caller.

It hurts, Brandon.

"Hello? Who is this?"

It hurts.

He can barely hear her, the caller. "What? I can barely hear you."

167

"My God, Brandon, it HUUURTSS!" The voice is a guttural scream and the clock flashes brilliantly and there is the smell of ozone and Brandon Verity checks his closet for monsters in the darkness. Then there is nothing but the digital readout: 12:00... 12:00... 12:00... 12:00... 12:00...

"Hello?" He begs the phone to answer. "Please... are you there?" Silence. "What hurts?" The line clicks dead in his ear. It feeds dial tone to his brains.

A flash, then nothing.

From the Seattle *Post-Intelligencer,* Sept. 4, 19–:
Gates dies: First woman in Walla Walla chair in 40 years
WALLA WALLA, Wash. — Convicted murderer Sharon Ashley Gates was put to death in Washington's electric chair for the 1993 killing of her boyfriend and his parents in Grays Harbor County. Gates, who was 29, was declared dead at 12:02 a.m. PDT by Walla Walla County Coroner Dewey Naismith.

Relatives and neighbors were stunned in 1993 when Gates, a vivacious, successful college graduate...

From the Seattle *Times,* Sept. 5, 19–:
'Power & Light' spokesman killed in home fire
RENTON, Wash. — Brandon Verity, longtime company spokesman for Pacific Northwest Power & Light Co., died at his home in Renton in the early hours yesterday, Sept. 4. He was 41, an apparent victim of a fire that started in his bedroom and spread to consume most of his home.

Verity, widely known for his dependable, friendly reports on power company issues, was discovered in the home's wreckage after fire crews battled the blaze for nearly three hours. Forensics experts with the Fire Department have issued a preliminary statement that they believe the fire started in a short-circuited alarm clock that sat on a bed-stand near Verity's bed.

Early reports of a second body in Verity's home were not substantiated, and the coroner's office called them "unfortunate rumors that responsible journalists would not broadcast or print."

Verity, who was single and had no relatives living in the area, will be buried in his boyhood town of Grays Harbor, according to another power company spokesman.

ABOUT THE AUTHOR

Brian Ames writes from St. Charles County, Missouri. His work appears in numerous magazines, anthologies and on the World Wide Web, including *Glimmer Train Stories, The Edge: Tales of Suspense, The Massachusetts Review, Red Rock Review, Weber Studies, Darkness Rising, South Dakota Review, Sweet Fancy Moses, Carriage House Review,* and *Unusual Circumstances: Short Fiction From Around the Globe.* Pocol Press of Virginia published his first story collection, *Smoke Follows Beauty* in 2002. He is a former editor of *Wind Row,* Washington State University's literary journal, and today edits fiction at *Word Riot.*

Made in the USA
Coppell, TX
19 December 2020

45141548R00105